# COCONUT WIRELESS

*A Paradise Crime Cozy Mystery Book 1*

TOBY NEAL

*COCONUT WIRELESS*
*A Paradise Crime Cozy Mystery Book 1*
*By Toby Neal*

*In memory of Royce Piro: beloved reader and friend*

Copyright Notice

This is a work of fiction. Names, characters, businesses, places, events, and incidents are either the products of the author's imagination or used in a fictitious manner. Any resemblance to actual persons, living or dead, or actual events is purely coincidental.



http://tobyneal.net/

ISBN Ebook: 979-8-9857068-4-0

Print: 979-8-9857068-8-8



Cover Design: Jun Ares

Format Design: Neal Enterprises, INC.

COCONUT WIRELESS

"Isn't it nice to think that tomorrow is a new day with no mistakes in it yet?"
— L.M. Montgomery

# I

"This can't be happening." I clutched the armrests of the tiny ten-seater plane headed for Hana, Maui, as it bounced crazily in the updrafts coming off the cliffs of the island. Those cliffs were close enough to skin my nose on, and my nose wasn't even my biggest feature.

My feet were.

Size eleven, to be exact. And if you've ever tried to find women's shoes in an eleven, you know it's like finding a pearl in an oyster shooter—not gonna happen.

The woman in front of me was still wearing her wedding dress and it filled the aisle, as big and poufy as the parachute I'd once used to deploy over Paraguay.

"We finally did it!" she shrieked with excitement. Her hair, dyed the exact shade of a stop sign, bounced atop her head with matching enthusiasm. Her husband, in the seat opposite, beamed at her across the aisle. One look was all it took for them to begin canoodling, not at all bothered by the way the plane was bucking like a pissed off bull with a cinch on his boy parts.

I didn't mind either, to be honest. I'd flown missions much hairier than this little commuter flight to a remote corner of paradise.

What I minded was that I was now the new postmaster of a town called Ohia. Until today, I'd spent my professional career in Washington, D.C., as a Secret Service agent, guarding some of the most important people in the country. The most I'd seen of the Aloha State was a high-rise in Honolulu where one of my favorite clients, Ambassador Frank Smithson, had lived.

I'd also tried a drink once called a Blue Hawaiian. I do not recommend.

And now, I was in my supervisor's idea of a witness protection program. Indefinitely.

"Behave, Kat! This is the best I can do for you. It's a government job! You'll even keep your pay rank." He'd handed me a driver's license with a rainbow on it. "And don't make waves. You need to keep a low profile until this situation blows over."

The "situation" was that my latest client, a U.S. Congressman from a state with a lot of inbreeding, made a pass at me. When I kicked him in the balls, he'd gone after my career with an assault charge and had his yes-men hop on the bandwagon to get me fired.

Talk about unfair.

I continued to white-knuckle the armrest as I stared out the tiny window at the rugged green cliffs. In the distance, they gave way to a bamboo forest and a junglelike tangle of green. *Very nice.* The ocean sparkled a ridiculous turquoise, with little empty beaches and waterfalls enlivening the already dramatic coast. We approached a hill dotted with cows and palm trees, a worn white cross perched atop the crest.

Then, we landed.

*Boom!*

Literally.

The moment we touched down, one of the tires on the little turboprop blew out, causing the plane to go into a nasty spin. The newlyweds and the other Hotel Hana guests in the front of the plane screamed their heads off, sure they were going to die.

I spun in my seat, grasping at the fire extinguisher, my eyes searching the tail for an emergency exit. There. Right where it should be. I popped the handle on that puppy before we even fully stopped, jumped out, and landed on the tarmac in my size eleven Nikes, extinguisher locked and loaded.

A small fire had erupted from the spray of metal-on-asphalt sparks. Globs of white foam launched from the red canister, coating the landing gear. I finally released the handle when nothing but smoke rose from the blackened wheels. I dropped the canister to the ground with a clunk and turned my attention to the fuselage.

Passengers flooded the front of the plane as the crew attempted to open the doors. All but one. I turned to see two legs and a wad of white tulle dangling from the hatch I'd just exited. Panic is the enemy—we learn that early in the Secret Service. Yet somehow this bride had made it to seventy-something with all the composure of a turkey with Thanksgiving on its mind.

I rushed to the hatch, dodging satin bridal shoes until I was close enough to duck under and prop her up on my shoulders. Clouds of fabric tumbled into my eyes while her top half, still inside the plane with most of her massive dress, struggled to get loose. During this graceful moment, the pilot arrived at the back of the plane.

"What's going on back here?" Of course, he had to be a good-looking Hawaiian guy clad in a tight white uniform that I imagined didn't hurt his prospects with women any.

I grunted, struggling with the increasing load of satin and tulle as the slippery material oozed out from under where it wedged the bride. Above me, she called upon various deities, including her new husband, whose name was apparently Gary. "This passenger decided to exit the fun way, and the door is too small. Feel free to jump in anytime. We might have to cut the dress to get her out."

"And what the heck are *you* doing outside the plane?" Hot Pilot raised his voice, and not because I was buried under a wedding dress the size of a small sedan. I freed a hand to lift the fabric and look at him. His face mirrored my look of irritation, his hands on his hips.

I was so done with dudes yelling at me. "I exited to put out the fire." I pointed to the empty canister on the ground and scorched, melted tire that had wrapped itself around the strut. "Would you rather I sat in the tail cone while we all went up in flames?"

He turned and looked at the smoking mess of metal and rubber. "Holy crap. You prevented a . . ."

"Disaster. Yep. You're welcome. Now, I could really use a little help here." The woman's thighs kept squeezing my head as she struggled to push herself up. Not exactly comfy around my head and shoulders.

The copilot helped the rest of the passengers out of the plane as the staff from the tiny airport came running over with a set of rolling stairs. They placed it beneath her, freeing me to wiggle out. I swiped at my sweaty, beet red face. Thankfully Hot Pilot was nowhere to be seen.

It felt good to breathe fresh air again, free of bride and billowing fabric. A moment later, she disappeared back into the aircraft; arms in white sleeves with striped cuffs hauled her back inside the tiny hatch opening. She then made a proper exit through the side door.

The other guests surrounded the bride and clucked and cooed over her. I stayed at the back of the plane, dusting myself off and waiting for the hullabaloo to die down so I could go back inside and get my carry-on bag.

But Hot Pilot was a step ahead and emerged with it in his hand. He approached and looked me in the eye. Most men can't because I'm a petite six foot one.

"I owe you a big *mahalo*," he said. "Sorry for yelling like that."

"*Mahalo*. That's thank you in Hawaiian, right? Well, either way, 'sorry' is universal. In that case, I accept." I took my bag and turned to go.

"What's your name?"

I paused my departure and turned to look at him. This guy had a lot of really shiny white teeth to go with his big muscles and handsome face. He took my silence as a green light to continue. "Mine is Keone Kaihale. I fly for this airline."

"Yep, you sure do. I saw you get into the cockpit." I spun on my heel and set off for the baggage claim. The man with a lot of Ks in his name was pretty enough even without the uniform gilding that lily. The last thing he needed was one more woman falling over herself to talk to him.

The "baggage claim" turned out to be a rickety metal trailer hitched onto a golf cart. I found my suitcase in the pile and hefted it out. Massive, ancient, and built to withstand a fall from the cargo hold at cruising altitude, the thing had been around the world more times than years I'd been alive. I felt a pang as I grasped its handle and began towing it across the asphalt. I'd thrown all my worldly possessions into it with only a few hours' notice to board the flight to Maui, my government-issue apartment in D.C. already reassigned.

Was this suitcase and its contents all I had to show for my life, looking down the barrel at thirty?

I didn't even freakin' know where I was going.

Where was Ohia, anyway?

It didn't really matter. I'd just walk until I got there. It couldn't be that hard to find a town of less than five hundred people just outside of Hana. There was only one road, and it went all the way around the island according to the map I'd memorized. I'd use the time getting there to clear my head and wrap up my pity party. At least I still had a job . . . even if I didn't have the first clue about working for the Postal Service.

The road to Hana didn't have a shoulder. Deep grass grew on either side of a narrow, two-lane road, puddles hidden in the wild overgrowth. The wheels on my suitcase didn't like it.

A big white shuttle with HOTEL HANA on the side, its windows filled with the familiar faces of other passengers from the flight, dodged around me, overcompensated, and hit one of the puddles, dousing me with mud the color of rust.

"Son of a toadstool!" I'd been raised by my Aunt Fae, who didn't hold with swearing—so early on I'd gotten in the habit of making up my own cusswords. But if both hands hadn't been occupied with luggage, I would've flipped the bird for sure.

The big white refrigerator of a shuttle bus glided to the side of the road, and Hot Pilot Mr. K opened the doors. "Need a ride somewhere? Least we could do to thank you for saving our lives."

I spat out some mud and headed for the bus. "Maybe you can get me partway to my goal. I'm headed for Ohia."

His eyebrows rose. "What are you doing in Ohia?"

"None of your business." I hefted my suitcase on board.

Mr. K sat down in the driver's seat, shook his head, and pulled the lever to shut the doors.

The bride and groom waved at me from the back row of the bus. "Come sit with us! You're our heroine!"

I stowed my case in the luggage rack and worked my way to the back. The troublemaker gown protruded into the aisle up several rows, shockingly still white after all it had been through. I made it to the back and gestured to my jeans and shirt front, spattered with mud. "I better stand. I'll get your fancy dress dirty."

We wound our way down a road loaded with wild, exotic growth on either side and more hairpin turns than a jigsaw puzzle, eventually pulling up in front of a huge fountain with a koi pond at its base. The turnaround drive was lined with pretty, tropical plants. We had arrived at the low, gracious entrance of the Hotel Hana.

Oh, how I wished I was getting off here, headed for a soft bed and a hot shower, maybe even a glass of wine and some room service. But this place was way too pricey for Kat Smith on a government salary. I'd taken a quick look on my phone during the ride and was still a little queasy at the astronomical price of a room.

I waved goodbye to the bride and groom as everyone piled off the bus. When I was the only one left, I tugged my massive case out of the rack and mentally prepared myself to hitchhike. Despite having to stand, the lift had spoiled me, and I'd also peeked at rideshare options. Zilch.

I was rolling the beast to the edge of the steps when Mr. K

climbed back on. "I can give you a ride the rest of the way to Ohia. It's the least I can do to thank you."

"I can just grab a bus or taxi from the lobby. But thanks anyway," I replied, positioning myself to scoot past him and down the stairs.

"Neither Hana nor Ohia have a bus service or taxis. Come on, let me repay you."

I sighed, resigned. "In that case, I'll take it." I slid my suitcase back into the rack. "*Mahalo*, Mr. K."

I walked to the bench at the back of the bus where the bride and groom had been and sat down for the ride to my new home—my stomach churning with hunger and apprehension.

So far, my posting in paradise left a lot to be desired.

"Things can only get better from here," I told myself, but I'd been wrong before.

# 2

The Man with Ks in His Name drove the shuttle out of town, beyond a little grocery mart called Hanzawa Store, and past a series of food trucks that seemed to mark the end of Hana. The next ten miles were made up entirely of hairpin turns, with vine-draped trees and brightly colored tropical flowers flying by in a blur. Every now and then little roadside stands would appear, selling mangoes and leis to passersby. Mr. K slowed for a barely visible turnoff and we bumped along, the jungle scenery gradually opening up to waterfalls and gemlike bays. I'd just figured out how to brace myself on the seat in front of me when we arrived at a little village.

"WELCOME TO OHIA, BEST LITTLE TOWN ON MAUI" declared a new, carved wooden sign mounted on a pile of lava rocks. I stood up to see better, grabbing the dangling strap for balance, and craned my neck to see out the windows.

A half-moon of bay with a pier on the left and a few rows of square, tin-roofed, plantation style cottages on the right seemed to make up the town's main area. The shuttle slowed, turned, and bumped across a dirt parking lot pitted with puddles. We rolled to a stop in front of a green and white storefront with a sagging wooden porch labeled "Ohia Grocery, currently CLOSED."

On the other side of the shuttle, rusted red gas pumps from the fifties also declared they were "CLOSED."

Directly beside this unprepossessing edifice stood another building—and this time my heart gave a jump of excitement. Or trepidation, I wasn't sure which.

A white, official-looking "Ohia Post Office" sign hung above a weathered porch that sheltered floor-to-ceiling, old-fashioned brass mailboxes secured by paneled glass doors.

"You have arrived," Mr. K said, in a perfect imitation of a phone's GPS voice. Then, in a more serious tone, "I hope you know where you're going from here."

"I do." I glanced down at my Nikes—they weren't going to like the mud, but it couldn't be helped. "Thanks for the ride."

I walked to the front of the shuttle and reached for my bag, but he beat me to it, pulling it out of the rack and opening the double doors in a gentlemanly way. "Where can I take this for you?"

I cocked my head. "You're dying of curiosity, aren't you?"

Hot Pilot hit me with his killer smile, a dimple revealing itself just to the right of his wide grin. Not that I noticed. "Let's just say I have a lot of relatives in this town, and there aren't many places you could be going. Unless, of course, you're headed for New Ohia." He pointed through the open doors. "Though, I didn't think anything but the model homes were completed yet."

I peered past his nicely muscled arm to where he pointed.

Over the antique looking cement bridge, a high lava rock wall ran alongside the narrow road and curved around a bluff. Nearby, an artificial waterfall pumped spray over an enormous, carved stone sign that read "NEW OHIA." Smaller, golden letters spelled out "Luxury Living in Paradise" beneath.

"Nope." I wrinkled my nose. "Not my style. It's a good thing, too, because I couldn't begin to afford anything over there." Since Mr. K had a lot of relatives here in Ohia, I realized that it would behoove me to sweeten my attitude. I could do that. After all, I was trained to make friends and influence people. I stuck out a hand. "My name's Katherine Smith. You can call me Kat. I'm the new postmaster in Ohia. I hear the previous one left."

He stiffened. "Disappeared, you mean." He shook my hand. "Keone Kaihale, in case you didn't catch it the first time."

"Right. Keone, got it." I really had missed it. Those Ks and vowels were slippery as heck. "Disappeared? What do you mean?"

"As in, took off. Made like a rabbit and ran. *Hele'd* on home. Slipped on a banana peel and split."

I straightened up to my full height. This was the last thing I wanted to hear. "Well, I'm not a quitter."

"Too bad. Might be a good idea."

I bristled. "I've spent my entire career in government service." Not the Postal Service, but po-tay-to, po-tah-to.

He turned, ignoring my assurance. "You'll be going to the little *'ohana* in back then. Watch the puddles."

"What's an *'ohana*?" I picked up my backpack and followed him out of the shuttle. Sure enough, the doors opened directly over a large puddle. I hurdled over, colliding with his back. "Whoops."

He grunted at the impact. "*'Ohana* is a Hawaiian name for an in-law style cottage. It also means family. Speaking of, Auntie Pua is going to eat you alive."

"What?" I hopped over another puddle. "Who's Auntie Pua?"

"You'll find out soon enough," Mr. K said grimly, without further explanation.

The situation was beginning to feel hostile, and I needed to do a threat assessment. If I could tease info out of this guy, it would help me form a strategy to deal with what may come. "Listen, Keone. Anything you can tell me about the current situation would help me a lot. I really want to make a good impression." I was still talking to his back, and what a fine back it was.

"Like you care about that."

His tone shocked me. He was right—I didn't care. But I'd been careful not to convey that. So why the sudden change in attitude? He'd been nice to me at first. Now, I was getting a chill off him like wind blowing off the Russian steppe . . . and I've been there. It's not warm.

"Hey, Mr. K. I was a little grumpy when we first met. I'm sorry. It was a rough landing, what with the fire and the bride ending up on my head and all. And I was hangry. I'm even more hangry now—I'm not a girl you want to keep away from food," I joked, hoping to lighten the moment. He didn't respond.

We'd arrived at the back of the building, and I pulled up short in front of a tiny green shack. It was modestly embellished with white trim and a rusty, red tin roof and—not even kidding—a small coconut palm growing out of the rain gutter. The porch was the size of a postage stamp, and a big, round rock from the nearby beach served as the front step.

"Hmm," I said.

He glanced at me, searching for a reaction. "It's a bit rustic. Where did they say the key was?"

I frowned. "They didn't."

Mr. K shrugged and grabbed the janky door handle. It swung open with the kind of creak that wakes the dead. The hair on my neck rose with primal terror; a shiver rippled over my skin.

"Looks cozy." I was not about to show this guy that I was put off.

I brushed past him and confidently stepped inside, immediately tripping over something alive. That something gave a screech and a yowl, grabbing my leg in its powerful talons and applying its teeth to my shin.

"Mother trucker!" I recoiled, my hand dropping to my nonexistent weapon and my body falling into a fighting stance as I kicked the thing off my leg—and it wasn't small. "There's an animal in here! Maybe a raccoon or even a small bear!"

"We don't have raccoons or bears in Hawaii." Mr. K reached across my shoulder and grabbed a string dangling in the dim light that I couldn't even see. A bare bulb jutting from the ceiling bloomed on and blasted my irises.

He chuckled. "Oh, it's just Tiki. The post office cat," he said casually, as if I should know this. "I bet she got inside when Auntie Pua cleaned the place for you." He squatted and extended a fist to the hissing, spitting bundle of rage hiding under the battered Formica table. "Hey, Tiki-girl. Whatchu doin' in heah?" His voice had gone soft and melodic. I'd heard the pidgin dialect on my trips to Oahu to visit my detail, Ambassador Frank Smithson. Former detail, I should say. Dang it.

I shook out my pant leg. I wasn't about to show him the blood Tiki-girl had drawn. Hopefully it wouldn't leak through and stain my jeans. "Can you catch her? I'm not a fan of cats."

"Kind of ironic that your name is Kat." He looked over his shoulder from where he'd crouched. "I'm no cat whisperer. Tiki does what she wants."

"I guess I have an intruder, then." Hands on my hips, I inspected my new place.

The cottage consisted of a single square room with a kitchen sink and counter on one side, and a Murphy bed (currently folded up) on the other. In the center near the galley sat the aforementioned table, which still hid the large and belligerent cat. Two doors loomed opposite us, one open and revealing a small closet and the other closed, presumably the bathroom.

Or so I hoped. The place looked like plumbing would have been an innovation when it was originally built. I draw the line at no bathroom in any workplace. Well, except overseas. Overseas, anything goes.

Ohia, Maui, was another world all right, but technically it was not overseas.

I walked the three steps across the room to the closed door and turned the old-fashioned porcelain handle. Another string dangled inches from my face. I pulled it, and it lit up a rust-stained toilet, an old sink with clearly original fixtures, and a tiny shower stall. "Oh good. I was wondering if this was going to be an outhouse."

"It used to be. Back when Auntie Pua started here."

I shut the bathroom door. It looked better that way.

I needed to know more about this mysterious Auntie Pua. "You keep mentioning this lady. I'm intrigued. Tell me about her."

"She's not actually my auntie, but everyone calls her that." Keone kept his hand out toward the cat, but his pretty brown eyes on me. He wiggled his fingers. Tiki lashed her tail in response but sidled a little closer. "Auntie Pua has been the clerk here for close to thirty years and keeps getting passed over for promotion to postmaster. Oahu keeps sending over people like you, instead."

Ding ding ding. The sudden tension made more sense now. I probed cautiously. "People like me? White people? Outsiders?" His expressionless stare confirmed it. I felt my jaw tighten and my body tense for a fight, but I forced myself to take a breath. "Does Auntie Pua have a college degree? Any certifications?" I had no idea what was needed for the job, but it seemed to be a good start.

"No. Just a lifetime of service in the town where she was born and raised."

*Oof.* I felt my entire being deflate. Despite only being here because I was a victim of sexual harassment, it hit me like a punch to the gut to realize I might be a pawn for institutional racism. Crap!

I took a deep breath and steadied myself. I could feel Keone's eyes on me while I gathered my thoughts. "I'm sorry," I said sincerely. I yearned to explain how it wasn't my fault, but I hardly knew this guy. "Listen. I'm tired. And hangry, as I mentioned before. This cat doesn't seem to be going anywhere any time soon, and the grocery store is closed. Any chance you could help me find a bite to eat?"

Keone studied me for a moment, then rose to his feet. Some of his tension had faded, too, and my stomach did a tiny flop as he stood. The dude had no right looking that good in a uniform. "You asking me out?" he challenged, the sparkle back in his eye.

Tiki chose that moment to save me from answering by coming out from under the table. She was huge, easily the size of a raccoon. She was missing an ear, one eye seemed swollen shut, and her tail had a kink in it that spoke of being run over. She switched on a purr that sounded like an outboard motor on the verge of running out of gas and wound her patchy calico body around Keone's leg like a pole dancer.

I pointed to the lascivious feline leaving hair all over his pants. "Looks like you made a friend. Want to take her home?"

"I'd rather take *you* home." His dimple was back. "But I'll settle for a trip back to the food trucks in Hana."

## 3

I woke to the sensation of being watched. My body went on high alert when I realized there was something heavy and warm beside me. Or someone.

I was not alone in my lumpy Murphy bed with its musty sheets.

I was sure I hadn't drunk enough last night to have forgotten if I'd invited the handsome pilot home with me. I'd been tempted. We'd driven back to the food trucks outside Hana, had a beer and some "local grindz," and then he'd driven me back. He'd been a perfect gentleman the whole time. So who was beside me?

I lay perfectly still, keeping my breathing even, and let my training take over. I performed a quick threat assessment, mentally cycling through my senses to size up my current situation.

I'd locked the door last night, such as it was. The windows were closed, but they didn't lock, so someone could have easily opened one and climbed in. There were no sounds in the room, except for what came in through the thin walls. The raucous call of a mynah bird echoed through the air, and not too far away, a bullfrog that hadn't got the memo that it was morning croaked incessantly. A soothing shushing sound could be heard coming from above, likely the fronds of the palms in the breeze.

I felt a stirring beside me in the bed. Whoever was there was way too close.

My hand crept slowly up to slide under my pillow. I wrapped my fingers over the cool, pebbled grip of my service weapon, a standard-issue Glock 19.

That's when my attacker made a move. Claws dug into my bare skin and my head was suddenly gripped like a hairy bowling ball.

My finger tightened on the Glock's trigger before my brain could get the message to my hand that Tiki had leaped on me with all the savagery of a semi-feral, hateful cat whose territory had been invaded.

Glocks don't have an external safety, but they are perfectly inert as long as the trigger isn't depressed all the way. You can even drop one or hit the thing and it won't go off.

But pull that trigger?

Yep. It's gonna go.

The weapon fired so close to my ear that I was momentarily deafened.

Tiki launched several feet straight into the air and disappeared.

I sat up and gripped the gun two-handed, my heart thundering and my arm and head bleeding. "Tiki? Are you okay?" I couldn't even hear my own voice, my ears were ringing so bad.

Tiki had withdrawn to her cave under the table. She glared at me with one fierce yellow eye that glowed in the dim light. She hadn't been shot, thank goodness. I hadn't been either.

I strained my ears, but they still weren't working enough to be able to tell if anyone was coming to investigate a gunshot at dawn on the first morning the new postmaster moved in. What a rookie mistake! *Gah.* I turned to inspect the damage.

The wall of the cottage near my pillow sported a nice round hole. Through it, I could see that it was drizzling outside—probably why the bullfrog was still going strong, although the gunshot had shut him up.

Despite being very early, I was now wide awake.

"Smooth move, Kat. You could have killed yourself or that dang cat. This is clearly not a place for firearms."

I tossed the shabby comforter aside and got out of bed. The wooden floor felt damp and cool on my feet. I swung my arms in the darkness until I encountered the light string and gave it a tug. After scanning my tiny quarters, I crossed the room to the closet and opened it. A bar with a few dangling hangers and some built-in drawers littered with cockroach droppings seemed to be the extent of the storage. It would do. I put the gun in one of the drawers and shut it. I'd clean up the bug droppings later, before I put away any of my other personal items.

I turned and saw Tiki pull in deeper under the table. I squatted down in my skimpy sleep tee to address her. "I thought you were gone last night. How'd you get in?"

When Keone and I went to get food, we'd left the door ajar for her hoped-for departure. I'd checked all around and hadn't seen her inside when I got back, so I was sure she had taken her leave. I couldn't have slept as soundly as I had with her baleful presence anywhere near me.

"I'm going to have to find out how you're getting in and put a stop to it," I told her.

Tiki blinked her open eye; the other one looked weepy and infected. She let out a mew that sounded like the squeak of the attic door in a haunted house, protesting my insistence on throwing her out. "Oh yeah? You're hungry, as well as in need of a vet?"

I knew I shouldn't feed the beast or I'd never be rid of it, but I felt guilty for almost shooting her head off. Maybe I could use last night's leftovers to lure her outside.

"I've got something for you," I sang as I opened the rusty fridge and took out the goods. The Styrofoam carton was filled with the leftovers from the Hawaiian food truck that Keone had recommended: a heart-stopping platter of barbecued pulled pork called "kalua pig," macaroni salad, and two scoops of white rice.

I removed a chunk of shredded pork and waved it around in front of Tiki. "Here, kitty kitty."

She came out from under the table, and I quickly opened the door and launched the piece of meat into the wet hibiscus bushes beside the porch. Tiki went after it like a tiger on the hunt and never looked back.

Now that the door was open, I peered around in the early morning light. The bulk of the post office obscured my view, but if I remembered correctly, the beach was right on the other side of the road. I could hear waves from where I stood.

I was up, my hearing was coming back, and I was jet-lagged. I didn't see any coffee in the tiny kitchenette, so I decided I might as well explore the beach.

I ducked back inside to tug on my jeans and shirt from yesterday, with a hoodie for warmth. After shoving my feet into my Nikes, I stepped back outside the cottage. A growl from the bushes told me that Tiki had found her prize and wouldn't appreciate any interruption. I just had to get past her.

I thought about locking the door of the shack, but what was the point? Nobody but Tiki was around, and the door was next to useless.

Tiki growled again but I circled wide, stepping off the rock that made the front step. I picked my way past the main post office building and around the deepest and most egregious puddles in the parking area.

I frowned. The general store was still closed. When did it open? I needed coffee, and I needed it badly. I needed food too, but coffee was priority. Other agents I worked with used to say that I was most lethal when deprived of my caffeine.

I crossed the narrow two-lane road grandiosely named "Hana Highway" and followed along the overgrown shoulder until a path appeared. It was only a short distance through some bunchy shrubs to the beach. The sand stretched before me, and I realized it just wouldn't be right to wear shoes for my first beach walk at my new home on Maui.

I bent, undid the laces, and slipped the Nikes off, hiding them behind a nearby coral head. You never knew when there might be another woman desperate for a pair of size elevens.

The sand was cool on the soles of my bare feet, and slightly damp from overnight dew. Off in the distance, over an ocean the color of a blued steel revolver, a golden glow had begun. Suddenly the sun popped up, lighting the underside of the clouds with the pink of a flamingo's breast.

I choked up. I admit it. "The first day of the rest of my life," I said aloud.

I hadn't asked for the sexist attack that had led to this abrupt change in my life. I hadn't asked for the machinations of my agency that bumped poor Auntie Pua, a deserving civil servant, out of her hoped-for job. And yes, I felt like a flamingo myself, completely out of place in this village that probably had more factions than a mafia convention in Las Vegas.

But here I was anyway. The sunrise was glorious, and I was standing on a beach in bare feet.

Contemplating the horizon, with delicate waves bathing my feet in foam, my mind flashed to my favorite client, Ambassador Frank Smithson. A big, handsome fellow in his sixties, he'd recently been laid low by cancer. Then his ex-wife, a world class assassin who'd been on the lam for years, attacked and stabbed him. Luckily, I'd been able to visit him in the hospital on Oahu before my banishment to Ohia.

Sitting at his bedside, holding his ashy brown hand, and listening to his rough breathing, I'd known in my bones that life was short, fragile, and every second needed to be appreciated.

Maybe this weird detour in my life was about learning to do that even more.

Fortunately, it seemed like Frank was going to make it, but I made a mental note to call and check on him.

When I could get a phone signal.

Or a landline.

Or a ham radio.

Smoke signals or carrier pigeons?

Something had to work out here for communication. I turned to assess—the road was lined with rickety phone poles. There was probably a landline inside the post office. I would call once I was at work.

I walked the short horseshoe of golden sand. I explored an old cement pier in the center of the bay, peering over the sides to the sandy bottom. Built-in, rusted ladders led into the crystal clear water. Perhaps there had been a time when the pier was the heart of the town, an important site for the import and export of pineapples, sugar, taro, or beef. Now, it was probably just a fun place for kids to jump into the ocean.

I glanced back at the row of vintage plantation cottages that lined the road, then over at the stone wall that separated them from the influx of gated community luxury homes. Right here in front of me was a classic setup for conflict. How would the town adapt to this big, upcoming change?

I had grown up in Maine, on the coast, and we called outsiders "from away." Here, I was "from away," but the homeowners in New Ohia were likely even more so.

On my way back, I spotted a round glass ball caught in a nest of twigs, leaves, and debris. The orb was heavy and thick. The glass itself was filled with bubbles and looked old. Tiny barnacles pocked its sides. About the size of a baseball, it seemed like a fishing float of some kind—we certainly got our share of plastic floats washing up on the beaches in Maine, but I'd never seen one like this.

I slipped it into the pocket of my hoodie. I didn't know what it was exactly, but it would look nice on the windowsill of the shack. My first beach find! And now, it was time to go "home," find a way to get some coffee, and get ready for my first day as postmaster of Ohia.

# 4

I turned on the shower and was pleased to discover that the bathroom was equipped with a modern gas water heater, the kind that heats the water as fast as you use it. So despite being short on soap, my washup was piping hot.

Afterward, I wrestled my thick brown hair into a tight ponytail and donned a pair of black dress pants and a white button-down shirt. I wanted to look official for my first day on the job as the hamlet's new postmaster. Such an occasion also called for a dab of lipstick and a swipe of mascara, the most makeup I ever bothered with. Lastly, I wiped the mud and sand off my Nikes. Not the most professional footwear, but the quick cleaning improved them immensely. By eight a.m. sharp, I stepped onto the back doorstep of the post office, ready for work.

The handle didn't budge.

Unlike the cottage door yesterday, this door was locked. A quick check revealed no key in the usual hiding spots under the mat or on the door ledge. I circled the exterior of the building, looking for clues as to how I was supposed to get in.

The front door had a stout, shiny new lock that sent a clear message to anyone who might have thought of raiding the old-fashioned brass postal boxes lining the front porch: the U.S. Postal Service took security seriously, and I was not getting in without a key. I plunked down on the steps and waited.

Eight o'clock turned into eight fifteen, which turned into eight thirty.

Suddenly, I heard the rasp of something unlocking. The front door of the general store across the parking lot opened with a bang. I looked up from my phone, where I was trying and failing to get a signal. I wondered who I could even call to get the building open—I knew nobody in town. I stood up and trotted over to the general store to investigate.

The store owners must have a similar living arrangement to mine and live behind their place of business. I hadn't seen anyone arrive while I sat on the porch steps. I hoped they would have some information, but even if they didn't, there was now the possibility of coffee. Things were looking up.

I stepped up onto the wooden porch and stopped in my tracks. A woman started back from the doorway with a cry of surprise. She wore a tent-like gown in a bright Hawaiian print featuring large, splashy flowers, and bright pink Crocs. Her hand clutched a handful of amulets dangling across her significant bosom. "Whoa! You scared me!" She leaned over to peer past me. "How did you get here? The parking lot is empty."

"I'm Katherine Smith, but I go by Kat. I'm the new postmaster. I'm staying in the shack behind the building, so I didn't have far to come." I extended a hand. "And you are?"

"Opal. Opal Pahinui." She pumped my hand twice, briskly. I suppressed a wince at her grip. She eyed me up and down. "You're unexpected."

Was it my height? My extreme shoe size? Both were often unexpected. "How so?"

"I thought Auntie Pua would finally get promoted," Opal said, with an unmistakable disapproval.

I lifted my hands in a surrender gesture. "I'm sorry. I know nothing. I go where I'm sent. In fact, I know so much nothing that I can't even get into the building. I saw from the posted hours that I was supposed to be open at nine, but there's no key. I'm waiting for someone to open the place and show me the ropes."

A gleam appeared in Opal's pale blue eyes. "Auntie Pua's probably out 'sick,'" she said, her fingers hooking air quotes around the last word.

"Well, it's the post office, so neither rain nor sleet nor . . . um, anything else will keep us from making sure people get their mail." I cleared my throat. "But first, do you have any coffee? I'm dying here."

Opal put her hands on her hips and studied me for a moment, eventually deciding to take pity on me. "Come on, I'll put on a pot. There are always a few poor unfortunates who take this road to work in Kahului and stop in for a cup. I even have an espresso machine for the yuppies we're expecting when New Ohia opens up."

"When is that?" I said, trying to make casual conversation. In reality, my mind was deeply concerned with the fact that Auntie Pua had not shown up and I had no key to open the post office. This would not look good when customers started arriving to pick up their mail. But what could I do? Clearly the woman already had it in for me and was setting me up for failure.

We stepped into the dimly lit store. An impossible number of shelves filled the space, holding a little bit of everything. "July," she replied. "Just a couple more months of quiet as we've always known it. Except for the construction, of course." As if on cue, the little country store shook with the sound of a heavy vehicle passing by. She gestured toward the road. "There goes Charlie. He's the cement guy, and lemme tell you, that place is going to be filled with cement."

I trailed Opal as she wove her way through the musty-smelling aisles. Damp was clearly an issue here on the eastern side of Maui, as if the stain blooms on the ceiling of my shack hadn't already told me that.

"How long have you been here, Opal?"

"Twenty-seven years. Been here since I married my husband, Artie Pahinui." She stopped in front of a large, industrial-size coffeepot and stood up on her toes to reach the basket of grounds at the top. "Artie is one of the slack-key Pahinuis," she bragged proudly. "The whole family is famous in the slack-key scene. Especially known for fingerpicking and slide work."

I didn't understand a word she said, but I did understand that Opal was too short to reach the top of the coffeemaker. "Here, let me help. Being tall is useful once in a while."

I took the coffeemaker's lid off and retrieved the basket of used grounds and handed it to Opal. She banged it empty into a nearby trash can. "You haven't heard of the Pahinuis, I take it."

"Not sure," I hedged. "Sounds familiar."

"They're a big deal here in Hawaii."

"I bet. They sound impressive. I could sure use a fingerpicking expert to help me with the lock on the back of the post office door. If my coworker doesn't show up, I'm afraid the mail won't be accessible today."

Opal grinned, showing off the gap in her smile where she was missing a side molar. "You really are a *malihini*."

"A what?"

"Newcomer, in Hawaiian." She used a flexible hose from the nearby utility sink to fill the big canister. "Actually, you're a *haole malihini*. Even worse. Don't expect folks to open their arms to you until you've proved yourself. I'd say to give it . . . ten years or so."

I pinched my lips against a rebuttal. I was tired of being the bad guy when I hadn't asked to be posted here in the back of beyond. Ohia postmaster was as far from a career goal as I could get! But keeping my mouth shut was a survival skill in my line of work, and I'd learned how to do so the hard way.

I did a yoga breath in through the mouth and out through the nose. "I just want to make sure people get their mail."

She glanced up at me. I mentally upgraded Opal's water-colored eyes to "blue steel." This lady was sharper than she looked, despite her tent dress and Crocs.

"I'll see what I can do about your key." She bustled away, exiting the front of the store through a door marked PRIVATE.

Maybe she'd track down a key for me. I hoped I wouldn't be forced to use my lockpicks to break into federal property on my first day on the job. I had them with me, of course—you never know when you're going to need to get into something. "Getting into something is what you're good at, Kat," my boss always said.

If only the famous Auntie Pua had shown up for work the way she was supposed to—but as it often happened to me, I'd stepped into a pile of poo without noticing the smell until it was too late.

While I waited for Opal to investigate my key situation, I wandered the dimly lit aisles of the Ohia General Store, filling a plastic shopping basket with the basics that my shack so desperately lacked. Thankfully, the store was one of those mom-and-pop deals that carried a little bit of everything for those living in this back end of nowhere.

I liked to start my day with protein and fill the rest of it with abundant carbs. I picked up a carton of eggs for that virtuous start to the day, a stick of butter to help 'em slide down, a loaf of King's Hawaiian sweetbread (it smelled heavenly through the plastic bag), a jar of extra crunchy Jif and one of guava jelly, a head of iceberg lettuce in case I needed fiber, and several cans of tuna. I paused in the pet food area, staring at a bag of cat food.

Tiki seemed to have adopted the shack as her home. And now that I'd shown weakness by giving her a bite of kalua pig, she'd likely be attacking me on a regular basis. I still hadn't figured out how the dratted feline was getting in.

Opal appeared at my elbow. "I see you've met Tiki."

"I have. So far, not good." I turned to her. "Whose cat is she?"

"Tiki appeared out here about six months ago. Someone probably dropped her off. She attached herself to the post office and hangs around hoping for handouts, but she's too nasty for any of us to adopt. She's been known to attack."

I pointed to my arm and forehead, where Tiki's scratches blazed red against my skin. At least they had finally stopped oozing. "That's from this morning. You don't want to see the puncture marks on my leg from our first meeting."

"We should probably call the Humane Society. They don't have animal catchers on Maui, but they'll loan you a trap and you can take her in if you can catch her. No one around here would cry over it." While in the back room, Opal had wrapped an apron around her waist. She produced an old-fashioned feather duster from its gaping pocket and went to town on a nearby shelf. Her demeanor had changed, from cautiously friendly to prickly as a sea urchin.

"Help me out here, one *malihini* to another," I said. "Where can I get a key?"

She gave me another of those penetrating looks. "I'm a *kama'aina* now, and you'll have to look up what that means for yourself." She tucked the duster in her pocket. "Coffee's ready."

She bustled off.

I decided to preserve a little dignity and finish my shopping without pressing the issue. Maybe spending some of my few available dollars in the store would sweeten her mood.

I tossed a bag of Purina into the basket. I didn't like the idea of catching Tiki and taking her to the Humane Society to be put down. That's usually the fate of aggressive animals. What a bad way to start out this new chapter! Trying to make friends with Tiki might be the wiser choice. It was worth a shot—I could always do something else if it didn't work.

I grabbed paper towels, toilet paper, soap, a box of Ziploc bags, a fire extinguisher, and a citronella candle for the mosquitoes. An endcap caught my attention, and I added a tube of sunscreen in case I got more time on the beach. Since I decided to befriend Tiki, I ducked into the first-aid section and put together a small medical kit to treat my injuries, both from this morning and those likely to come.

I also grabbed a bottle of aspirin for the headache that was brewing since I hadn't had a drop of coffee in over twenty-four hours. And the *pièce de résistance*—a bag of Kona coffee to prevent such headaches tomorrow.

I set the plastic basket on a counter beside an old-fashioned metal cash register and went to the coffee urn, which had ceased its bubbling. I filled up the largest cup there, put a lid on it, and returned to the checkout.

Opal took an iPad on a stand from behind the register. "Cash or credit?"

"Credit."

She took my card and ran it through one of those little readers, then scanned my goods without a word. "Need a bag? They're twenty-five cents."

"Sure."

She shoved my items across the counter to me and slapped the bag on top of them. "Anything else?"

"What changed?" I asked, making eye contact at last. "I thought you were going to help me find out about opening the post office so people could get their mail."

"I called Pua, that's what changed," she said. "And Pua is the only one with a key to the building."

I winced. "I'm really sorry about the situation, truly. I had no idea. I'd like to go talk to her if you don't mind sharing her contact info."

"I will not." Opal turned to dust the shelves behind the counter. "Her contact information is for her alone to give out. Besides, Pua's ill today."

I began bagging my groceries to keep my hands busy. "I don't have any phone signal at my shack—I mean, the *'ohana* cottage. I think I should let someone at the main post office on the island know that this location is closed." The main office is probably in Kahului or Wailuku, the capital. I'd studied a map of the island and memorized the two main civilized areas—always know your surroundings was a creed in the Secret Service. "May I use your phone to make that call?"

Opal's mouth worked like she was chewing her dentures. "Nope. Pua says there's an automated phone tree that's alerted when she calls in sick, because she's been the only one out here for six months. You'll just have to wait for her to get well enough to come back to work." Opal popped the register open with a jingle and sorted a few bills, turning them so they faced the same direction. "Whenever that might be."

"Okay." I forced the word out. "Guess I've got a day off, then."

"Guess you do."

I picked up my bag of supplies and tucked the cat chow under my arm. I somehow freed up a hand to lift the Elixir of Life to my deprived lips. Tromping back to my hovel with my groceries, I sipped the hot brew as fast as my mouth could tolerate it. It was delicious.

As I crossed the empty parking lot, I contemplated the odd interaction with Opal. Why didn't I feel better about a completely free day off? Didn't I deserve one, as much as long-suffering Auntie Pua did? I hadn't time off in so long I'd forgotten what to do with myself should such a thing occur. But then again, here I was in Maui, with a tube of sunscreen and a beach nearby. Surely, I could come up with some way to pass the time.

Turns out, finding a body creates enough drama to take up most of the day.

# 5

Groceries and coffee filling my arms, I headed for the haven of my porch. Hopefully Tiki was appeased by my offering and wouldn't attack me, but either way, I'd soon find out.

My thoughts conjured Tiki like a bad burp reminds you of last night's pizza. She sat square on the porch, blocking the door, licking a paw. Hearing me approach, she shot me a glance like she'd done something worth mentioning in the local news.

Lying on the big round rock serving as a step to the porch was a strange branch—maybe? I was too far away to distinguish what it could be. Maybe a super weird tuber of some kind? As I got closer, I settled on a rootball. That's what it was, crusty with dirt and protuberances.

"Nice Tiki. You brought me a present. Good girl. Now, please get out of the way so I can go in?" I approached warily.

Tiki put her paw down and eyed me with disapproval. Clearly, I'd failed to appreciate what she'd brought me in exchange for that scrap of tasty kalua pig. Maybe she'd move from the doorway if I picked up her offering, symbolically accepting it.

"Okay, Tiki. We're going to be friends, okay? This marks a turning point in our relationship. I even bought you some food." I set down my bags, took another restorative belt of coffee, and squatted to inspect what the cat had literally dragged in.

As soon as I got within a foot of the thing on my doorstep, I recognized it.

"A hand," I said aloud, through the buzzing in my ears.

Tiki burst into that rumbling motorboat purr of hers, pleased that I had finally appreciated her gift. I stood back up so fast my head spun—after all six foot one is a long way to travel for a brain that has had very little coffee. "Oh, crab on a cracker."

I looked around wildly. No one to call for help but grumpy Opal back at the store. I pulled my phone out of my pocket—no signal. I had no choice but to use the store's phone. I decided I wasn't going to engage with Opal at all, just make the call. This was a genuine crisis.

Or, there had been a crisis back when that hand was buried, most likely still attached to a missing person.

I was about to leave when I realized I couldn't take a chance that Tiki would make off with her prize while I was phoning for help.

"Shoo!" I made a big gesture waving her away. Tiki narrowed her eyes and turned off the purr. "Scat! Bad cat! Go, you grave robbing beast!" I shouted at her. At last, Tiki stood up. She glared at me unblinking, clearly offended by my epithets, and hopped off the porch into the bushes to plot her revenge.

I turned and ran back into the nearby store.

Instead of going to the beach, lying in the sun, reading a romance on my phone, and enjoying my forced day off, I was still sitting on my porch over an hour later, guarding Tiki's gruesome bounty. I'd been watching the road for any response to my 911 call. I'd managed to sneak in and make the call on Opal's old-fashioned dial phone behind the counter while she was occupied in the front of the store. I didn't want the famous "coconut wireless" gossip train to get going if she overheard my discovery.

The coffee began its work on my bladder almost immediately. Finally, when I'd begun to get restless enough to consider running inside for a quick pee, a jacked up purple Toyota pickup pulled into the dirt parking lot. The lurid vehicle passed the locked post office and stopped in front of my cottage, a light on the dash spinning alternating blue, white and red.

I eyed the vehicle—from its chick silhouette mud flaps to the miniature feathered Hawaiian warrior helmet dangling from the rearview, the thing screamed "local boy." But there was nothing boyish about the large Hawaiian man who jumped down from the cab.

A woman got out of the passenger side, using the chrome step like a sensible human. She had curly hair scraped into a ball on top of her head, tilted brown eyes, level brows, and a nose dotted with freckles. A detective's badge clipped to her belt and a buff-colored cotton blazer semi-concealed the Glock she wore in a shoulder holster.

The driver of the truck switched off the light on the dash and shut his door. He was a good head taller than his female partner and probably double her weight, most of it muscle, though there was a bit of a dad bod forming around his waist. He had black hair in a buzz cut and Oakleys that hid his eyes. A dent formed in the brown flesh above his ears where the shades pressed. A bristle of mustache tried to hide a mouth that looked like it did a lot of smiling when he wasn't in cop mode. And right now, he was in cop mode.

I stood slowly, keeping my palms open and hands visible at my sides. "Hello. My name is Katherine Smith, and I'm the new postmaster for Ohia. You must be the homicide detectives I asked for when I called to report a dead body. Over an hour ago."

The two came forward, their attention already on Tiki's little gift displayed on my front stoop rock. The female detective looked up and met my eyes at last. "Sergeant Lei Texeira. This is my partner, Detective Pono Kaihale."

Wasn't that Hot Pilot's last name?

The male cop gave a serious head nod, his gaze still on the item in question. "Where did you find this?"

"The cat left it there, right where you see it."

Both of their heads shot up. The man who must be related to Mr. K the pilot laughed, a sudden boom. "Nice present."

"I'd have preferred a dead rat, thanks very much. Do you have a relative named Keone Kaihale who flies for Pacific Wings?"

The detective used a thick brown finger to push his Oakleys up onto his head, the better to look me over. "Did my cousin hit on you?"

"Possibly." Heat warmed the skin under my collar. "I try not to speculate too much about those kinds of things."

The detective opened his mouth to ask me more, but Sergeant Texeira held up a finger and shushed him. She'd taken out her phone, and she aimed it at the thing on the rock. "I'm going to take a few pictures of the—the item *in situ*."

"I'm guessing six months to a year since it was buried in an iron-rich soil somewhere nearby, indicated by the staining on the skin." I gestured to the discoloration. "The burial site was either protected from or outside the range of the frequent rain this area gets, since it is more desiccated than decayed. The small bone size makes me think the victim was female."

Both detectives straightened. I had their full attention.

"Who did you say you were again?" Texeira asked.

I shouldn't have shown off. I was supposed to be keeping a low profile! "Katherine Smith. Postmaster."

"Huh," Kaihale said skeptically, cocking his head.

I pointed to one side of the hand. "It's possible the cat—ahem—removed it from its owner, and the owner is somewhere nearby." Both cops bent to examine Tiki's offering once more, paying close attention to the area I was indicating.

Texeira took a few more photos, then lifted her chin toward her partner. I could see some invisible communication pass between them, and she strode back to the truck and opened the door, removing a crime kit.

Meanwhile, Kaihale reached in his back pocket and took out a crumpled notebook. "I've got a few questions for you, if you don't mind."

"Of course."

He began asking me the usual background stuff: name, date of birth, address, social security, yada yada. I knew they'd use that to run a background on me.

I watched Texeira out of the corner of my eye as she covered her hair with a ball cap and rolled on gloves beside the truck. She shook out a paper evidence bag and wrote on it with a Sharpie, then approached the item and picked it up gingerly with a pair of plastic tongs. She held it up for a moment, examining it from all directions before dropping it into the bag. She sealed the bag and put it back inside the truck, locking the doors. She then returned to the rock and produced a vial of fingerprint powder from the crime kit.

"How long have you been in Ohia?" Kaihale said, his voice a pleasant, almost hypnotic rumble.

"Arrived last night. That's when I met your—cousin, is it?"

"Cousin, yes. Is the cat yours?"

"Tiki? No. She's a stray who's apparently attached herself to the post office. Not the friendliest. She attacked me twice, and I haven't even been here twenty-four hours." I indicated the scratches at my temple, arm, and the puncture marks on my calf. "You don't want to piss her off with an interrogation about where she found the—the item. Trust me on this."

The two exchanged an eyeroll.

Texeira swirled dusting powder over the rock. Immediately a large cat's pawprint appeared beside the blot where her trophy had rested.

She grunted. "Looks like your story checks out. Did you go

looking for the body around the cottage?" Texeira's pretty brown eyes were narrowed at me. I had a feeling they didn't miss a thing.

"I resisted the temptation and sat here waiting for you to arrive like a good civilian." I indicated Kaihale's notebook. "When you run me, you'll see I'm Secret Service, not Postal Service. But I'm here on the down-low, so I'd appreciate if that didn't get out."

Neither Texeira nor Kaihale reacted to what should have been a bombshell—my disclosure about being with the Secret Service. I wasn't sure whether that confirmed to them that I was completely nuts with delusions of grandeur, or reassured them that they were dealing with someone with a law enforcement background.

"Interesting," Texeira said. "Not sure it's relevant." She made that gesture with her chin again, and Kaihale gave a slight nod. She moved off around the side of the house, clearly going to hunt for the body that might have yielded Tiki's discovery.

Kaihale held his pencil above the notebook. "So. What brings you to Ohia, Secret Service Agent Katherine Smith, here on the down-low?

"Kat. My friends call me Kat."

Kaihale had a way of conveying meaning with just a lift of his brow. His barely discernible wiggle said, *we'll see if we become friends.*

Honesty was necessary. These two would find out my background, anyway. I sucked in a deep breath and sighed. I told him the thumbnail version of what had gotten me assigned to the official back of beyond. "I would be behind the desk inside the post office right now if I had a key to the building. But the clerk who's been here for years called out sick, and she's apparently the only one with a key."

"Interesting." Kaihale made a note on his pad. "What's the name of that employee?"

"I've only heard her referred to as Auntie Pua."

"Oh, Auntie Pua Chang," Kaihale said. "A bit of a local legend. So is her family."

I shrugged, my hands open to convey my total lack of an agenda. "I've already been informed, in no uncertain terms, that I took the promotion she expected. Honestly, finding a piece of a corpse on my front doorstep is par for the course since my arrival here."

We were interrupted when another jacked pickup, practically a twin to the purple one already occupying the space in front of my house, pulled up in a splash of mud. This version was a more reasonable dark green color, but the replica war helmet dangling from the rearview was the same as his cousin's. Someone had probably given that same item to all the men in the Kaihale family for Christmas.

"Cuz!" Mr. K approached Detective Kaihale to engage in the ritual back-slap man-hug. "Whatchu doin' out heah?"

"Brah," Kaihale said. "I'm on a case."

"What case?" Mr. K's eyes widened, then narrowed, fixing on me where I sat on the porch. "What, she's in trouble already?"

"And what makes you think she'd be in trouble?" Kaihale was suddenly all cop once again.

Mr. K rolled his shoulders back, clearly regrouping. "I actually came out here to see if Kat wanted to go surfing, if she wasn't busy with work today. I thought I could show her a few moves." That darn dimple reappeared to punctuate his statement. I was saved from having to respond when he continued. "Kat saved our flight from a worse disaster than the blowout you heard about on the news. She's handy with a fire extinguisher, it turns out."

"I heard about that." Kaihale turned to me. "That was you? The passenger who hopped out of the tail of the plane and prevented a fire?"

I shrugged. Didn't see a point in explaining further.

"Something's happened and Ms. Smith here is going to be tied up with an investigation," Kaihale told his cousin. "Hate to say it, but you need to *hele* on."

This is the second time I've heard that phrase. "What does that mean?" I asked.

"Means we can't hang out, and I've got to get moving," Mr. K said. "Bummer." He turned to address his cousin. "But you guys can't go back around to the other side of the island without coming over to Mom's house for dinner. Bring your partner." He leveled a finger at me. "And bring Kat."

"What if I don't want to come?" I sounded as surly as a two-year-old who'd missed a nap. I didn't do relationships. And now, I was going to his house for dinner and to meet his mother. Before we even went surfing, no less.

Both men frowned at me. Kaihale turned back to his cousin. "Will do."

Mr. K addressed me over his cousin's shoulder. "We'll go surfing another time. See you at Mama's with Lei and Pono." The man hopped into his truck, backed up, and rolled away with the unbridled power of a big engine with a bad muffler.

Kaihale regarded me for a moment. I fought the urge to squirm. "You seem to have made an impression on my cousin. He likes you."

I shrugged. It was becoming my new habit. I didn't know how to put into words that I was feeling mighty put upon. I had not asked for any of this. I just came here and tried to do my job, and even that was a nonstarter.

"I found something." Texeira came around the side of the shack, her eyes bright with excitement. "Come see."

Kaihale turned to go, then remembered I was a person of interest and not one of them. He held up a hand.

"Stay here," Kaihale said. "And don't follow us."

Of course, I took that as an invitation.

# 6

Tracking and surveilling a suspect in a variety of settings is a skill I've always been particularly good at. Even with my height, I knew how to blend with my surroundings—appearing to be window shopping, getting a pedicure, or otherwise engaging in mysterious female activities that seemed to throw off suspicion. But following two trained detectives into an unknown jungle without being seen was a new challenge.

I waited a bit until the two had made it to the rear of the shack. Texeira spoke rapidly in a low voice, thwarting my ability to make out her words. I slipped out of my Nikes, tiptoeing after the pair in my stocking feet. I mentally pitched the socks into a trash bin post-adventure.

The detectives made no attempt to disguise their progress past my tiny cottage and into the depths of a seemingly solid wall of vegetation. Thick bushes and tall trees trailed vines worthy of a Tarzan movie—there was nothing but a real, honest-to-goodness jungle growing behind my dwelling. Once I made it past the overgrown brush, the gaps between the trees made keeping out of sight more difficult.

I made like a giraffe and flattened against a tree trunk, watching

Texeira and Kaihale examine something behind a large log lying on the jungle floor. The log was sheltered by an even bigger black volcanic boulder hanging over it.

"There was a natural overhang at the edge of this log that kept rain off the body," Texeira said, her voice now carrying clearly to me. "And the rock outcrop created a further shelter. The doer just rolled the body into the depression under the log and threw some dirt on top of it. Look here, where the hand is missing." The two squatted down behind the log. Dang, I wanted to see what they were seeing! I strained to hear.

"Female victim. See any ID?"

"There's her purse and what looks to be a suitcase down by her feet. Someone made it look like she took a trip, but this woman never left Ohia."

"Yeah, we haven't had any missing persons reports from this town or I would've seen them before coming out here. The place is so small."

"Got her wallet. And her phone. Name's Frances Borland. Her address is here in Ohia—a post office box. I've never heard of her."

"She wasn't reported missing, which is definitely odd. And I don't see any obvious cause of death. Hopefully her body will tell Dr. Gregory something more when he comes to do the post."

"Got any signal?"

Texeira popped up from behind the log like a jack-in-the-box, holding her phone up in the air. "Nope."

"Ok. I'll go call the ME's office from the general store," Kaihale said. "Even the radios barely work out here."

That was my cue to skedaddle.

And skedaddle I did. I tiptoed back on soggy socks, picking leaves out of my hair as I went. Quickly pulling on my Nikes, I arranged myself just as I'd been and exhaled, controlling my breathing. Nothin' to see here, folks. Just a civilian sitting on her front stoop rock, waiting to be summoned for questioning.

When Kaihale appeared, I waved at him. "Can I go inside and wait for you in my cottage?"

"Just don't go anywhere. I'll be back to talk to you soon."

"Like there's anywhere to go," I muttered.

He booked it toward the general store. Busybody Opal was going to be agog about the body. I bet she knew who Frances Borland was.

A chill tickled up my spine like a wet feather. I suddenly felt homesick for Washington, D.C., a town filled with worse sharks than patrolled the waters of Ohia Bay.

Or so I'd thought until now. I stared out across the street at the beach. It looked like it was going to be a long time before I was able to get into that beautiful aqua water.

What a day it had been—things had to get better from here. Didn't they?

Once inside, I peeled off the soggy socks and tossed them in the trash. After replacing them with a fresh pair, I swung the door of the cottage wide to make myself available to the detectives, but also to better hear what was going on outside.

I opened the half-size refrigerator. Thankfully, it had been plugged in and left on. There was only a little bit of mold growing in the rubber edging around the door. I put away the groceries I'd bought at Opal's and turned to face the stove. Another apartment-size appliance, the little gas number hadn't fared as well as the fridge in the rustic environment. *Ew.* Rust, mold, and droppings from some kind of critter arrayed the surface.

I pulled on a fresh pair of rubber gloves from my grocery run, unwrapped a virgin scrub pad, wetted it with dish soap, and went to work taking out the metal burners and scrubbing down the entire thing. I kept one ear cocked toward the door. Sure enough, it wasn't long before I heard the arrival of several more law enforcement vehicles.

They didn't have the sirens on. There was no emergency here—the body had been dead for months. But I was "nosier than a coonhound" as my Aunt Fae used to say, so I went to the door to see who'd joined the murder after-party.

The ME's van had pulled up along with a blue and white Maui Police Department cruiser. The uniforms were already out of their vehicle, dickering with crime scene tape and the sign-in log. The ME team climbed out and opened the side of the van, producing white hazmat suits from inside and beginning to don them right there in the parking lot.

Sergeant Texeira reappeared from the jungle and directed the uniforms back to the crime scene with the tape. Kaihale, his notebook still in hand, arrived from the store. He'd probably been getting Opal's statement.

The male medical examiner appeared to be having trouble fitting into the zip-up white coverall. A lurid aloha shirt decorated with parrots covered a soft paunch that was getting in the way. The female medical examiner tucked his belly in and drew the zipper up to his chin, a distinctly coupley gesture. "There you go, hon. I told you we need to cut back on the malasadas."

"We all need to cut back on the malasadas, Dr. Gregory," Kaihale said, patting his midsection. "Except you, with your nonstop metabolism, Dr. Tanaka."

I made a mental note to look up malasadas and get myself some.

Texeira spotted me lurking in the doorway. The dripping scouring pad still in my hand, I immediately began scrubbing the jamb as if that's why I was standing there. She gave a little head jerk to Kaihale and the two approached. "Is there any reason we can't search your dwelling?" she asked bluntly.

I straightened up to my full height and looked down my long nose at her. "There are several other ways you could ask to search my current habitation that are less confrontational."

Kaihale smiled, waving his hands in a "calm down" kinda way. "No offense, Ms. Smith. May we search your cottage?"

I stepped inside and made a grand welcoming gesture, complete with a half bow. "Please, come in. Welcome to my current abode.

I've been here approximately twelve hours. You will find a gun in one of the bottom drawers in the closet. Service issue standard Glock 19, loaded with one in the chamber, and a separate fully loaded ammo clip. You will also note a missing round from the loaded magazine, and a hole in the wall above the bed. I was alarmed by the attack cat that lives here and accidentally fired off a round into the wall."

Texeira's flinty brown eyes narrowed at me, but I plowed on. "I have a concealed carry permit. I'll show it to you once you have secured the weapon." I pointed to the bottom drawer where I'd stashed it earlier this morning. "But after I almost shot the cat's head off, I decided this town was probably safe and I wasn't going to need it. Clearly, I was wrong about that last part. Feel free to take it in and check it against any ballistics you find. I guarantee they aren't a match to whatever did the victim in."

Texeira removed an evidence bag from her back pocket and picked up my Glock, dropping it in without comment. She clearly thought I was a person of interest.

Kaihale cleared his throat and shifted from foot to foot. "Do you mind waiting outside, Ms. Smith?"

I blew out a breath. "Okay if I go to the beach? That was my plan for the day until Tiki brought me the gift that keeps on giving."

"Stay within visual range," Texeira said. She was clearly the "bad cop" of the two.

"You got it," I said with fake cheer, and stripped off the rubber gloves I'd been cleaning with, tossing them into the sink. "Feel free to help clean this place while you're at it. I inherited a lot of strange insect droppings."

"Geckos," Kaihale said, pulling a flashlight out of his pocket and running the light beam over the top of the stove, still decorated with little black nuggets.

"What?"

"Hawaiian geckos. Little lizards. They can be a pest when they get in the house, dropping poop everywhere, but they keep down the mosquitos. If you hear a chirping sound, it's them."

"So, in addition to an attack cat, this place comes with a brigade of interior house lizards. Nice." I stepped into the tiny bathroom. I shut the door and stripped down, changing into my bikini and trying to ignore the sounds of two detectives rifling through my meager possessions and sad living quarters. I had no towel, but I'd brought a terry cloth robe with me. I shrugged it on before stepping out of the bathroom. "Give a holler if you need me."

I walked past the two cops searching my place with all the dignity I could muster, snagging my backpack off the wall as I walked out the door of the shack.

That's what I'd call it from now on. Forget euphemisms like "*'ohana*" and "cottage." The place was A Shack with a Coconut Tree Growing Out of the Gutter and a Rock for a Stoop, with an attack cat that lurked under the table and geckos that pooped on the appliances. I was done sugarcoating my living situation.

A cop stood guarding the tape that stretched from the corner of the shack into the jungle. My presence garnered stares from both him and the gaggle of locals who'd arrived at the general store and were gossiping on the porch with Opal.

I crossed the street, glad I had a robe on as several sets of eyes followed me. "This place is the biggest fishbowl I've swum in since the Inaugural Ball in D.C.," I muttered.

Once at the beach, I found a tree shaped like an umbrella and positioned myself beneath it. It was shelter from the village rubber-neckers but still within line of sight of the shack should the grouchy detectives need to verify my whereabouts.

I took off the robe and spread it on the sand in lieu of a towel, then dug into my backpack and produced my new tube of sunscreen. I generously slathered it on my face, chest, shoulders, and arms. The rest of me, I'd crisp like bacon. I liked that look.

I settled back on my elbows and stared out at the restless ocean, turning my situation over in my mind. Things could be worse. I could be arrested right now, for no other reason than being a resented *malihini* in a tiny town that disliked outsiders. Texeira and Kaihale seemed competent, but I had no doubt they'd be facing pressure to nail the killer, and I was a random newcomer with a slightly shady story. The perfect fall guy.

Who could I call who might be able to vouch for me?

Sophie Smithson, the Ambassador's daughter, knew people. An amazing tech whiz and the CEO of a private investigation firm, she'd mentioned having friends in law enforcement on Maui. It couldn't hurt to give her a call and see if I could get her to vouch for me.

I took my phone out and held it up. Miracle of miracles, three bars appeared. Hallelujah! Maybe the ocean was the signal amplifier I needed. Good to know.

I pressed Sophie's speed dial and held the phone to my ear, closing my eyes and praying she'd pick up.

"Kat?" Sophie's familiar husky voice and British accent made me smile. "What gives me the pleasure of a call from you?"

"Sophie. Thank goodness. Who do you know in the Maui Police Department?" I didn't have time for pleasantries. "I might be in some trouble."

"What's going on? I'll get to my keyboard." Sophie's favorite place was behind her trio of screens, and I'd seen her pull off some amazing discoveries from that cockpit.

I blew out a breath, wondering where to start. I darted a glance over at the scene across the street. Texeira and Kaihale were standing outside my shack, discussing something. The hairs rose on the back of my neck. "I've had a change in circumstances since I saw you last. I'm in the little town of Ohia, on Maui. I'm the new postmaster—today's my first day on the job, actually. But then the cat dragged in a body. Or a piece of it, I should say."

"Great welcome! Ugh. Finding a murder can be very disrupting."

"No kidding. I mean, catting."

"Ha!" Sophie said. "You were making a joke." Sophie was very literal, but she was getting better at noticing my quips.

"Indeed. I do that when I'm nervous."

"Why would you be nervous?"

"The detectives are treating me . . . as a person of interest."

"Things must have really changed for you. The last time I saw you was at my dad's bedside in Honolulu when he was stabbed. You were still with the Secret Service."

"Yes. Well, since he retired, I was reassigned to another protectee. My new posting didn't go so well." I brought her up to speed on current, disheartening events. "Now these two detectives, Sergeant Texeira and Pono Kaihale, are searching my shack for evidence related to the body they found in the jungle behind it."

"Lei and Pono?" Sophie's voice went alert. "They're good friends of mine. What could they be looking for in your place?"

"I don't know, but Texeira was pretty hostile. Told me to stay in sight, and not to go anywhere."

"I'll call her." Sophie clicked off.

I slowly lowered the phone, still watching the two detectives as they hunched over something on my stoop rock. Texeira's phone rang on her belt. I watched her take the call, then look across the narrow road at me.

I glanced away quickly—it was time to go for a swim. I was overdue for washing the stress off my body and cooling down in that beautiful blue water. Hopefully, by the time I got out, the detectives would have had a change of heart toward me. Sometimes in life it wasn't what you knew but WHO you knew that made things easier, and I wasn't too proud to lean on the friends I still had.

The difference in the detectives' attitudes when they approached me was startling. Texeira was actually smiling, and Kaihale had unloaded his investigation gear and pulled on a pair of swim trunks at his purple truck.

"What happens in Ohia, stays in Ohia," he admonished his

partner just as they reached me. He tugged his loose aloha shirt off over his head, tossed it on the sand beside my "towel," ran down the slope of the beach, and cannonballed into the surf with a yell.

I had just come up from swimming and could vouch for the refreshing feeling of the water. It seemed to cleanse my soul-deep discouragement. "I like that. What happens in Ohia, stays in Ohia."

"Sometimes you just need to jump into the water and wash it all away. The ocean helps Pono cope. Did you know his last name means House of the Ocean?" Texeira sat on the sand beside me. I rested on my elbows, drying off. She too had a dimple when she smiled. "Sophie speaks highly of you. Says you've been a part of her family for years."

"I have been. The Smithsons are good people."

"Sorry if I was a little—"

"Rude. You were rude, Sergeant Texeira."

"Yeah, I was. 'Bad cop' gets to be a habit." Texeira extended a hand. "Call me Lei."

We shook. "Kat."

She looped her arms around her raised knees.

We watched Pono frolic in the surf like an overgrown puppy. The sight was the antithesis of the sad discovery we'd made. That would have to be addressed sooner rather than later.

Lei seemed to read my mind. "The victim was the postmaster before you," she said. "Her name was Frances Borland."

My stomach tightened involuntarily. Lei glanced at my midriff—the bikini didn't hide much. "You have a four-pack, Kat. Do you work out?"

"I don't use weights, but I do sit-ups when I'm stressed. Push-ups too. I swim and jog."

"I like to run. Pono body-surfs." As she spoke, Kaihale slid down the face of a jumbled wave, one arm extended as he made his body into a human surfboard. "Keone, his cousin, likes to surf too. He's a good guy. You could do worse."

"I'm not into relationships." The last thing I needed right now was to deal with a dude. I'd just learned that my predecessor had been murdered, and I had no idea how long I'd last in Ohia myself. "I'm guessing whoever killed Frances Borland made it look like she left voluntarily. Keone told me she made like a banana and split."

"Yes. There was a suitcase in the dump site with her. The killer must have disposed of her car somehow." Lei had taken an object made from pale bone or ivory out of her pocket, turning and smoothing it with her thumb. It was shaped like a crude fishhook. "Rough that this has landed on your doorstep, but better to know right away, yes?"

I suppressed a shudder at the thought of the body in the jungle, so nearby. "I guess."

Pono came up from the ocean and toweled off with his shirt. "Back to work," he said, sitting down on the other side of me. "Did you give Kat the bad news about the previous postmaster?"

"Yep."

"I've got concerns about this famous Auntie Pua Chang," I said. "She called in sick today, I think to send me a message that I wasn't welcome." I filled the two detectives in on what I'd been through with Opal and the missing key. "I'm not looking forward to meeting her at this point. But I have to put as good a face on it as I can."

"Is Auntie Pua one of the Big Island Changs?" Pono narrowed his eyes in a glance at Lei.

"Probably. I'll put out some feelers on that." Lei took out her phone and began texting. "This seems to be the only spot with any phone reception, even for text messages."

"Let's go out and meet her. Find out what she knows about Frances Borland," Pono said.

"That seems like the next logical step." Lei agreed.

"Can I come along?" I asked. "Just to meet her and get the key. I was supposed to open the post office today. Opal wouldn't give me any contact info for her."

Lei slanted me a sympathetic glance. "This is the kind of place where you need to prove yourself first to be accepted."

"So I've heard." I was sick of hearing that.

"I guess we can take you out with us, but we have to interview her privately," Lei said. "You can get the key and then wait in the truck. His name is Stanley, by the way."

"Who?"

"The truck. His name is Stanley."

That surprised a smile out of me. I glanced over my shoulder at Pono's jacked purple pickup. "That ought to be entertaining."

Lei rolled her eyes. "You have no idea. A ride in Stanley is an experience to be remembered."

"Hey," Pono grumbled. "We could be driving one of those cruisers, and those sedans don't like the roads around here at all." He shrugged into his damp, wrinkled shirt. "Might as well check in with the medical examiners, and then get on the road to Auntie Pua's."

My heart did an odd little flip-flop—I was finally going to meet the woman who'd made my arrival so difficult. Would arriving in the company of a couple of cops improve our relationship, or be the death of it?

I suspected the latter.

In a manner of speaking, of course.

# ⁂ 7 ⁂

I stood back unobtrusively, observing the scene with both ears cocked "like a bat," as Aunt Fae used to say.

With the help of two uniformed officers, Dr. Gregory and Dr. Tanaka lugged the zipped-up black body bag out of the trees. The four of them hefted it onto a gurney waiting for them at the edge of the jungle. With some difficulty, they trundled the gurney over the rough, weedy ground to the van, sliding it into place and strapping it down.

Lei and Pono were including me now. They seemed to have concluded that having me on the team would extend their eyes and ears. Whatever the reason, I'd take it. I wanted to find out what happened to Frances Borland as much as they did. Maybe more, since Tiki had brought me her "treasure."

"The body tell you anything right offhand?" Lei asked Dr. Tanaka. "From your visual examination?"

"Not much." The petite Japanese woman was rosy with heat. She pushed the white head covering off and blew out a breath, lifting the hair damp with sweat off her forehead. "No obvious cause of death."

"Could it be natural causes?"

"We'll know more after the post," Dr. Gregory said. Once more, his tummy interfered with the hazmat suit's zipper. Dr. Tanaka fiddled with it until it moved past the tight spot. He sighed gratefully, shedding the garment, and stepping out of it. "Whatever her cause of death—and I hope we can find it given the state of the body—someone wanted people to believe Frances Borland left Ohia voluntarily."

"We got that impression from the scene, too," Pono said. "We'll focus on the why, if you focus on the how."

"I'm looking forward to being back in the air conditioning before digging into that," Dr. Tanaka said. "Literally." The medical examiners hopped into the van and slammed the doors, waving a cheerful goodbye as they drove off.

Lei and Pono turned to me. "Do you still want to go out to Auntie Pua's with us?" Pono asked.

"I do." I nodded toward the general store, where a group of onlookers sipped sodas and beers, watching us like a sports game. "Did you get all the statements you need from the looky-loos?"

The two glanced at each other, then at the locals on the porch. "Might as well deal with them," Pono told Lei. "We'll go do a canvass and then visit Auntie Pua."

"I'm sure everyone knew the victim's identity seconds after you made the call on Opal's store phone," I said. "I tried to keep the discovery under wraps when I made my call by waiting for her to be out of hearing range."

Pono grinned. It reminded me of his cousin's smile. "You think I let the victim's identity slip to Ohia's best coconut wireless operator? Heck no. I sent Opal to the back room before I called it in."

Relief relaxed my shoulders. I shook my head. "I'm sorry. I'm a control freak, and this is your investigation. I'm just the poor sap whose cat dragged in a piece of the body."

"According to my friend Sophie—and she knows a thing or three —you're a lot more than that," Lei said. "Listen, we have to check in with our commanding officer and take these statements. And I bet you could use a rinse after your swim. We'll be back to pick you up and go see Auntie Pua when we're done."

"Perfect. Thanks." I stared after the detectives as they walked purposefully toward the store. Immediately, the onlookers began to disperse toward their cars.

"Hold up," Pono boomed. Everyone froze. He continued toward the porch, advising them that they all needed to wait and give statements. Lei cut toward the cluster of cars in the lot, whipping out her phone and photographing license plates in case anyone tried to make a getaway.

Everyone wanted to know what was going on, but no one wanted to get involved with a murder investigation. Wasn't that always the way? Human nature in a nutshell.

I had to pause just inside the door of my shack to let my eyes adjust to the dim light after being out in the sunshine. It turns out that brief halt saved my bare legs from an encounter with Tiki's revenge. The cat, parked in the doorway like she owned the place, backed away from me with a hiss. She took up her favorite spot under the table to sulk.

"How did you get in here?" I asked her again. Tiki slitted her single yellow eye in response, her body hunched to spring and her tail lashing. "Never mind. You have no plans to tell me. I get it."

Moving slow, I stepped fully inside and shut the door. "Remember I told you I brought food?" Keeping a wary eye on the attack cat, I sidled into the kitchen area and found the bag of Purina where I'd left it on the counter. I pulled the string on the corner and opened the bag. Tiki emitted a noise that sounded like the turning of a rusty windmill as the smell of cat chow filled the room.

"You're hungry. I know." I dumped some food into a battered plastic bowl I found in the bare cupboards, then set it on the floor a safe distance from her makeshift cave. I filled a second bowl with water and set that down, too. "Since I don't know how you keep getting in here and can't keep you out, we might as well be friends."

Tiki growled.

"I'll give you some privacy and go take a shower. I hope you're done eating and gone when I get back. If not, we'll need to talk about getting you to a vet."

Tiki didn't reply, but I had the feeling she understood me perfectly. Sure enough, when I came out wrapped in my multipurpose terry cloth robe, Tiki had vanished, and so had the food.

Riding in Stanley was indeed an experience, if an uncomfortable one. The purple truck may have looked huge from the outside, but once I crammed all six feet of me into the compact seat behind the detectives, it seemed a lot less impressive. Pono clearly loved his over-the-top truck, and I found the shiny chrome skull topping the gearshift to be a classy touch.

In my narrow space, a soccer ball took up half the footwell on one side, and a bag of kids' gear, including shin guards and shoes, the other. I turned sideways, my long legs pulled up and my gaze drawn repeatedly to Pono's replica Hawaiian war helmet swinging from the rearview mirror.

It took an hour for Lei and Pono to take everyone's statements and come back to the shack to get me. They were both silent upon their return, their closed expressions giving me no clue as to what they had learned—except maybe that this wasn't likely to be an easy investigation. How could it be? The victim had been dead for at least six months, and it appeared that no one had missed her.

Who was Frances Borland?

Where was her family?

Why hadn't her loved ones come to look for her?

These questions gave me an uncomfortable pang as I realized the previous postmaster's situation was distressingly similar to my own. My parents died when I was 9, killed in a car crash that had landed me as Aunt Fae's ward. Aunt Fae and I remained close, but she wouldn't miss me until Christmas—we had a standing date to spend the holidays together in Maine.

In all my peripatetic wandering of the globe with the Secret Service, I'd always tried to return "home" to her annually for the holidays. "I need to know I can count on seeing you at least once a year," Aunt Fae had declared, and I'd done my best to honor that. She deserved it, too. She'd given up a lot to take the sad, traumatized, baby giraffe of a girl I was and raise me with so much love.

I'd grown into a competent woman who lived for her job as a Secret Service agent, and sacrificed everything for it. I had no siblings and no boyfriend. The only person who might check in on me occasionally was my boss in D.C., and after placing me in Ohia, he wouldn't expect to hear from me for anytime soon either. The sad truth was, I too could disappear off the face of the earth and no one would come looking for me.

"Wallowing is for cowards," Aunt Fae used to say when my grief got the better of me. "Walk it off, run it off, shoot it off." She took me moose hunting in the Maine woods when I got tearful. I'd learned that firing a gun and sweating out in nature was great therapy. Her bootstrap brand of encouragement was what pushed me into a career that challenged me to protect others.

I shifted in my tiny seat and rolled my shoulders back. "Anything you'd like to share about the interviews?" I asked. Pono navigated Stanley away from the booming metropolis of Ohia, population 750, according to a sign we just passed.

"Can't discuss it with you." Lei's tone wasn't brusque exactly, but definite. "I will say this much—we've checked in with our captain about the case, and she's assigned another set of detectives in Kahului to run down background on the victim. We're curious why no one has missed this woman."

"Captain Omura doesn't want you in the loop," Pono admitted, glancing at me over his bulky shoulder. A tattoo wrapped around his big bicep; the series of interlocking triangles marred by the jagged track of a bullet scar. I had seen enough of those to recognize one when I saw it.

"I could help you out here in Ohia. I'm sure the post office is as big a clearinghouse of information as the general store," I protested.

"You're going to have your hands full learning your new job," Lei said. She couldn't make eye contact from her angle in the front passenger seat. "This murder must be a little close to home for you, considering that the vic was occupying the cottage and postmaster role before you."

"Yeah. It's a little spooky." A lot spooky, to be honest. I planned to get a stout lock for the shack's door and figure out a freakin' way to close the windows. I also planned to keep my Glock primed for action once I got it back.

We drove on silently. I occupied myself with staring out the window at the variegated landscape we were passing through. The heavy jungle, with its dangling vines and lush ferns, seemed to hit a change in climate zone. The heavy vegetation dwindled off to shrubby bushes, then changed to windswept grass and open space studded with large volcanic boulders.

"Quite a change in the scenery," I commented.

"Yeah. The rain doesn't wrap around the coast this far," Pono said. "Good fishing this side of the island. Good hunting out here, too."

Hunting for what? Clues? The landscape was open grassland, steep gullies, and washes—not at all the lush Hawaii I was used to.

The GPS on the dash squawked out directions and Pono hung a right, heading up a single-lane, graveled road that followed the track of a dry streambed through a steep canyon. The walls of the canyon were the red, oxide-rich soil I was becoming used to, sprinkled with more of the volcanic stone common to the area. I spotted movement at the top of the ridge and gasped, pointing. "Is that a mountain goat?"

Pono slowed, rolling his window down and craning his neck to look out. “Nope. Just regular wild goats. Told you there was good hunting out here.”

“And what are those?” I pointed to a small, spotted, reddish deer standing near the cluster of shaggy wild goats.

“Axis deer,” Lei said. “Pretty, aren't they? Native to India and Nepal, they were first introduced in 1867 as a gift to King Kamehameha V and released for sport hunting on Molokai in 1868. Over time, they spread to the other islands like the Hawaiians’ goats, pigs and chickens did. These non-native species compete for resources with the few endemic species here—mostly birds—and do a number on their habitat. But that’s a topic for another day.”

I wanted to ask more, but we had arrived.

A wooden gate supporting a large NO TRESPASSING sign barred the driveway. A small, hand-lettered notice directed delivery drivers to ring a button hung beneath a metal shield on a plinth.

Pono rolled up to the structure and rang the button. A few minutes later, the gate grumbled inward, swaying on its long arm. We drove forward to a cluster of buildings surrounding a pleasant looking plantation house encircled by a wide, covered porch. The house was dark green with white trim. A flowerbed of cosmos and marigolds, bordered by silvery driftwood logs, bordered the porch.

A petite woman came to the door as we pulled up. Pua Chang was younger than I thought she would be. Even at home on a sick day, her perfect face was made up and her long black hair hung in an unbroken sheet to her hips. She wore what I'd expect to see on a country club matron: a neat madras button-down and a pair of black capri pants. A small, fluffy white dog bounced through the open screen door and barked at us from beside her.

“Hush, Sassy,” she said.

As I climbed out of the truck's narrow side door, our eyes met. A flash of awareness and recognition showed in her expression. But how could she know who I was? I brushed the thought aside—the coconut wireless was always crackling in Ohia. Someone probably called her to let her know that two cops and the new postmaster were headed out to pay her a visit.

Lei and Pono approached, flipping open their credentials. "Maui Police Department," Lei said in that no-nonsense tone she reserved for official business. "May we come in?"

Pua Chang still had not broken eye contact. She raised a finger to point at me. "Who is she?"

I stepped forward with a confidence I didn't feel, reminding myself that I towered over her in every possible way. She should not intimidate me. I would not let her.

"My name is Katherine Smith. I was appointed the new postmaster. I caught a ride with the detectives so I could meet you." I extended a hand to her.

She waved her fingers limply, refusing to shake, and covered her mouth with a hand. She emitted a patently fake, delicate cough. "Germs. I'm not feeling well."

"Of course. I'm sorry you're under the weather. I was looking forward to meeting you this morning, but Opal told me you were sick." I stuck my hand in my pocket to hide my embarrassment. "The detectives were kind enough to let me come along to meet you in person and tell you how much I look forward to working with you." I smiled. My cheeks protested, feeling stiff and reluctant. "I'd like to open the post office today so people can get their mail. May I borrow your key?"

"Afraid that's impossible. Each key is issued directly to an individual. You will have to contact the main Kahului Post Office for yours." Her dark brown eyes were hard. "I may not be well tomorrow, either." She gave another pathetic cough.

Lei's and Pono's heads whipped back-and-forth as they watched our exchange. Pono took pity on me and stepped forward. "Perhaps you can wait in the car, Ms. Smith," he said. "I'm sure you and Ms. Chang will have plenty of time to get to know each other when she's feeling better."

I gave the woman a single nod of acknowledgment. "I look forward to seeing you tomorrow at work, Ms. Chang."

She said nothing. As I walked back to the shelter of Stanley, I felt her stare between my shoulder blades like a wasp poised to sting. She waited until I'd opened the door and settled myself into my tiny seat to open her screen door for the detectives to enter. I watched as the trio disappeared inside.

The small white dog, too fluffy to be a poodle and too bad-tempered to be anything but evil, waddled down from the porch to yap fiercely at me until I closed the truck door. I reached forward and rolled down the manual crank window for some air circulation.

"Hey, Sassy," I said in a friendly voice. "Tell your mama I'm a friend." The dog yapped once more, then lifted a leg to decorate Stanley's tire before trotting away with his tail aloft like a victory flag.

In the opening skirmish of Kat vs. Auntie Pua Chang, I'd been trounced.

# ☙ 8 ❧

The retreat from Auntie Pua afforded me a quiet moment of privacy to lick my wounds. I took out my phone, hoping for a signal to call the Kahului main office. Of course, there wasn't a single bar to be had. Maybe I could talk the detectives into taking me into town after they interviewed Ms. Chang.

That woman was never going to be "Auntie Pua" to me.

Fortunately, the detectives didn't take long. Less fortunately, their stony faces suggested Ms. Chang had not been very informative. They both got into the truck and shut the doors with a frustrated slam.

I waited until we were back on the road to speak. "Can I catch a ride into Kahului with you? I need to go to the main office and see about getting my own key. It sounds like Ms. Chang may call in sick again tomorrow."

"I was going to suggest that" Lei said. "Though, I don't know how you're going to get back out here."

"I was thinking a taxi? They have taxis in Kahului, right?"

Lei turned and raised an eyebrow at me. "You're kidding me, right? A taxi to Ohia would cost more than you make in a month.

That is, if you could even get someone to bring you out here." She settled back into her seat. "You'll see."

I did see.

The one-lane road was unpaved and so rough that my head hit the top of the cab several times. I wedged myself between a couple of soccer balls to keep from getting bruised. We navigated multiple hairpin turns with signs advising "Blind Curve, Honking Advised," which Pono never did, not once. Stanley the Purple Truck was way too cool to honk going around a curve. He did, however, have to swerve several times as cars came from the other direction. Angry honks sure happened then.

But who was I to criticize? I was getting a free ride around the famous backside of Maui!

Even if I had to grit my teeth to keep my fillings from rattling out, the trip was a beautiful sight—wide-open slopes of windblown grass and the sight of humpback whales blowing and breaching off the rugged black lava coastline. Seabirds seemed to twirl by in the strong wind like white confetti, and cattle dotted the arid hills.

It was starkly beautiful and reminded me of South Africa, not Hawaii. We passed a strange, orange toned, smooth-barked tree with a bulbous trunk and very few leaves.

"What the heck is that?" I pointed.

"A rare native *wiliwili* tree," Pono said. "Has lightweight wood like balsa."

"Kind of reminds me of a baobab tree from Africa," I said. "And those tall, thorny scrub trees along the road—I keep expecting to see an elephant nibbling their feathery tops while a lion stalks from the long dry grass. This isn't like the Hawaii of the brochures, is it?"

"Nope," Lei replied. "The height of the volcano traps passing clouds and rain on the eastern sides of the island, so the western sides are always drier. You'll see a variation of that weather pattern on every island, but Haleakala on Maui is over ten thousand feet tall, so things are exaggerated here—the rain seldom makes it to this side of the island."

We eventually circled a cinder cone and wove through more undulations—thankfully paved now—and then came upon a cute ranch with a winery and a general store. "Wish we could stop for an ice cream," Lei said longingly.

"We still on 'what happens in Ohia, stays in Ohia'?" Pono grinned at her.

"We could flash Frances's photo in the store. See if anyone remembers her," Lei said.

"Two birds, one stone." Pono cranked the wheel, and parked Stanley beside the Ulupalakua Ranch Store. The historic-looking, wooden establishment sported alarmingly realistic, carved wood cowboys on the porch and advertised bison burgers on a sign above the door.

"I'm starved," I told the detectives. "Do you mind if we take a little longer to grab a burger?"

The three of us ended up eating thick, juicy bison burgers at an outside table, followed up with cans of POG, an overly sweet concoction of passion fruit-orange-guava juice. Lei and Pono bought several mochi ice cream balls for dessert, insisting I eat one too. The thing was dreamy, creamy, and only big enough for two bites.

After our epic meal, Lei chatted up the woman behind the counter and showed her Frances Borland's driver's license photo. "Do you know this woman?"

"Oh yeah. That's Fran, the former postmaster at Ohia." The cashier had skin the color of teak and thin, cottony-white hair. She scowled through thick specs as she counted change in the old-fashioned register. "Haven't seen Fran in ages. Thought she finally took her skinny butt back to the mainland where she belonged."

"Did she stop in here often?"

"She liked the alcohol section." The cashier pointed to an array of wines, including Ulupalakua Ranch's own "MauiWine" label. "Didn't eat much, but she liked to drink, that's for sure."

Pono leaned on the counter. "Sounds like she was a regular."

"A regular boozer. Real piece of work. She'd sit out on that rock in front of her shack and sing. We thought a coyote had moved into Ohia!" She snorted a laugh. "Fran was nothing like Auntie Pua. Now that lady knows how to run a post office." The cashier nodded sagely.

My bison burger had turned into an indigestible ball of lard in my stomach. I belched behind my fist as I lurked by a rack of carved turtle key chains. "Excuse me."

The cashier glared at me for my rude interruption, then continued. "We were all glad when Fran got the hint she wasn't wanted and took off. Between Auntie Pua and Opal, things run smooth as clockwork in Ohia—until those mainland *haoles* arrive to take over the new development. None of us are looking forward to that day."

"So, you live in Ohia?" Lei asked. "Can I get your name and address?"

"Liholani Maka. I live behind the general store, three blocks up from the main road. I'm the one with the big mango tree. Plumeria Place." She rattled off a phone number.

Lei jotted the older woman's info into her spiral notebook as I took a mental note. "Thanks, Ms. Maka. We might be in touch for a follow-up."

"What's this about, anyway?" For the first time, the garrulous lady peered through her glasses at Lei and Pono. She leaned forward and whisper-shouted. "And who's that really tall *haole* girl with you? She a basketball player?"

I steeled myself and turned away from the fascinating array of Hawaiiana tchotchkes. I put on my best smile and advanced. "Hi. I'm Kat Smith, the new postmaster at Ohia. Looking forward to delivering your mail to you." It was a treat to see Ms. Maka at a total loss for words, though I was sure I'd feel the backlash of her embarrassment sometime soon.

After the bison burgers, introduction to mochi ice cream, and the interview of Ms. Maka at the Ulupalakua store, the rest of the drive to Kahului was downright anticlimactic. The detectives filled the time brainstorming ideas about what could've happened to the victim.

"She didn't have any clear physical trauma on her body. What if she just passed out drinking one day and died of a heart attack?" Lei suggested. "She was approaching sixty. That's in the heart attack range, especially for an alcoholic."

"But why hide her body and her stuff?" Pono countered. "Why pretend she left of her own accord?"

"That's the question of the day," Lei said. "We need to know more about the victim—her life before Ohia, her relatives. What's in her will."

"She couldn't have had much. She put up with living in that shack," Pono said. He flicked a glance at me in his rearview mirror. "No offense, Kat."

"None taken."

They continued to bandy theories back-and-forth, but I stayed silent. While I felt my input would have been welcome, I had no ideas about what could have happened to the victim. It was evident that Frances Borland had not been liked in Ohia, and the thing that bothered me most was that I was being primed by Pua Chang to follow in her footsteps.

Pono waved a hand in front of my unseeing gaze. "We can drop you off at the Kahului Post Office. It's on the way to our station. But you'll have a problem getting back out to Ohia. I could call my cousin and see if he'd like to give you a ride? We're obviously not going to be able to make it back to my auntie's house in Hana for dinner tonight."

"That's silly. Mr. K won't want to drive two hours out here to provide me a taxi service, and then drive all the way back," I argued.

"Mr. K?" Lei smiled.

My cheeks heated up. "I couldn't remember his name at first, just remembered the K's. Now that's how I think of him."

"Sounds like a porn star," Lei chuckled.

My cheeks were burning. Now that she mentioned it, it sounded naughty to me, too.

Pono laughed. “Keone will love that nickname. As to whether he wants to come out and give you a ride . . .” Pono shrugged, and his muscles rippled. “He's a big boy. He can decide for himself. All I know is that he complains about getting bored out there when he's not working, especially when there's no surf. Says he never has a reason to come back into Kahului between flights, and when he is in town, he doesn’t have his wheels because he’s just done a flight from Hana. Maybe he has errands here and could use the trip. It can't hurt to ask.”

I shook my head in protest, but Pono hit the side button on his phone and told the phone to call “Cuz KK.”

“Hey Cuz!” Keone’s upbeat voice blared clearly through the speaker. “Auntie's firing up the imu. We’re hoping you two want to spend the night out here.”

“You’re on speaker, Keone. Sorry, but Lei and I had to go back to Kahului to work on our case. We brought Kat out here with us. She has some business at the main post office to take care of, but she doesn’t have a ride back to Ohia. Any chance you want to come out to Kahului and get her?”

A short silence.

I covered my hot face with my hands in embarrassment. It was so much to ask and I barely knew the guy.

“Kat, you there?” His voice was softer, gentler.

“Yes, I'm here,” I said through my fingers.

“Want me to come to get you? It’s no problem. I need to grab some things in Kahului anyway, and I never get a chance when I'm flying.” I didn't reply, but he went on quickly. “Mom was really counting on some folks to eat her cooking tonight. You won't be sorry if you come eat dinner with us. I'll run you back out to your place after.”

Both Lei and Pono turned in their seats to glance at me expectantly. Pono lifted that eyebrow of his, giving me a thumbs-up. Lei grinned, showing off her dimple.

The truth was I hated asking for help, and I'd had to keep doing that since I hit this island. I forced myself to lower my hands. “It’s too much. I’m so embarrassed . . .”

“It's no prob, really. I like driving. I’ll see you at the Kahului Post Office in a couple of hours. There are stores around there you can reach on foot. You can pick up a few things for your place while you wait.”

“That's a good idea. I don’t know how to thank you.”

“*Mahalo* is fine,” he said.

“*Mahalo*, then.”

There was a click as Mr. K ended the call.

The relief of knowing I had a ride back home was undeniable, although the thought of riding in a truck with Mr. K for an extended period made me feel like my skin was too tight.

Pono bounced his brows suggestively. “I thought that might be the way it went. He digs you, Kat.”

“Whatever,” I said, fanning my face with a plastic shin guard.

Lei laughed. “I'm looking forward to seeing what happens with this. Mr. K is going to have to try a little harder than he's used to, I'm thinking.”

# ☙ 9 ❧

Lei and Pono dropped me off in front of a large, busy post office building in the middle of downtown. It was painted the usual industrial gray and built in the popular government style I privately call "urban ugly." The only thing that suggested the building was in Hawaii were the pair of palm trees on either end, gyrating in Maui's brisk wind.

I got out but leaned back into the cab to address the two detectives as they prepared to pull away. "You'll keep me up to speed on things?"

"As much as we're able to, considering you don't have a phone or Internet," Lei said. "But remember, you're a civilian and a witness. We will probably be back out to Ohia tomorrow to do more canvassing."

"Can I get your cell phone to call in case I find anything of interest?"

"Sure."

Lei and I exchanged numbers. I stepped back and patted Stanley's shiny purple fender. "I appreciate all you've done."

"Just the job, baby! All in a day's work." Pono grabbed the

chrome skull and put the truck in gear. “And don't forget. What happens in Ohia, stays in Ohia.”

I gave them a grin and a salute, and they rolled out.

I turned, squared my shoulders, adjusted my backpack, and headed into the post office.

After the hazing I’d experienced in Ohia, I was prepared for any kind of resistance. But the postmaster in charge of Maui, a kindly man named Phil Hanoi, seemed very pleased to see me. Turns out he had been expecting me to check in before I went to Ohia, not after.

He was sympathetic to my plight, and promptly handed over a ring of keys and a manual detailing my responsibilities. “Glad to have you aboard, Agent Smith—we don't get too many transfers from the Secret Service to the Postal Service. Didn't know it was done, to be honest.” He shook his head. “Until it happened.”

“Me neither. I want to do the best job I can, given the circumstances.” I hefted the heavy procedural binder and cleared my throat. “Mr. Hanoi, why wasn't Ms. Chang promoted when the last postmaster disappeared?”

Hanoi stroked a swatch of a gray goatee on his chin with his forefinger as if it were a pet. The plush hair was a contrast to his shiny, bald head. “Well, you know, Auntie Pua's one of the Big Island Changs. Not that you heard it from me.”

I blinked, playing dumb. “I’m not sure I know what you mean. Everyone seems to think she's more competent than Ms. Borland was.”

His shiny brown pate gleamed with sweat. Hanoi grabbed a nearby paper towel roll, ripped off a few, and mopped the area in question. “Pua is well respected. As far as I know, she's not involved with criminal activities. But you never know what kind of pressure she might come under from her family to tamper with the mail. That’s a felony. ‘Better to be safe than sorry’ is my motto, as head postmaster.”

“Thanks. I’m new here. I wouldn't know a Chang in Hawaii from a Smith in Washington, D.C.,” I joked.

My attempt at humor flopped like a fish out of water. Hanoi looked at me blankly. "I suppose they're both common names." He lowered his caterpillar-like brows and leaned forward to whisper as if the walls had ears. "They're behind almost everything illegal that goes on in the Hawaiian Islands. Scratch any dirty surface, and you're likely to find a Chang in the background pulling strings."

"Good to know. Thanks for the warning."

I eyed him, considering. Blocking Pua Chang's advancement up the postal ladder had to be illegal on his part, unless she'd actually done something wrong. Regardless, it looked like I'd found the reason Pua never got promoted—she was a Chang and tarred with their black brush by association.

"I was wondering, what brought you to the backside of Maui?" Hanoi steepled blunt fingers stained with ink from the various stamp pads littering his desk.

I ended up filling him in on a thumbnail sketch of my abrupt career change.

"They should have had you come straight here instead of going out to Ohia when you first arrived," he said. "I could have gotten you all set. Your landing wouldn't have been nearly as bumpy."

I flashed back to the blowout on the little plane Mr. K had been piloting. What if I hadn't been there to put out that fire because I was here instead? "Everything seems to be working out okay, except for the discovery of Frances Borland."

"What?" Hanoi's fuzzy brows climbed his forehead. "She's been gone for months—left abruptly for the mainland. Don't tell me she's back in Ohia!"

"She was found dead in the jungle behind the postmaster living quarters."

I was treated to a view of Hanoi's tonsils (rather large) as his jaw dropped.

I hoped I was doing the right thing by seeking more answers about Fran's death. "Please don't let on that I told you about the discovery. The detectives don't want her name getting out yet. But since I'm inheriting her job, her house, and even her sheets, I've got a few questions about her."

"I do, too. Did she pass out in the jungle?" Hanoi ripped off two handfuls of paper towels this time and patted his head with them. "She was a drunk, you know."

"So I've gathered." I described Tiki and her offering, and how the discovery of Borland's body had unfolded. "Is there anyone or any reason you can think of why someone would kill Ms. Borland? Or, if she died of natural causes, hide her body and her suitcase so it appears she left town of her own volition?"

"She was generally good at her job. I mean, her reports came in on time and the office out there ran smoothly, even with the increase in deliveries from online ordering." He waggled a paper towel at me. "You're going to hate that, by the way. All those Amazon packages pile up at our little outposts more than anything else."

"I imagine." I wasn't home enough to do much online shopping myself, but I'd seen the piles of boxes in the halls of my D.C. apartment building. "How do I put this . . . are you sure that good performance was Ms. Borland's doing, or Pua Chang's?"

He cocked his head, removing the damp paper towels from his shiny dome and folding them carefully. "Fran occupied her position for three years. When she came to Maui, she told me she was near retirement. She applied for the posting in Ohia, saying she wanted to end her career in paradise. She passed her performance reviews. I only know about the drinking because of the gossip. I know Opal and her husband at the general store, and they frequently complained about her singing too."

"Ah, the singing." I nodded.

"Yeah. They talked to her about it several times. Apparently, she was inspired to sing by the loneliness and the light of the moon." Hanoi's smile was sad. "I'm still digesting the fact that she didn't leave on her own . . . that someone took her out. Fran was a good person, if a bit of a troubled soul."

I fidgeted with the keys in my hand. "I am sorry to have brought that bad news. If you think of anything I should know about Fran—about her disappearance—let me know."

"There is one more thing."

"What?" I tried not to prick my ears and point my tail like a hound on the hunt.

"She had a friend in Kahului. She'd spend the night in town here with someone." He shook his head. "But I don't know the name, or even if it was a man or a woman."

"That's good. It's something. Maybe someone else knows who this is, too. I'll pass it on to the detectives," I reassured him.

"I'm sure they'll come to speak to me." He winked, looking a bit like a sleepy tortoise as he did so. "And I'll pretend to be surprised when they tell me Fran is dead."

"Thanks." I schmoozed him a bit with some eyelash fluttering that probably looked ridiculous. "It's good to know I have a friend."

He bought it hook, line, and sinker. "Take my number." Hanoi handed me a card. "Call me anytime you need a pep talk or help solving problems. Unfortunately, I can't speak to whether Pua Chang will make your job easier or harder."

"I suspect the latter," I said. I left with an undeniable spring in my step, having gained an ally in high places. In my little war with Pua Chang, I gave this round to Team Kat.

Outside the post office, I glanced at my phone to check the time. I still had about an hour to find a Walmart, Target, or some other store to buy myself a few necessities for the shack.

I ended up at a drugstore I'd never heard of called Longs. It was the only retailer within walking distance that wouldn't take me too far afield. Once inside, I loaded a cart with towels, kitchen and personal items, and some new bedding in a cheerful Hawaiian print that I hoped would scare away Tiki. I headed over to the clothing section and grabbed a hat and a pair of black flip-flops like I had seen other locals wearing. On my way to the register, I spotted a folding beach chair peeking out from one of the aisles.

I needed that chair. I needed it to erase the image of lonely, drunken Frances Borland, seated with her skinny butt on the front stoop rock, singing at the moon like a coyote doing karaoke. I was not going to suffer Fran's fate, whatever it had been.

By the time I got all my loot repacked into my backpack and a couple of auxiliary bags so I could carry it all back to the post office, it was time to meet Mr. K.

He drove up in that green truck much like his cousin's right when I'd expected he'd get there. I didn't give him time to get out and open the door or perform any other gentlemanly gesture. I tossed my bags and the beach chair into the truck bed before he was fully stopped, then hopped up into the passenger side. "I can't believe you came all the way out here just to give me a ride all the way back."

Mr. K shrugged big shoulders. He looked just as tasty out of his uniform as in it, wearing a Maui Built tank top that showed off his guns. "No problem. Like I said, mama was cooking for an army and expecting Lei and Pono, too. You'll have to be her consolation prize." His warm brown eyes twinkled.

I wasn't used to seeing guys with a twinkle in their eye. Most of the men I dealt with were semi-dead on the inside, a hazard of our job. Or they were politicians, a whole other kettle of fish. Well, "sharks" would be more like it. The twinkle in *their* eyes was faker than two-carat cubic zirconium and usually meant trouble for me, as my current situation demonstrated.

I pointed to the miniature war helmet dangling from his rearview. "Pono has one of those too."

"Yeah, our cousin gave them to all the men in the family for Christmas. The ladies got those hula dancers you fix onto your dash that shake their hips," he said, wiggling in illustration. I snorted a laugh.

"Need anything else in town?" He put the truck in gear and we roared loudly out of the parking lot and onto the main road, Hana Highway.

"Nope. I loaded up on supplies for the shack at Longs. I was looking for a Target or a Walmart, but Longs was all I could find."

"They're a local drugstore. Been in Hawaii forever. CVS bought them out, but everybody had a fit when they tried to change the name, so they kept it Longs in Hawaii."

"I'm getting a feeling Hawaiian people do a lot of things differently."

"We take pride in that." He treated me to a dimple.

I was definitely getting the better part of this relationship, such as it was. But maybe he could help me with more than a ride. "Does your cousin ever talk to you about his cases?"

Mr. K sobered. "Not usually. But I'll be honest, I'm pretty curious about what they found back behind your cottage."

"Can I swear you to secrecy? If Pono finds out I spilled the beans . . ."

"My lips are sealed." He made a kiss sound with his lips instead of the usual zipper motion, and it made me think inappropriate thoughts. "What was back there?"

"Did you know a woman named Frances Borland?"

Mr. K's eyes widened, and his brows flew up. "Everybody knew Fran. But I doubt very many people actually knew her personally. Other than drunken escapades around the area—never while on duty at the P.O. by the way—she pretty much kept to herself."

"So, you told me she made like a banana and split. Turns out she didn't get very far."

"No way!" His foot lowered on the gas pedal as he turned to gape at me. A huge pineapple truck, loaded to the brim with big, golden fruit, loomed in front of us.

"Look out!" I shouted.

He braked and we fell back to a safer distance, but an intense, heady pineapple smell filled the cab anyway—that truck was potent.

"Sorry. I'm pretty shocked to hear this." Mr. K opened and closed his big hands on the steering wheel. "What happened?"

"Well, it started when Tiki left a treat for me on my doorstep." I told him about my discovery just this morning. "It's been a long, rough day—trying to start my job and getting blocked by Ms. Chang, and then finding the body of the woman who had my job before me."

"Things can only get better from here." He patted my leg.

HE PATTED MY LEG ABOVE THE KNEE!

FIRE! FIRE! FIRE!

Panic zinged like electricity all over my body, worse than that time I had to do sensory input training to prep for torture. I kept my gaze on the horizon and focused on breathing normally.

He gave my leg a friendly squeeze, the way you do when you're testing a tomato to see if it's ripe. He removed his hand, and I sighed loudly with relief, concealing it with a cough.

"I did find something nice today, though. A glass ball, maybe some kind of fishing float."

"Eh, sweet!" He grinned. "Those are so rare these days. They're major good luck. Maybe one thing will cancel out the other."

"I can hope." I jingled my new handful of keys. "I've got my own set of keys now so the post office will be open tomorrow, come heck or high water."

"Good on you. Meanwhile . . ." His brow furrowed and hands flexed on the wheel as we re-entered the curves and dips of the back roads. "I'm sure Fran's name will be circulating soon, if it isn't already. I'll keep an ear out for anyone who might have had it in for her. She was a notorious drunk, but never did any harm that I heard of—other than singing outside at the full moon, which drove the neighbors crazy."

"I heard about that from Ms. Maka at the Ulupalakua Store."

He shook his head. "For being here one day, you've sure got your finger on the pulse of trouble, Kat."

"You don't have to tell me that. Some say Trouble's my middle name."

"That can be your nickname. K.T. Smith. It has a ring."

"A fine thing coming from you, Mr. K," I teased.

He frowned. "Who?"

"I'm not the only one with a nickname."

He rolled his eyes. "Oh, you *malihini* you. Now, you ready to meet my mother?"

# 10

Mr. K's mother was tall and statuesque, with the scent of coconuts and tropical flowers permeating the air around her and a hug strong enough to take my breath away.

"Mom, this is Kat. Kat, this is my mother, Ilima Kaihale."

She straightened and held me out at arm's length. "Let me get a look at the first girl that Keone drove all the way to Kahului and back for, just to bring home for dinner." She held my face in her warm palms and gazed into my eyes, then leaned forward and placed her forehead on mine. She was tall enough that I only had to incline my head a little.

We stood there, her hands were still on my cheeks, our noses and foreheads lightly touching. Our breath mingled—I was glad I'd chewed that piece of dried ginger Mr. K offered me when I started getting carsick.

Being close to her this way felt like being probed with a Vulcan mind meld, and it went on long enough to be excruciating. Just when I thought I might wrench myself away and run for the door, screaming at the intimacy, Ilima Kaihale let go and stepped back.

Her smile was as bright as a full moon. "Welcome to our *hale*. When I found out Lei and Pono weren't coming, I invited a few other family members from around the area." I looked around and saw at least ten people crowded into the room. "And please," she said, "call me Auntie Ilima."

"Thank you—Auntie." I dug in my backpack and brought out a round, blue bottle of Ocean Vodka. "I brought a little something."

"Eh, nice!" Without missing a beat, she turned and walked across the crowded living room, twisted off the lid, and emptied the entire jug into the punchbowl. "Now it's a party!"

The family cheered.

Nobody was interested in shaking hands—I was swamped in hugs. When it was time to eat, we sat at a long folding table in an open, lean-to garage that faced Auntie Ilima's lush backyard. The food was authentic Hawaiian fare: poi, fresh fish cooked over coals and wrapped in ti leaves, and more of that delicious kalua pig. I sneaked a large chunk and wrapped it in a napkin, stowing it in my pocket for Tiki.

Everyone wanted to meet me. Everyone wanted to know how long I had been on the island and what I was doing here. And most of all, everyone wanted to know what made me so special that Keone brought me to meet the family. Thankfully, Mr. K stuck to my side and took over, embellishing the story of the plane rescue and adding his own humorous twist to it: "I knew I wanted to get to know her better when I saw she was strong enough to hold up both the bride *and* the tail of the plane."

They continued to pepper me with questions, eager to get to know me. When I mentioned that I was the new postmaster at Ohia, the noisy room grew silent. Speculative looks appeared on their once laughing faces. It seemed Auntie Pua had been here too, but I hoped that maybe I would have a chance to make some new friends with Mr. K paving the way. The moment softened and passed quickly, for which I was grateful.

Much later, after the punch was long gone and the party settled down, Keone drove me back home to Ohia. "Your mother is a beautiful human," I told him, sneaking a look at him while he drove.

Moonlight reflected off the ocean in the distance, and the dim light from the dash lit his smile.

"She is. You had a rough welcome to Ohia. I wanted you to know it can be very different here."

I rubbed my nose at the memory of her greeting. "That was certainly different, what she did when she said hello."

"It's a traditional greeting called *honi*. We exchange the divine breath of *ha*. It's where "*aloha*" really comes from."

A beat went by. It had been a very long day, but it ended well because of him. No other reason. I was woman enough to admit it.

"Thank you for everything. For giving me a ride, and the food . . . so *ono*." I rubbed my distended stomach and said my new favorite word proudly. "Delicious."

He patted my leg. "You'll be *kama'aina* in no time."

HE PATTED MY LEG AGAIN.

OMG OMG OMG

. . . and then it was over.

Whew.

I rolled down the window and stuck my head out like a dog, letting the wind cool down my flaming face. It was going to be a bummer when I had to push him away and give him the "I'm not into relationships" speech. I decided it should be sooner rather than later. I dreaded it, but it had to be done—and I'd lose a valuable friend in the process. But it was better that than leading him on.

His mother would kill me if I hurt him—that's what her Vulcan mind meld told me.

We pulled into the dirt parking lot beside the post office and general store. The lot was dark—no streetlights or floodlights on the buildings—and misty rain had begun to fall. I was grateful for the latter, which forestalled any ideas about a moonlit beach walk or other shenanigans that might have crossed either of our minds. I was so tired that all I could think about was throwing my new sheets on the Murphy bed and falling asleep.

Nevertheless, my hands were sweaty as I reached for the door handle. “I’ve got to get my stuff out of the back.”

“Let me help you,” Mr. K offered, reaching to tug off his seatbelt.

“No, I got it.” I opened the truck’s door and stepped directly into a mud puddle. “Son of a goat herder!”

“Yeah. You learn to look before you leap around here.” Despite my protest, Mr. K joined me at the truck’s bed and hoisted out one of my loaded shopping bags. “Got a flashlight?”

“Nope.”

He switched on a powerful beam. “Got you covered.”

I retrieved the rest of the bags, the folded chair, and my backpack, and we headed for the front door. My heart was pounding in an uneven rhythm. My attempts to ditch him at the truck hadn’t panned out. And the worst thing was, I didn’t want to say goodnight—but I had to before something bad happened.

I opened my door. Tiki hissed and growled from under the table, making it clear I wasn’t welcome in my abode.

“Hey, attack cat. I brought you something.” I set my bags down and squatted slowly so as to not aggravate the testy feline. I dug in my pocket and removed the morsel of pork I’d taken from the Kaihales’ table. I unwrapped it, crept forward, and set it on the floor just under the table. “Here’s my fee to cross the doorstep.”

Mr. K pointed the flashlight’s beam down at the floor, so it provided some light but didn’t blind Tiki. She blinked at us, and I was pleased to see that her weepy eye looked better. It was even open a bit now. She lurched forward abruptly, grabbed the pork, and withdrew back into the shadows under the table.

I turned to Mr. K. “I don’t know how she’s getting in. Everything is closed when I leave, but she keeps appearing.”

“Probably a hole in the floor somewhere. Want me to look around?”

He was too close. He was in my space. Panic seemed to wrap

around my throat and strangle my vocal cords. "No thanks," I choked out. I grabbed the heavy bag he was still holding and yanked. The flimsy plastic split, and out tumbled a number of personal items, first and foremost a box of environmentally friendly Tampax.

Tiki bolted out from under the table and zoomed between us to disappear into the dark.

I whirled to face Keone. Fear had risen full force and set my skin on fire. "You need to go, now." I flapped my hands in a shooing motion. "Thanks, but you need to go."

"Okay." He reached past me, the heat of his arm making me jerk aside. He pulled the dangling string for the overhead bulb, and light bloomed around us. He stepped back across the threshold, flashlight in hand.

He was outside. I was safe.

"I need you to go," I babbled. "Right now. Go." I flapped my hands some more, unable to look him in the eye.

He stepped back further, all the way to the stoop rock. "It's okay, Kat. I'm not going to hurt you. I'll leave, that's fine. But I thought we were having a good time. Did I do something wrong?"

His voice was gentle, his movements slow.

I was Tiki.

He was me, trying to calm me with a verbal piece of pork.

Now that Keone was far enough away from me, I managed to look up and see his worried eyes and raised hands.

Shame flushed over me. I'd overreacted. I was still messed up.

I'd thought I was getting better. I'd tolerated all the hugging at his family's house, I'd been able to stand there when his mother *honi*'ed me . . . but the thought of a man I liked touching me? All I wanted to do was grab my gun and run for the hills.

"I have PTSD from . . . something," I said. "Please, don't touch me."

His eyebrows drew together—not in judgement, but in concern. "No problem. Got it."

My eyes stung. I opened my mouth, my speech ready, but he

shook his head and held up a finger. I closed my mouth and shivered with mortification. I wrapped my arms around myself and looked at the worn boards of the porch near his feet, wishing I could disappear.

"Hey. I'm sorry I freaked you out. I didn't know, but I do now." He eased back off the stoop rock and into the mist. "I'll be back Saturday morning to take you surfing, okay? Day after tomorrow." He paused for a moment, waiting for me to say something, anything.

I couldn't. My vocal cords simply refused to move. I gave a tiny nod of acknowledgement.

He mirrored my nod. "Goodnight, Kat. I've got your back. Sleep well." Mr. K turned and disappeared into the dark, the flashlight beam bobbing as he moved through the misty rain. A minute later, I heard the truck turn on and pull away.

Still shaking, I closed the door and turned to survey the mess on the floor. The basic toolkit and locks I'd found at Longs lay scattered on the floor amid the personal items and kitchen gadgets. Now seemed like a good time to make the changes to the shack's security that I'd planned to—maybe then I'd be able to unwind enough to rest.

I picked up the stout hasp and lock kits and went to work.

What a difference a set of keys makes! Unlocking the back door to the post office the next morning, I felt energized despite a short, rough night's sleep.

I'd had coffee, made fresh in my own little hovel, on my own gecko-poop-free stove. Tiki had returned to spend the night under the table, but didn't attack me in bed OR in the shower. And, she only growled a little bit as I passed by her while getting ready this morning.

Progress.

The back door opened smoothly at the turn of my very own key, and I stepped inside my new workplace. A loud beep and a red flashing light to my left shattered my sense of peace. Hanoi had not told me about an alarm system. I had ninety seconds to input a code before the police were called and everything went berserk at six-thirty in the morning in quiet Ohia.

"You could have mentioned this, Ms. Chang," I said aloud as I dug in my backpack for my Leatherman. "But nooooo, you had to set me up for more fun, instead."

I used the knife to pry off the plastic cover and the snips to cut the leads and power cables. I doubted this was an official system or Hanoi would have told me about it. This was Pua's doing, and I'd fix it if Hanoi wanted it reinstalled.

Deactivating the alarm would likely still send a passive signal to Maui Police Department that power was out to the system, but I wasn't worried—the response time had been an hour for a dead body. How fast would MPD arrive when they got a notice that something had malfunctioned with Ohia's post office alarm?

Not very fast, I was betting.

Considering my rocky start yesterday and that small hitch today, I took a bit of time to look around for other booby traps. The place was neat as a pin. All the counters and surfaces gleamed when I turned on the lights.

Rows of mailboxes, clearly marked with last name and number on the back, invited me to fill them. A single, large counter space had plenty of room for packages; rows of stamp pads, sorting racks full of forms, and the gizmos for paying and printing postage were laid out along one side as neatly as a surgery bay. The front reception area matched the orderly back room. The floors, counters, and the front side of the brass mailboxes gleamed brightly in the slanted morning light coming in through the glass doors.

I sensed Pua Chang's touch in every tidy corner.

I returned to the back room and investigated a windowed door marked POSTMASTER. Through it, I could see a clean desk with an old-fashioned business phone. The door was locked, but I tried keys on the bunch Hanoi had given me until I found one that opened it.

I smelled Pua Chang the minute I opened that door—a light, tropical floral fragrance like a whiff of plumeria on the breeze. The office was as bare and neat as the rest of the space. I scanned for the source of the perfume and located a plug-in scent dispenser shaped like a small, tasteful lotus in pale yellow ceramic. When turned on, it probably puffed steam like a tiny scent volcano.

This was my chance to send a message to Pua Chang. Whether right or wrong, for good or (more likely) bad, I was postmaster in Ohia. I unplugged the dispenser, picked it up, and carried it to the office beside mine, neutrally labeled STAFF.

I unlocked it and deposited the dispenser on a tidy desk identical to mine. I then went back and cleared every personal item I could find out of the postmaster desk: a lipstick (Pink Orchid by Estée Lauder), a tube of hand cream (also Estée Lauder), and a tin of Altoids. I opened the last drawer and was surprised to find a worn copy of *People* magazine with dog-ears and hearts drawn on pages featuring pictures of Chris Hemsworth.

My brows flew up. "My, my, my." Apparently, Ms. Chang had a celebrity crush.

I arranged the magazine and the rest of the items neatly on the Staff desk and relocked the door. Ms. Chang could make whatever she wanted of this change, but I'd been in Washington, D.C. long enough to know that possession was nine-tenths of the law. I unpacked a few things from my backpack and arranged them in my office space, then returned to the shack to get another (totally necessary) cup of coffee.

Tiki had spent the night with me in relative peace. She'd only growled when I got up to pee during the night, and only in a "just letting you know I'm here" kind of way. Now, she sat up in the warm morning light and let out a mew that sounded like rusty scissors cutting burlap.

"Hungry, are you?" I filled her food and water bowls. "Keep an eye on the place, okay? Rip the legs off anybody who tries to get into our shack. I'm off to work."

Tiki didn't reply but approached the bowl and hunkered down to eat. I took that as a sign of trust and locked the door behind me. She'd come and go in her mysterious way, and who was I to interfere?

I returned to my office. I was ninety minutes early for the P.O. opening, but I had a lot of reading in the official binder that Hanoi gave me, and a phone call to make. I sat down at the desk and savored the sense of anticipation as I surveyed my new workplace. I might not have the faintest idea how to function in this job, but I was smart and adaptable. I could do this.

"But first, coffee." I took a big swig and shut my eyes to savor the taste of locally grown Kona beans.

I pulled the big plastic desk phone over to me. I could call Lei's cell phone number—she'd given it to me. But I decided I'd try the Maui Police Department main line first. When I asked for Lei, I was surprised to be connected so early in the morning. "This is Sergeant Texeira."

"Lei, it's Kat—Kat Smith. In Ohia."

"Like I could forget who you are." She chuckled. "Hey, Kat. Any new discoveries on your stoop this morning?"

"Thankfully, no. And, I'm calling you from the desk phone in the P.O., so mission accomplished on getting into the building."

"Good. What's up, then?"

"I . . . picked up a tip. About the victim."

"Oh yeah? Where?"

"From the head postmaster in Kahului. When we were chatting, he said Frances Borland had a friend in Kahului she would spend the night with. Didn't know if the person was male or female, just that she had someone to see and a place to stay when she came to town."

A pause ticked by. "Okay. Anything else?"

"Nothing too useful. Just confirmation of things we already knew, like her drinking. But he might be a good person to interview further."

I took another sip of my steaming hot Elixir of Life as I admired the view through my office window. I could see across the parking lot and the street, beyond the beach, and all the way to an ocean burnished by sunrise and framed by palm trees. I was looking at a freakin' postcard view right now, and this was my place of work. I, Kat Smith, had landed on my very large, very lucky feet with this new job.

"So, anything new you care to share with me?" I asked Lei.

"Nice try, Kat." I heard the smile in her voice. "You know I can't discuss an ongoing investigation. I wish I could tell you more. However, I will let you know what happens with the tip you just gave us." She paused, and I heard a voice in the background. "Pono just rolled in. He says hi and that Auntie Ilima likes you. Nice touch with the Ocean Vodka at the family dinner."

"Wow. Word gets around."

"That's why they call it the coconut wireless."

I rubbed my forehead and scrunched my nose. I sure hope Mr. K didn't tell anyone about my freakout. What a debacle that was last night!

I heard a rumble in the background. Pono was asking a question.

"Pono wants to know if Pua came to work."

"Nope. Not so far."

"Good luck, then. Have a great first day. We'll swing by if we go out to Ohia for more interviews."

"Thanks." I hung up and lifted my size elevens onto the desk. I had an hour to get caught up before I had to unlock the doors and be ready for business. Dropping the huge procedural manual on my lap and opening the first page, I settled in to read.

I made it all of one paragraph before I heard someone trying to break into the back door.

## 11

The binder and my shoes hit the ground simultaneously. I groped for my sidearm, belatedly remembering that it was at MPD to check ballistics. The door handle rattled but held. Fortunately, I'd remembered to lock the door behind me after returning from my coffee run to the shack. The sound stopped, and for a brief moment there was silence. I waited. Then, the sound of a key sliding into the lock.

There was only one person other than me who had a key to the back door of the post office: Pua Chang.

I stood up, fortifying myself to greet my nemesis, then sat back down with the manual. Better to seem unruffled and cool than overeager.

Pua paused just inside the back door, no doubt spotting the way the alarm had been disabled. Her high heels tapped on the linoleum floor as she walked. She did not hang a left to my office, as I expected. She turned right, and I once again heard the sound of a key as she unlocked the STAFF office.

Another pause. I remembered the neat pile of her things I'd placed there earlier this morning. I kept my eyes down, sightlessly scanning black squiggles on the page under the heading "Procedures for International Mail."

Once again, Pua's heels clicked across the floor, and she appeared in the open door of my office. I pretended to be fully engrossed in my studies. Eventually, she made that delicate coughing noise from yesterday, which I found tremendously irritating. "Good morning, Ms. Smith."

Only then did I drag my eyes from the book to look at her and give her my frostiest half-smile. "Well, hello, Ms. Chang. Glad you could make it in today. I hope you're feeling better."

We locked gazes like bulls lock horns.

She was the first to glance away. "I see you removed the former postmaster's personal items from your desk and brought them to mine. Were you wanting me to dispose of Frances Borland's personal effects, Ms. Smith?"

"Oh. I thought the items were yours," I said, a flush suffusing my face. I'd misread the situation. Pua Chang had NOT been occupying the postmaster's office inappropriately. Of course she hadn't. She was not the type to be inappropriate—I was getting that message loud and clear.

Also, those Chris Hemsworth pages in *People* should have told me the stuff wasn't hers. She also wasn't the type to have a celebrity crush. Too bad. I wanted to like her when I saw that marked-up magazine.

Meanwhile, triumph brightened Pua's eyes, and they glittered like mean, black diamonds.

She was immaculately turned out in a Lilly Pulitzer flowered sheath with big, fat, creamy pearls around her neck. Genuine, of course. Her (excellent) legs were set off by low-heeled Ferragamo pumps. Despite not having any interest in such things, my time in D.C. and metro centers around the world had familiarized me with women's battle armor—aka fashion. Next to her aesthetic perfection, I looked like a giant frump in my cat-hair-covered black slacks, semi-muddy Nikes, and a none-too-white polo shirt.

Pua spoke to the wall over my head. "That's all right, I'll just take the items to the trash. Along with the alarm console . . . looks like you had a bit of trouble with it." (Translation: I see you're an idiot, and I raise you my total competency.)

"No trouble. I simply wasn't briefed on the alarm's existence by our director in Kahului, Mr. Hanoi." (Translation: I only take orders from the BOSS, not YOU, Pua Chang.)

"Ah. Well, a few adaptations were necessary while I solely occupied a position meant for two people, until the next postmaster was appointed." (Translation: I am indispensable. You are not, and you won't be here long, Kat Smith.)

"Of course. You did what you had to do. You may bag up Ms. Borland's private effects for her next of kin. She won't be back to claim them." (Translation: Did you kill that poor woman to get her job?)

"Should I hold her belongings for the police?" (Translation: I know she was murdered, and I'm cooperating with the investigation.) Pua shook her head in faux pity. "Poor Fran. She tried so hard." (Translation: Fran was a worthless drunk who I had to cover for constantly, but I didn't kill her. Murder is beneath me.)

I slapped the giant binder shut and stood up. "Just put Fran's things in a bag. I'll figure out what to do with them. You might as well show me the ropes around here, so we can serve the public together." (No translation.)

"I will, just as soon as I tidy up." (Translation: It looks like I will have to clean up your messes, too.) Pua spun and walked back to her office.

I heard her tossing Fran's sad leftovers into a bag. I waited in the doorway as she handed the plastic bag to me and walked on by, trash can in hand, to where the alarm console dangled from the wall.

With unexpected violence, Pua ripped the remainder of the device out of the stucco and dropped it in the trash, setting the can by the back door. "I have been collecting the rubbish from the post office to take to the dump in Hana once a month. I will do so with this too, unless you'd like to take that duty over?"

"No thanks." I cleared my throat and shifted from foot to foot, starting to feel bad and like maybe I'd jumped to some inaccurate conclusions. "I don't currently have any personal transportation."

"That must be inconvenient." Pua strode past me to the front counter, and I smelled her subtle tropical perfume. Out of the corner of my eye, I spotted the lotus dispenser still on her desk. Perhaps it had been a gift to Fran?

"Why don't you sort the mail today and I'll run the counter?" she called back. "There will be double the usual number of bags to distribute since the office was closed yesterday."

"That will be fine," I said, feeling a bit cowardly. I was happy that I wouldn't have to interface with the curious denizens of Ohia on my own, while doing functions I had no idea how to do.

Nine o'clock rolled around and Pua unlocked the front doors of the post office. The only person to arrive in the next hour was Chad, the young, pimply-faced dude who drove the mail truck. He hefted four large, zippered, padlocked canvas bags of mail out of the van and onto our front porch. He disappeared back into the white, windowless van and returned with a dolly full of boxes. After a few trips, he tossed us a salute, hopped in the driver's seat, and took off again.

Pua glanced at her manicure. "Since you're dressed for it, I'll let you bring in the deliveries."

She click-clacked out of the enclosed porch area and sashayed across the parking lot, taking care around the puddles. Opal stood waving on the porch of the general store. "You're back!" Pua reached her friend and they embraced, disappearing into the store.

I stood where she left me, in the company of the old brass mailboxes. I rolled my shoulders back and reached for the bag handles. She didn't need to be here; I would figure things out myself.

I dragged all four bags of mail into the back-office area in one go, and then moved the packages to a corner. I set out to look for the keys to the mailbags on my ring from Hanoi, and soon discovered a half-sized key that fit.

I had the bags open and had begun sorting by the time Pua came back from the store. She stood for a moment on the other side of the counter and watched me.

I had no system. I had no idea how to do what I was doing. I just reached into the bag, grabbed a handful of letters, and scanned the backs of the boxes for the name they were addressed to. It had taken me fifteen minutes to slot four pieces of mail. This was going to take all day.

Pua flipped up the counter and joined me in the sorting area. "It's easier if you dump the bag onto that table and spread them out. I also recommend a pair of gloves." She pointed to a box of disposable nitrile gloves. "You never know where the mail has been, and it will save you from paper cuts."

"Thanks." I snapped on a pair of the gloves, picked up the bag, and dumped it out on the table, spreading the letters so they were easier to sort through.

"The boxes are arranged numerically, so focus on the P.O. Box number in the address, not the name of the recipient," she said. "Then scan for the row it will be in. There are ten rows of ten at this post office."

"Okay." This was a huge breakthrough—I'd been bogged down looking for last names. While those were listed on the boxes, there appeared to be no rhyme or reason to it. "Are all of the boxes assigned?"

"Yes. There are over five hundred people living in Ohia, and only a hundred boxes here. We have a waitlist." She reached under the counter and activated a couple of machines that hummed to life. "Oh, and I brought you a coffee from the store. Opal says hi."

I spotted the large Styrofoam cup of steaming coffee resting on the counter. My mouth fell open in shock at this olive branch. "Oh! Thanks." I took the coffee, gazing down at its glossy brown surface. Was this some kind of trick?

Pua seemed to read my mind, and shook her head a little, but said nothing.

I took a sip, set the coffee aside, and got back to sorting with renewed vigor now that I understood the system. Once her area was prepped for customers, Pua slipped on a pair of gloves and joined me without a word. We worked in a strangely companionable silence.

The bell over the door tinkled as a man walked in. He wore a battered cowboy hat and had a white beard so long that he'd tucked it into his belt, presumably to keep it from trailing everywhere. "Auntie Pua!" He bellowed. "I hear Fran's dead, buried out back behind the new girl's shack!"

Pua tugged off her gloves and walked over to the front counter. "How can I help you today, Kermit?"

Kermit! I'd just seen that name and it stuck out to me. Box 227. I stuffed a letter in for him, and I'm pretty sure I'd seen more mail with his name on it. I rustled through the pile spread out on the table and found another, shoving it in his slot as I flapped my bat ears to hear how Pua handled this.

"What's the skinny on Fran?" Kermit hollered.

Pua made a "keep it down" gesture with her hand but raised her voice—Kermit must be hard of hearing. "I'm sorry, Kermit, we don't have any news to share. This is Kat Smith, our new postmaster."

I stuck my head around the wall of boxes and waved a purple-gloved hand. "Hey, Mr. Kermit. We're a little behind with the mail since we were closed yesterday, but I think you have a few items in your box already."

"Welcome to Ohia," Kermit said dubiously, then leaned toward Pua and whisper-shouted, "You didn't get the promotion again?"

"Afraid not. It's always something, isn't it?" Pua tinkled a fake laugh and patted the old man's hand where it rested on the counter. "Now, I know we're all upset about Fran, but don't go stirring things up, okay? You need to keep your blood pressure down."

"Nice to meet you, Kat!" the old man yelled into his postal box when he retrieved his letters. The small metal space amplified the noise and I winced but managed a wave at him through the little square tunnel.

"Have a nice day!" I called back.

When Pua came back to join me in sorting, I groped for words to apologize. Despite our rough start, I still felt terrible about taking the job she no doubt deserved, but I couldn't figure out how to broach the subject. Anything I said was bound to only hurt more, and I couldn't reveal what I learned about her situation from Mr. Hanoi without serious repercussions. So instead, I marveled at the speed and accuracy with which she distributed the mail, slotting three items to my one.

A few more customers came in throughout the morning, and Pua knew every single person's name and introduced me. After the third or fourth customer she said, "You're doing very well, Kat. I can tell I'll be leaving the post office in good hands."

My eyebrows flew up so high they were in danger of leaving my forehead. "What? You can't leave, Ms. Chang! I can't do this without you!"

Pua Chang continued to sort the mail, her purple-gloved hands a blur of motion as she stuffed the boxes. "It's been a good run. I held on for a long time, hoping for the promotion to postmaster. But with your arrival, I've realized my time is up. I'm going to put in for early retirement."

I reached for the now-tepid cup of coffee she'd brought me from the grocery store and took a big swig . . . then chugged down more. Maybe caffeine would help me deal with this situation—my brain seemed to have gone on hiatus.

Pua went on. "I've got enough years in the Postal Service that I'm vested in the system. I can retire with an okay pension. I was hanging on, waiting, hoping—and I also wanted someone smart and competent to take care of this post office. Ohia is a special place." She paused and met my eyes. "I hope you think it is, too."

I found my voice at last. "Ms. Chang. You barely know me. I

haven't even been here one day. How can you know I'm the person for the job?"

"I can tell." She looked me in the eye. "You're hard working, resourceful, and determined. You found a way to get your own keys and access the facility even with the alarm on . . . .and frankly, you did it all with the deck stacked against you. You'll be good here."

"You were testing me." I sucked in a breath and gusted it out. "You can't leave because I won't be here long. There's something you should know." I could be shooting myself in the foot right now, but if Pua quit . . . not only would it be a grave injustice, but I might end up trapped here. "I have never worked for the Postal Service before. I'm a Secret Service agent, and that's what I want to be again once the coast is clear and I can go back to my old position."

Pua's forehead scrunched delicately as she frowned. "I don't understand."

"This whole thing is messed up. What's happened to me, what's happened to you . . ."

Just then, the bell over the door tinkled. We stuck our heads around the row of boxes to greet the latest customer, a little Filipino grandma with three kids under three in tow. She was babysitting for her daughter who worked in Kahului, and the little procession had walked over from Tutu's house, towing the baby in a red wagon. The kids were adorable. Apparently, a trip to the post office was the highlight of their day. Pua gave them each a sugar-free lollipop.

Once they left, we resumed our task and our conversation.

"So, I don't understand," Pua said. "You're telling me you didn't apply for this job?"

My cheeks heated. "No, I did not. I was . . . caught in a bad situation with my last protectee, and then assigned here." I told her the circumstances as succinctly as possible. The memory of the congressman's hands still made my forehead sweat.

But then again, I'd had that reaction to being touched by men since I was a kid. Therapists who'd worked with me after I moved in with Aunt Fae said it was a reaction to the accident when my parents died. I'd been in the car with them too, and had no memory of any of it. I'd been rescued by EMTs who'd had to manhandle me out of the wreck with the Jaws of Life, and I'd been screwed up ever since. So yeah, here I was, almost thirty, with no relationships under my belt. Literally—a virgin, and likely to remain so.

But Pua didn't need to know that much. In fact, I'd probably overshared already. I sneaked a glance at her, worried. If Pua'd set out to pry the truth from me, she'd done it as easily as an automatic can opener peeling open a tin of albacore.

"I'm sorry for everything that is going on with you and your career, but what you've told me is just confirmation. I'm never going to be promoted," Pua said sadly. "I have no future here." She stepped away from the sorting area. "I need a break. I have some spreadsheets to complete." She ripped off the gloves, dropped them into a nearby receptacle, and went into her office. She shut the door and pulled a cord, the blinds dropping to cover the window.

I was on my own, and now it seemed I'd stepped in it and made the situation worse.

For the rest of the day, Pua only came out of her office when the bell dinged over the door. I had plenty to do with the sorting, and I figured she needed her space. So did I. How was I going to convince her to stay? From a logical point of view, she was right. I had nothing to offer. Sharing what our boss said about not promoting her because she was a Chang certainly wasn't going to help—but maybe I could change his mind? I needed to get in to see Hanoi again and try to get him to give Pua my job before I was stuck out here, too.

I breathed a sigh of relief at the sight of the MPD detectives entering the office and bellying up to the counter. I stepped out to greet them. "Lei! Pono! You're here!"

Pua had come out of her office at the sound of the jingle. She turned to go back in, but Lei extended a hand in a STOP gesture. "Please wait a moment, Ms. Chang. We need to speak with you. Official business."

Pua gave no sign she was bothered by this. "All right. Come into my office, please."

My curiosity antennae were aquiver as the three went into her office and shut the door. Fortunately, the office was empty of customers, so I was able to plant my ear against the old-fashioned keyhole, which provided clear, unobstructed sound.

My eyes widened when Lei Mirandized Pua. Whoa! Something big must have happened. "Do you understand these rights?" she said in closing.

"I do," Pua replied calmly.

Lei began her interrogation. "Where were you six months ago?" She named a date.

I heard pages ruffling. "That was a workday, a Friday, so we closed at four p.m. per usual. I would have gone home and been there through the night."

"Is there anyone who can corroborate your movements that day?"

"Most likely my nephew can verify that. He's an adult, but he has pervasive developmental delays and would not make a good witness." Her voice was dry and cool.

Pua Chang lived alone on that farm in the valley, with only that evil white pooch and a cognitively disabled nephew for company?

"Then I'm afraid I must place you under arrest for the murder of Frances Borland," Lei said, the shock causing me to lose my balance.

# 12

I heard Pua gasp and so did I, falling over onto my butt when the office door opened. I crab walked out of the way as Lei and Pono, holding a white-faced Pua in handcuffs between them, came through the door.

I scrambled to my feet. "She didn't do it!"

Pono looked away, clearly uncomfortable. Lei met my eyes. "We have new information that says she did, and she has no alibi."

Pua stopped in front of me. "I need you to do me a favor," she spoke rapidly. "Go tell Opal what's happened. She will take care of Sonny Boy and my animals out at the farm. And call my cousin on Oahu. He's the Honolulu District Attorney—his name is Alan Chang."

My gaze skittered back and forth between Pua and the detectives. Pua's earnest eyes implored me for help. Meanwhile, Lei and Pono looked surprisingly miserable, considering the fact that they were holding Fran's murderer between them.

"Okay. Anything else?" I asked, committing the details to memory.

"That is all, thank you. Alan will get me legal help," Pua said.

She wriggled her cuffed arms out of the cops' grip. "Please respect my personal space, Detectives. I'm not going to run away." She strode to the front of the office and waited in front of the counter for me to flip it up, then led their little procession out through the doors and straight to a blue and white cruiser parked out front.

I watched open-mouthed as Pono guided Pua into the backseat. He turned my way, his kind eyes hidden by mirrored Oakleys, and mouthed "I'm sorry." Then he got in beside Lei and they pulled out of the lot and drove away.

Pua had just been arrested for Fran's murder and I was certain from the top of my head to the bottoms of my Nikes that she didn't do it.

I was going to have to find out who had.

I quickly made a hand-lettered sign that said "BACK IN 10 MINUTES" and taped it to the front door. The dust from the cruiser leaving with Pua in the backseat was barely settled as I jogged across the lot to the general store.

My mind was buzzing. What could they have found that was enough for them to arrest Pua for murder, just because she didn't have an alibi? It had to be something hard and sure. A witness, maybe? DNA evidence on the body? Both?

A few customers were browsing the ice cream and sunscreen aisle. I found Opal behind the old cash register. "Well?" she said, when she spotted me. "Did you and Pua work it out?"

"We started to, and then the MPD detectives arrived and arrested her for Fran's murder," I whispered, darting a glance at the customers. They were tourists by the look of them, in Bermuda shorts and aloha shirts. I didn't want the news spreading.

"What!" Opal's pale eyes flew wide.

"I know. They must have found something serious tying Pua to the crime. They took her phone, too. She told me to come talk to you, and asked if you could take care of her animals and Sonny Boy out at the farm. I'm assuming that's her nephew."

"Yes." After her initial shock, Opal rallied quickly. "I assume you agree she didn't do it."

"Honestly, yes. But I have no evidence one way or the other, and they must have something solid or they wouldn't have arrested her. They asked her about the night Fran disappeared and she had no alibi. She said she was where she always is after work—at home—and that her nephew wasn't a reliable witness."

"Poor kid will always be a kid." Opal said. "I have to see what the runes say."

"The what?"

"The runes." She patted a lurid purple velour scarf draped around her shoulders and secured by a rhinestone pin in the shape of an alligator. She pointed to a small sign on the corner of the counter. *FORTUNES TOLD; FUTURES READ. Donations gratefully accepted.* "We need to find out who did away with Fran so we can spring Pua from the joint."

The suspicious attitude she'd shown me before was gone. "Why have you changed your mind about me?" I asked. "I noticed Pua also had a different attitude when she came back from the store this morning."

Opal jiggled something that clacked musically in the pocket of her capacious caftan. "The runes told me you're here for a reason, and that you'll be good for Ohia. They're never wrong. I told Pua the good news. She bought you a coffee, and the rest is history."

"We don't have any history. We just had the beginning of a truce." I sighed. "Besides you, she asked me to call her cousin Alan Chang, who's apparently a bigwig district attorney on Oahu."

Opal snapped her finger and pointed to me. "You do that now. Use the phone in the back, not here. I'll get rid of the customers and close the store. This is an emergency. As soon as the coast is clear, we'll consult the runes."

"I thought maybe some old-fashioned detective work and deductive reasoning would be the way to go," I said. "You know, she threatened to quit her job at the post office today."

Opal's eyes bugged out for a second time, but the tourists had made their way to the counter to check out, their arms loaded with sunscreen, beach toys, and packaged ice cream.

I edged past Opal to the door marked PRIVATE and pushed open the portal to the Pahinuis' inner sanctum. The first thing I saw when I opened the door was a large, older man seated in a wide-bottomed wooden chair. His thick brown arms were wrapped tenderly around a guitar. One of his feet, encased in a compression stocking, was elevated on an upturned metal bucket.

He looked toward me with milky eyes—the man was blind.

"You're not Opal," he stated in a resonant voice that made you want to hear more of it.

"Hello there. You must be Mr. Pahinui," I said. "My name's Kat. Kat Smith."

"The new postmaster." He extended a hand that, when I took it, engulfed mine. "Welcome to Ohia."

"Thank you."

Mr. Pahinui didn't let go of my hand, and my heart rate ratcheted up. I glanced around to distract myself. We were in a small storage room lined from the ceiling to the floor with backup stock for the store: foodstuffs on one side, dry goods and fishing supplies on the other. This must be where they went to grab a quick restock of something that was low on inventory.

I tugged at my hand, feeling sweat spring out all over my body. "Um, Opal told me to come back here to use the phone. Can you tell me where it is?"

He released me at last, and I had the same feeling I'd had with Mr. K's mother—as though I'd been read and known, scanned by X-rays or something.

"Through the door behind me. I'll show you." Mr. Pahinui reached for a carved stick resting beside his chair and used it to heft himself to standing. "You're wondering what happened to me," he said.

"I wouldn't dream of asking . . ." I stuttered, but that was just what I'd been thinking.

"Diabetes." Mr. Pahinui indicated his swollen foot. "And cataracts with complications," he added, gesturing to his milky eyes. "Don't recommend either."

"I'm so sorry."

"Don't be. We all have our burdens to bear—even you."

"You are right about that." I shivered as his sightless eyes gazed into mine, seeing me more clearly than many with vision did.

"Opal has her runes, and I have my Sight." He turned and pushed open a swinging door behind his chair. Shuffling slowly, he led the way into a light, bright kitchen filled with the useful clutter of a lifetime. Along the top of a row of cabinets, a collection of ceramic roosters scratched and crowed, and pots of herbs crowded the counter by the window. Attached to the wall beside the door was an avocado-colored, button-front phone with a long, twisted cord. A second thin cable ran from the base to an old-fashioned answering machine.

"No sense fixing it if it isn't broke," Mr. Pahinui said, reading my mind again. "I'll just be in the living room if you need anything."

I was relieved that the room had a door, and that Mr. Pahinui tactfully closed it.

I faced the phone and the fat Yellow Pages open beneath it. I haven't seen a setup like this since I was at Aunt Fae's. Hers was identical—except her wall phone was beige. She would like the Pahinuis, and Pua Chang, too. In fact, she'd love the whole village of Ohia and its idyllic little bay. On the spot, I decided to bring Aunt Fae out to visit someday before I left for Washington, D.C. again.

The thought gave me an unexpected pang. Probably gas . . . that's what it was.

I pressed a fist to my sternum and started flipping pages in the book, first hunting for the section labeled *Government Offices*, then scanning the tiny print for the Honolulu District Attorney's office. It was a bit of a wrangle to be connected to Alan Chang himself, but after much name-dropping, I finally heard the lawyer's dry tone come on the line. "Who's calling?"

"This is the new postmaster in Ohia. I'm calling at the request of your cousin, Pua Chang. She's been arrested for the murder of a woman named Frances Borland, who occupied the position before me."

A long pause. "Who did you say you were?"

"Kat Smith, Ohia Postmaster. Pua has been arrested and needs your help. She said you'd know what to do and would send her legal representation."

Another pause. "I will certainly look into this. Where's a number I can reach you at, Ms. Smith?"

"Call me at the Ohia Post Office, please."

"Will do." He hung up.

"Well, that was warm and fuzzy," I said, and put the handset back in its cradle.

Mr. Pahinui hadn't come out, so I left the kitchen and headed back to the store. I was eager to see what "reading runes" was all about, and I didn't want Opal getting started without me.

I emerged from the door marked PRIVATE just as Opal was shepherding the tourists out of the store. She pushed a solid-looking wood panel shut behind them, turned a few bolts, and hooked the chain into its track. She turned and caught me watching her extensive closing ritual.

"Never know when some tweakers might try to bust in," she said, flipping the OPEN sign in the metal-barred window to CLOSED. "Thought those tourists would never leave."

I didn't comment on the fact that it was well before her posted closing time. "Are there a lot of meth users in this area?"

"Rumor has it there's a family or two cooking it out in the back valleys of Kaupo," Opal said. "You can't be too careful."

"I'm sorry you have to worry about something like that."

She sighed as she crossed the dimly lit store to join me at the counter. "Times aren't what they used to be out here. Not only do we have to worry about the yuppie invasion of New Ohia happening soon, but we have a drug epidemic going on in the background." She unpinned the large velour scarf from her neck. "I take it you want to see what the runes have to say about Pua's arrest."

"I'm so curious. I've never heard of runes before."

"They're Nordic in origin, though there are other cultures that use them this way. I made mine from kukui nut shells."

"What do you do?" I leaned forward, curious.

"This." She spread the bright velvety cloth across the glass countertop and reached into her pocket. She withdrew a handful of shiny, ridged, black nutshell halves. She held them in both palms, pressed her hands together, and shook them; her eyes closed, she brought them to her lips and breathed on them. Then she dropped them onto the cloth.

I leaned forward to see at the same time she did, and our foreheads knocked together.

Opal straightened up and laughed as I rubbed my sore noggin. "I guess you're interested in the ancient art of rune reading," she said.

"I guess I am."

We both studied the shell halves strewn across the shimmery cloth. She pointed to a shell that had fallen off onto the floor. "See the rune on the back of that one?"

I looked. A symbol had been carved into the back. "It's almost like a slanted F."

"Yes. This one represents a strong female energy. It's off the edge of the reading area, so I'd say this represents a presence that's no longer involved in the current situation."

"Hmm." I didn't know how to respond. Could that shell represent Frances Borland?

"This one?" She poked a shell that had somehow landed on its side. "It's neutralized because of its position." She plucked it out of the reading and set it aside. "What we have left is our message." She leaned forward again, and this time I stayed out of her way.

After a moment, Opal spoke in a singsong voice I'd never heard from her before. "There are forces working at cross-purposes. Some want to see old ways prevail; others want to usher in the new. Someone hopes to benefit from what was lost. Strong women must carry water. The cat is key."

She straightened up and blinked. "Well, that was about as clear as mud."

I couldn't agree more.

Opal reached under the counter and took out a spiral binder with blank pages and a soft lead pencil tied to the wire. Without a word, she flipped to a blank page and began sketching the shells and their symbols with a surprisingly artistic hand. "I need to spend some more time with this. I don't have a clear sense of the message," she said. "Once I get this drawing done, I need to get out to Pua's ranch and feed the animals and check on her nephew. You might as well go."

"Ah. Okay." I had been dismissed. "Is it all right if I leave the store door open behind me?"

"I'll follow you out and lock up. I have to finish this sketch."

I gestured to the phone protruding from the other pocket in her dress. "Why don't you just take a picture of the reading?"

"Because drawing it helps me with the interpretation. I feel meaning come through as I sketch the shapes," Opal said impatiently.

"Ah. That makes sense. Thanks for letting me watch." I briefly caught her eye. "I reached Pua's district attorney cousin, Alan Chang, by the way. He said he would look into the situation."

"I have no doubt." She had refocused on the runes and was absorbed in her task, barely paying attention to anything but the tumbled black shells and the quick artwork forming on the page. I turned and tiptoed across the store, leaving her to it.

The final sentence of her interpretation had caught my imagination: "The cat is key."

Was she referring to me, Kat Smith?

Or to my bad-tempered feline friend, Tiki?

# 13

Back at the post office, I discovered that the hours between three and four p.m. were some of the busiest of the day.

Having wrongly assumed Pua would be there to teach me, I had no idea how to work the front desk functions and thus had to turn away customers. The only thing I knew how to do was hand out General Delivery letters, of which there were surprisingly many since there weren't enough postal boxes for the townspeople.

Despite this, my encounters were mainly positive, until I met Mr. Ching ("not ever to be confused with Chang," he instructed me). Ching was a short, well-muscled man in his forties with a gray crew cut, and the project director of the New Ohia development nearby. "People in this town don't appreciate what New Ohia will do for them," he lectured me, leaning onto the service counter while I attempted to process the postage on his package for him. "New Ohia will put this town on the map. Make it a destination. Tax and investor money will be pouring in for new roads, new businesses, a shopping complex."

"Hmm," I said, noncommittally, handing him back the package that I was unable to process. I was glad I hadn't said more when an older lady wearing a shiny purple tracksuit and a red cowboy hat shuffled up and smacked Ching sharply on the arm with her cane.

"Do you think we want to be on the map?" She glared at him from beneath her scarlet topper. "You think wrong. We don't want a shopping mall or any of the rest of it. We like our village just the way it is."

"That's assault," Ching said, puffing up like a banty rooster. "I ought to have you arrested."

Ms. Red Hat turned to a gaggle of friends, all in scarlet chapeaux and varying shades of purple dress. Apparently, going to the post office was the big outing for the local Red Hat Society. "Did you hear that, girls? Big man here has been assaulted." She turned back to Mr. Ching and held up her scrawny wrists. "I'm into handcuffs, baby."

Her friends hooted and cackled. Ching, flushing dark with rage, whirled and stomped out.

I smiled at the Red Hat ladies, even as I felt a shiver of worry at the depth of anger I'd just observed in the New Ohia director. "Hello. I'm Kat Smith, the new postmaster here in Ohia. And you are?"

"Matilda Ramirez. I go by Mattie." The ringleader of the group gestured with her cane, pointing to each woman with its foot. "These here are Josephine, Pearl, Clara, and Edith. We're the local Red Hat Society."

"So I see." I smiled. "My Aunt Fae back in Maine is a member." I quoted the opening line of "Warning," the poem that inspired the movement, written by outspoken Englishwoman Jenny Joseph. "When I am an old woman, I shall wear purple, with a red hat which doesn't go and doesn't suit me." The ladies cheered my attempt.

"Pua Chang is an honorary member. Maybe you'd like to be one too." A Native Hawaiian woman tugged her oxygen tank over to shake my hand. Deep brown eyes gleamed beneath the brim of a handwoven palm frond hat dyed a deep red. "I go by Josie." She gestured to the woman closest to her. "Pearl would get up to introduce herself, but you know . . . she can't."

"Yes, I can! Brought my new wheels." Pearl, a tiny, wrinkled Japanese woman wearing a kimono and a simple *kanzashi* tucked in her bun, pulled a lever on the side of her wheelchair. The thing straightened up with a mechanical whir, depositing her on feet in tippy-looking traditional wooden platform shoes. She stepped off the footrests and fell forward to cling to the counter, extending a bony hand to shake the tips of my fingers. "Pleased to meet the new girl in town."

"Clara," said a tall, willowy Black woman, extending her hand as well. She wore a purple scarf draped around her head and shoulders, with a small, red cloche on top. Her garments were long and flowing, varying shades of deep purple. "You sure showed that rat Ching. I thought he was going to have a stroke and spare us all the hassle of the lawsuit."

My ears pricked up. "Lawsuit?"

"Yeah, lawsuit. We've got a class action going—the Citizens of Ohia versus New Ohia Land Development," said the remaining group member. "Edith Pepperwhite, Esquire, at your service." Edith was an exceptionally short white woman who somewhat resembled a lawn gnome. She wore a pointy, witch style red felt hat and bright yellow crocs that peeked out from beneath the hem of a purple, burlap-like pantsuit.

"Pleased to meet you as well." I had to lean forward on my elbows to see all of Edith on the other side of the counter. "This might be a bit odd, but would you mind telling me what kind of law you practice?"

"I work here on the East Side of Maui, so I've done everything." Edith smoothed a tassel dangling from her hat. "I can do anything from setting up your last will and testament to getting your ne'er-do-well cousin out of the clink."

"Like you did for me," Pearl said. "Someone gimme a hand back into my chair, will you?"

Josie stepped behind Pearl, caught her by the elbows, and hefted the tiny woman back onto the footrests of her wheelchair. Pearl once again pulled the lever on the side, and the chair folded back down until she was sitting once again.

"Quite a chair you've got there," I commented. "So, what can I do for you ladies?" I gestured to the hand-lettered sign I'd made that read "POSTMASTER IN TRAINING." "Not that I can do much for you. Pua's away and she didn't have time to train me on the equipment."

"Oh, what a shame." Edith put her fists where hips might be on her apple-shaped body. "Once a month, as part of our meeting, we all come over and buy up every stamp Pua has on hand with a woman featured on it. We are trying to create a shortage, so the USPS prints more."

"Though, I'm not in a huge hurry to load up on the new Nancy Reagan one," Josie said, squaring her hat firmly. "I'd like to see a few more women of color featured."

I glanced around the counter. "I have no idea where Pua keeps those."

"Under the counter in a locked drawer," Clara said, leaning over to point. "But if you don't know how to ring them up, I guess it doesn't matter."

"I have a call in to the main postmaster in Kahului. He's sending someone out Monday to train me," I said. Edith opened her mouth to ask about Pua's whereabouts, but I'd resolved not to answer anything to do with that topic. I headed her off by pointing to the clock over the door. "Oh dear. I'm sorry, ladies, but it's closing time."

"At least let us check our boxes," Pearl grumbled, spinning her wheelchair like a barrel racer and rolling it over Edith's yellow crocs.

"Ow! Watch how you're driving that thing!" Edith exclaimed, hopping on one foot. She lost her balance and keeled over, catching herself on Josie's oxygen tank. Mattie, Josie and Clara scrambled to help her up.

I busied myself straightening the already tidy space as the Red Hat Society ladies sorted themselves and checked their mailboxes. I followed them to the door as they made their way out, waving and making promises to see me again next week. I assured them I would be open for the business of supplying dedicated philatelists with all the featured female stamps of the moment, even Nancy Reagan. "I always liked her style," Edith the Lawn Gnome hollered back from the parking lot. "Save her for me, will you? I'll take all you have."

I closed and locked the door behind them, flipping the OPEN sign to CLOSED. Squinting through the glass, I watched the Red Hat Society slowly navigate the bumps and puddles of the unpaved parking lot. They were headed for Hibiscus Road, which led to the rows of little plantation houses that made up old town Ohia.

Mr. Ching still sat in his giant white Cadillac SUV that reminded me of an enormous chest freezer. He watched them go too, his expression suggesting he'd very much enjoy putting his gigantic car in gear and running over all of them. How had he felt about Frances Borland? I could butter him up—or antagonize him—and find out.

On impulse, I unlocked the door and stepped out, but the sight of me approaching seemed to activate the developer. He started the SUV, which made a sound like a tiger's growl as he put it in gear. He gunned it, spraying me with sandy mud, and headed for the entrance to New Ohia.

I might have made a powerful enemy by chuckling along with the Red Hat Society ladies.

I closed and locked the post office building for the weekend with a surprising feeling of regret. Yes, I'd been overwhelmed by not knowing the different functions, especially during the busy hour at the end of the day. But I'd also been stimulated by it all.

I loved the way the post office was the heart of this little community. All I had to do was be there, and eventually the whole town came to see me—or at least, that's how it felt.

If only Pua were at my side . . .

I'd already planned to take a run to unkink my muscles, but I decided I was going to jog around New Ohia. It was time to get familiar with it and see where "that rat Ching" lived. After, I'd go for a swim in the ocean. I was also looking forward to a relaxed evening, making myself a decent meal and reading a book before bed. I needed my rest, because tomorrow I had a surfing lesson to look forward to with Mr. K.

That shouldn't make me grin like an idiot, but it did.

I walked the few steps to my porch and unlocked the door of the shack. *Uh-oh.* I'd forgotten to fold up the Murphy bed. Tiki was curled directly on top of my pillow, and she slitted her eyes and hissed, lashing her tail. Clearly, she'd staked a claim.

I edged into the room, keeping well away from the bed. "Here's the deal, old girl. We have to coexist. I'll need that bed later, but you're welcome to it while I go out and do some things. I have to get my clothes, too. No attacking while I'm changing, okay?"

Tiki seemed reassured that I wasn't going to oust her from her chosen throne. She lifted a leg straight into the air and began licking her genitals.

"Well now, ahem, that's generally saved for private time," I said. She ignored me.

I opened the closet and took out my running clothes. Uncomfortable with Tiki's critical eye (though she clearly had no such inhibitions in my observations of her), I went into the bathroom to change, an athletic feat as always.

Getting into a jogging bra is a lot like putting a big tight rubber band over your head, pulling it down over your arms, and then arranging it around the necessary areas, all without punching yourself in the face. Somehow, I managed both it and my spandex shorts in the limited space. I pulled my hair into a ponytail and grabbed my socks and shoes to put on outside the bathroom.

I tossed my dirty clothes into the growing pile in the corner. I was going to have to figure out the laundry situation sometime soon and I wasn't looking forward to it. I eased open the door and left the sanctuary of the bathroom, only to discover that Tiki was gone again. How does she do that?

I took advantage of the cat's disappearance to shake out the pillowcase on the porch and fold up the bed tight to the wall, even anchoring it with the strap. I wouldn't put it past Tiki to have figured out how to fold it down. Better late than never. She would probably come in at dinnertime and sleep somewhere in the room, but if I could keep control of the bed, I wouldn't have to try to oust her from it—a battle I was sure I would lose.

Still feeling a little spooked from my hostile encounter with Ching and aware that I was heading into his territory, I put on my nylon webbing shoulder holster and loaded it with my Leatherman multi-tool. It would have to do as a self-defense weapon until Lei and Pono gave me back my Glock.

Shoes on, I headed out at a brisk walk down the Hana Highway. A few seagulls rode the gentle wind off the ocean. Mynah birds, much like the crows and blackbirds where I was from, hopped on the road and in the grass, scavenging for bugs and scraps and bickering amongst themselves.

As I got going down the road, several cars roared past, all tourist rentals tackling the "backside of Maui" after visiting Hana. They all drove much too fast for a road without a sidewalk or shoulder for pedestrians.

I was glad to turn into New Ohia's fancy entrance just to get off the narrow highway. There was no telling if one of those tourists would knock me off the road like a bowling pin while they tried to take a photo of the rainbow trailing over the bay.

Yep, the rainbow was doing that, and I was documenting, too.

I paused to study the pretentious sign. *NEW OHIA: Luxury Living in Paradise!* The golden letters glittered richly against the black lava stone. The artificial waterfall was a nice touch.

How had this development been built all the way to this point, with a lawsuit against it? New Ohia probably had powerful friends. Fancy places like this usually did.

I tugged down the brim of my reflective running hat and trotted through the entrance to check it out.

# 14

I took my time as I entered New Ohia, following the wide, smooth, freshly paved street. It curved through mounded, landscaped berms covered with tropical plantings. Large, mature coconut palms listed a bit at they tried to find their footing after being transplanted.

The lots appeared to be an acre or two in size, most of them not yet built on. Each was landscaped with neatly mowed grass and staked with fluttering bits of orange tape. Now and then I'd pass a completed house, usually marked "Model Home." These appeared to be occupied, judging by the cars visible through the garage windows. They were painfully neat otherwise.

Each of the streets ended in a cul-de-sac with a fan of lots at the end. I'd jog down each one, then backtrack to the main road and take the next street. All of them were named with Hawaiian names, beginning with A and going alphabetically from there, which seemed sensible.

I eventually happened upon a community center with a pool. The building was deserted, so I went inside. A brightly lit gym lined with shiny new machines took up one room and a dance studio with a barre and mirrors took up the other. The majority of the space was made up with a big dining area for events, and outside on the flagstone stood a row of shiny, new barbecues.

"Nice," I said to myself.

"It is, isn't it?"

Even though I'd only spoken with him once, I recognized Mr. Ching's voice immediately. I whirled and pasted a grin on my face. "Oh, Mr. Ching! I was hoping to speak with you a little more."

His smile lacked warmth but contained plenty of teeth. "The new postmaster, out from behind her desk." He looked me up and down. "What brings you trespassing into New Ohia?"

"I didn't know I was trespassing. I'm a possible resident." I tossed my ponytail like a horse flicking flies, hoping it seemed flirty. "I thought I'd take a look around, see what the buzz was all about. Those old biddies sure seemed to have their panties in a bunch about this place."

Ching stared at me for a minute, sizing me up; it seemed that for the time being, he chose to believe me. "They haven't taken the time to embrace all the benefits New Ohia will bring the community. But first and foremost, New Ohia is a gracious way of life." He gestured with an arm. "Picture an evening here with friends—using the pool, barbequing, fixing drinks, maybe even live music." He pointed to a small round pool at the end of the bigger one. "Perhaps coming here with a special someone for a little after-hours enjoyment of the jacuzzi."

"Lovely," I said in my gushiest voice. "How could anyone object to this?"

"Not everyone is ready for change. Progress. Prosperity." Ching's smile was practiced—he had his spiel down. "New Ohia is a place where families can embrace all the best things about Hawaiian life—the sea, the sun, the sand—and it's a great place to call home." He cocked his head, a challenge in his eyes. "Would you like to tour one of our model homes?"

"Sure," I chirped, bouncing on my toes. "Lead on, sir."

He turned and I followed him out of the center, surprised to see a golf cart pulled up outside the building. He continued his pitch as we climbed in.

"We have enhanced security in New Ohia," he said. "Embedded cameras with an AI that sifts for anyone not in our system. Very unobtrusive, but no one will be getting away with crime in New Ohia."

"So that's how you knew I was here."

"Yes. Thought I'd see what you were up to."

"Well, that's . . . interesting." Not creepy at all, Mr. Ching. I folded my hands demurely and tucked my knees under the golf cart's dash, but it was low and my long legs didn't really fit.

He started the golf cart with a lurch and I grabbed the dash for support, my knees bumping painfully as we peeled out of the community center parking lot.

"Did you know Frances Borland?" I asked, as we trundled down one of the side streets.

"Fran, the previous postmaster?" He slanted me a glance. "Sure. Bit of an oddball, that one. She was in the process of buying here."

"Is that so?" That was curious. Fran didn't seem like she'd have had enough money for New Ohia, but then again it didn't look like houses in Old Ohia came up for sale often. Maybe this was where she'd planned to retire.

I decided to take a chance. "Her body was discovered behind my shack."

He hit the brakes. My knees slammed against the dash. "Whoa!" I yelped.

"I'm sorry." Ching shook his head. "I was surprised. That's too bad—I've been sending her reminders that her next payment was due. That explains why I never heard anything back."

"She put money down on a house here?"

"Not a house. We have a planned apartment complex for seniors. All part of the multi-generational vision for New Ohia. She was one of our first buyers in that building." Ching seemed genuinely regretful. "I wonder who her heir is."

"Her body was just found, so I'm sure the Maui Police Department would like to help you out with that. I have the names and numbers of the detectives on the case. Let me help get the ball rolling for you." I whipped out my phone and before he could object, called Lei direct on her cell—I'd put her number in my favorites.

I'd suspected a cell phone tower was one of the perks of New Ohia. Sure enough, my call went right through. "Sergeant Texeira."

"Hi Sergeant, this is Kat Smith. The postmaster," I said into the phone as Ching glared at me.

"Hey." Lei seemed to be walking somewhere, she sounded out of breath. "What's going on?"

"I'm with Mr. Ching—what was your first name again?" I asked him.

"James. I go by Jimmy." Ching was scowling.

"I'll put you on speaker." I hit the button and held the phone away from my ear. "Sergeant Texeira, I'm with Jimmy Ching. He's the man in charge of New Ohia. He has some information about Fran that might be of interest."

"Oh yeah? Let me get somewhere a little quieter."

As we waited for Lei to move, Ching tapped his fingers restlessly on the steering wheel of the golf cart and fiddled with the rabbit's foot on his keys. "I wish you hadn't called them," he hissed.

"Really?" I widened my eyes. "Why not?"

"Excuse me?" Lei's voice came from the phone. "What was that?"

"Oh, Mr. Ching seems a little concerned that I called you about this," I said. "But I'm sure he's happy to help."

"Absolutely," Ching said. "Whatever I can do."

"Good," Lei said crisply. "Now, what's this information you've got?"

"Ms. Borland was an investor in New Ohia. She bought a unit in our pending Senior Living Complex," Ching said. "She signed contracts and put in a sizable down payment. But she hasn't responded to our requests for her second payment. Now I know why."

"Yes, Ms. Borland is deceased," Lei said. "Can we see your paperwork?"

"Happy to share it, but my understanding is that her obligation is inherited by her estate," Ching said. "That's in her contract. I need to know who her heir is."

"I think I'd like to formalize this conversation and speak more about the situation in person. Why don't you find Ms. Borland's contract and bring it down to the station in Kahului tomorrow? We can exchange whatever information is appropriate then," Lei said.

Ching's facial expression turned sour. "I'm a busy man. I have appointments tomorrow."

"And a murder investigation takes precedence over anything you might have scheduled," Lei said. "I'm sure your people will understand. I'll see you at ten a.m. tomorrow at the Kahului Police Station." She ended the conversation.

I slid the phone into my pocket. "Ready to show me that model home now?"

"I'm sorry, but I have calls to make." His sour expression had not lightened. "Need to clear tomorrow's schedule."

I flicked my ponytail again. "I hope you aren't upset that I called the detective. I assumed you'd want to assist."

"Of course, I want to help." He turned the golf cart and headed for the entrance. "I don't have time for your tour." He tossed me a sleazy smile. "Another time, though. I think New Ohia would suit a woman of your caliber much more than that shack behind the post office."

I bristled. I was becoming rather fond of my gecko-riddled shack, but I made an effort to seem ditzy and batted my eyes at him. "Oh, you're so right. I love what I've seen so far. New Ohia is going to be amazing."

He deposited me back at the entrance. "See you around."

"I'm sure you will," I said cheerfully. "The post office is eternal."

Ching gunned the golf cart as he left. It made a defiant farting noise and refused to speed up. I almost felt sorry for him—he seemed like a man with a world of problems on his shoulders. But I couldn't quite muster anything but suspicion about him. There was something fishy about this whole place, and Ching specifically. I also didn't like the feeling of unseen camera eyes on me.

Even so, their phone signal booster was working and I needed more info. I sat down on the black lava stone parapet that ran around the lip of the waterfall at the entrance, gazing across the road to the half-moon of beach. Sunset was gilding the poufy clouds over the ocean with pink. The rugged, corrugated metal roof on the shelter at the end of the pier almost glowed. Evening in Ohia was almost as beautiful as sunrise.

I took my phone out and called Lei back. Maybe she'd tell me what was going on with Pua now that I'd fed her another lead.

"Ms. Smith. Something else?" Lei picked up right away.

"I'm alone now, Lei."

"And?" She sounded like she was smiling. "What now, my post-master sleuth?"

"Ching wanted to scrape me off like I was something stuck to his shoe after your convo. I think you should look into New Ohia. There's something off about the whole place. I found out about a lawsuit against New Ohia brought by the citizens of the town, and yet the place is more than half-done and units are selling like nothing is going on."

"That's a heck of a can of *pilikia*," Lei said.

"What?"

"*Pilikia*. Trouble." Lei sighed. "I have to stay focused on the investigation and where it takes us. Maybe something will come to point us in that direction."

"I don't like Ching. He's a creeper."

"I respect your instinct on that." Her voice was sincere. "I'll dig into him, see if there's anything in his background."

I took a breath, gusted it out, and made myself ask. "Can you tell me what you've got on Pua that's so compelling that you had to arrest her?" I tried to keep the note of accusation out of my tone, but I could tell it crept in.

Lei sighed again. "She's about to be bailed out, so you can cool your jets—along with all the other people from Ohia who've called to tell us we're barking up the wrong palm tree."

"Her cousin Alan Chang must have gotten her some legal help."

"He did. Bennie Fernandez. Notorious defense lawyer."

"Good. I don't think Pua did it."

"Well. Kat, there's DNA evidence on the body that says she did."

# 15

"What? What DNA evidence?"

Lei didn't have to answer any of my questions. I was a civilian now. But after a moment she said, "Hair caught in her jewelry. There would've likely been more, but the material got degraded by the elements and decomposition. Pua Chang also has motive, you can't forget that."

My heart thumped. "What motive? Besides the fact that Pua wanted the job as postmaster?"

"Pua was dating Fran's cousin in Kahului. The 'friend' you said Fran had, that she spent the night with when she was in town . . . that's him. He's also Fran's heir. Turns out, Fran wasn't exactly loaded, but she wasn't broke either. She and her cousin co-owned an apartment building that they inherited from Fran's aunt. The cousin lives on-site and manages the units. Fran took her portion of the rents and invested all of it in the stock market, only living on her salary as postmaster. Those stocks have grown considerably."

"What does Pua say about all this?" I asked, still skeptical. Was it enough?

"Nothing. Even with her attorney present."

Good for you, Pua! I did a little fist pump. "Seems to me the cousin might have more motive than Pua did," I ventured.

"He has an alibi for the day she went missing."

"Ah. Well, in that case I hope talking to Ching shakes something loose. What's the cousin's name?" I was already planning a visit to his house with some excuse. I was good at getting people to talk, and I had the advantage of not being a cop.

"I gave you this info as a thank-you for the tips you've given us, but that's as far as it goes. No leaking any of this, Kat. I'm wise to your moves! And no more investigating. Who knows what will happen if you keep shaking the trees," Lei warned.

"That tells me you don't really think Pua did it," I said triumphantly. "You arrested her to flush out the real killer."

"Have a nice weekend, Kat. Enjoy your surf lesson with Keone," Lei said, ending the call.

I walked back to the shack with a lot on my mind. Tiki was still gone when I unlocked the door, so I changed into my swimsuit without interference and headed for the beach.

The wind had died down and the ocean was as calm as a lake, sunset colors slicking the surface of the water like oil paint. A couple of local families parked their trucks on the beach and were eating a picnic on the pier. The kids jumped off one side of it into the ocean, shrieking with happiness, and the men fished off the other, presumably the no swimming zone. The ladies sat talking around the picnic table as they managed the food.

I parked on my terry cloth bathrobe on the sand and watched for a while, then walked down to dive in myself. The water was too cool to hang out in for long, but fine enough for a quick dip. I swam back and forth across the little bay, my mind on what Lei had told me. I had to find out who Fran's cousin was. Maybe Opal would know, since Pua was dating him. I decided to forgo my quiet evening at home and go visit the Pahinuis instead to see what I could find out about this mystery man.

After a quick shower and change, I looked around the shack for something I could bring with me to the Pahinuis. It didn't seem right to go visit empty-handed. The only thing I had worth giving was the glass fishing float I'd found that morning. I reluctantly wrapped the glass orb up in a paper napkin and headed over to the general store.

Even after sunset, there was still plenty of light. As I crossed the parking lot, I marveled at the clouds on the horizon, pink and plentiful as cotton candy at a fair. The mynahs gathered on the fronds of the coconut palms, chattering away, their voices so loud I could hardly hear myself knocking on the back door of the Pahinuis' house.

Opal answered the door in an embroidered kimono robe and a long nightgown. "What's up? Did something happen?"

"Nothing serious, just a few things have come up that I'd like to chat with you about." I'd thought long and hard and decided to take the couple into my confidence about the case, at least as it related to getting Pua out of jail. "I brought you a present."

Opal's pale brows rose in surprise. "Really?"

"Yup." I handed her the float. "I found this on the beach this morning."

"Come in. The mosquitoes are right behind you," she said, accepting my gift and gesturing for me to enter. I stepped inside and shut the screen door behind me. She pointed at my shoes. "We don't wear those inside in Hawaii." I slipped my Nikes off and stowed them on a nearby shoe rack.

"You're just in time for dinner," Opal said. "We've got enough for Kat, don't we, Artie?"

"Sure," he said. "You're welcome to join us, Kat." The big man was swathed in a "Kiss the Cook" apron and held a wooden spoon in his hand.

My tummy rumbled a loud agreement to this plan. "Thank you," I said, taking a seat at their table covered with red-checked oilcloth.

Opal opened the crudely wrapped bundle I'd handed her. "Oh

my! This is very special. A sign of good luck." She handed the glass ball back to me. "I can't accept. The ocean meant for you to have it."

I couldn't help smiling as I received it. "I wanted to bring you something."

She flapped her hands. "You're helping Pua. That's enough for me."

My instincts about people had been honed by my work with the Secret Service. I knew I could trust Opal and Artie Pahinui, but I'd need to know that they wouldn't speak with anyone else about the information I was about to pass on from Lei.

"Speaking of helping Pua." I leaned forward. "I want to find out who killed Fran—really help with the investigation and clear Pua's name. Can I swear you both to secrecy? No sharing with friends or family. No coconut wireless updates."

Opal nodded. "Of course."

Artie blinked his milky eyes and inclined his head. "We want to help. Fran was a little *lōlō*, but she was a good woman at heart."

"Uh . . . what is *lōlō*?" I asked.

"Little bit . . ." He circled the air beside his ear. "Crazy."

"Right." I watched the blind man move confidently around the kitchen, preparing our dinner—which appeared to be a savory stew over rice. I addressed my next question to Opal. "Was Pua dating anyone? It's important."

Opal widened her pale blue eyes. "Yes, she was, for a time. But she dumped him. Said he wasn't who she'd thought he was."

"What's the guy's name?"

"I thought you were giving us information about the investigation, not the other way around." Opal shook the runes in her pocket. They made a musical sound like a rain stick.

"I promise it's relevant."

"His name is Gavin Peabody. He lives in Kahului. They met when he came out here and stopped by the post office a few times. He asked her out, they dated a while, then broke up."

"When did they break up?"

"About six months ago."

I raised my brows. "Around the time Fran disappeared?"

Opal frowned. "I guess so."

Just then, Artie turned away from the stove, a pair of steaming pottery bowls in his enormous hands. "Dinner's ready. Let's talk more after we've got something in our bellies."

The stew was delicious. I ate my whole bowlful and went back for seconds. Opal shook her head. "You've got a hollow leg, girlie."

"I worked all day without lunch and then went jogging," I said. "Besides, this is the tastiest stew I've had in a long time, Mr. Pahinui."

"Call me Artie." He hadn't eaten much of his dinner and was already finished. "How 'bout a little mood music?"

"Always," Opal said.

"I'd love to hear you play," I said.

Artie got up and fetched the guitar I'd seen before, a six-string acoustic. Pushing back a bit from the table, he began to play. He strummed softly, occasionally plucking out the melody, and began to sing. I listened, mesmerized, as he sang traditional Hawaiian verses in a deep, melancholy voice.

The music seemed to take me by the hand, leading me to the beach to walk in the sand alongside a warm, moonlit sea. Despite not knowing the meaning of the native words he sung, I felt the wonder and love of Hawaii in his music.

I clapped wholeheartedly when Artie finished and set aside the guitar.

"What is that?" I asked. "I've never heard anything like it."

"Hawaiian music is its own category," Opal said. "And the Pahinuis are the kings of it."

"Thank you, Artie. I'd like to download some songs on my phone to listen to, if you have any recommendations."

He told me the names of some "good starter albums" to listen to, and I took notes to order the music later when I had phone signal or computer access.

While Artie sang, Opal had quietly cleared the table, put away the leftovers, and washed the dishes by hand at the sink. Now she rejoined us, wiping her hands on a dishtowel. "Okay, Kat. What's your plan to clear Pua's name?"

"Well, I have some things to run down. First, did you know Fran was a buyer into New Ohia's senior living complex?" I told the Pahinuis about my visit to New Ohia and my conversation with Ching.

"Ching is a piece of work," Opal said, "but he isn't the big money behind New Ohia. He's just the project and sales manager of it."

I frowned. "So, whose land is it? And how did they get such a big development approved when the local residents oppose it?"

"That's the million-dollar question," Artie rumbled.

Opal picked up the thread. "The land belonged to the state, then suddenly we hear that it's been bought by a development group called New Ohia Vision LLC. There was one "community meeting" scheduled for it, but the notice was buried in the Maui News classified section on a Tuesday. No one out here saw it, and even if we had, the meeting was held in Kahului. So between the lack of adequate notice and the location, no one made it to represent the people of the town. Next thing you know, bulldozers showed up and they began building what you see now."

"That seems illegal," I said, indignant.

"Heck yeah, it was!" Opal said. "We rallied quickly, and the Red Hat Society ladies launched the lawsuit. It's slowed things down but hasn't stopped anything. They're actually at Phase Three, with individuals buying lots and condos for their own development."

"Exactly what do the Old Ohia townspeople want?" I asked.

"To fully stop the development because the due process of approval and the environmental and economic impact studies weren't done. If we can't get it stopped, then a new school, beachfront park, and proper infrastructure needs to be funded by the development, including some affordable housing units. They can't just add this huge luxury place out here with no services to support it," Opal explained.

Artie had begun plucking his guitar gently. I got the feeling the discussion was bothering him and playing calmed his nerves. I was grateful—it calmed mine too.

"Where do you think killing Fran might have been a part of all of this?" I asked.

"No idea." Opal shook her head.

"Did you know that New Ohia is bugged with hidden cameras? Ching made a point of telling me how safe the neighborhood is, with an AI security system embedded that's based on facial recognition."

"Whoa," Artie said in his soft way. "Big Brother is watching us."

"Sure is." I looked around the humble kitchen. Would the fancy folks who bought the homes in New Ohia frequent the dilapidated store Artie and Opal had poured so many years into? It didn't seem likely. My money was on the new shopping complex Ching mentioned. It would eventually squeeze the Pahinuis out of their home and business, as it happens in so many other gentrified places.

"What do you want to do next, Kat?" Opal asked.

"I am not sure how New Ohia fits in with Fran's death. Maybe it doesn't. But Pua's ex that you told me about? Turns out, he is Fran's cousin and heir. I have a few of Fran's personal effects that were left in the post office, and tomorrow is Saturday. Keone Kaihale is coming in the morning to take me surfing. I thought I'd ask him to give me a ride to Gavin Peabody's place afterward to give him the items. Supposedly, he has an alibi for when Fran disappeared, but it can't hurt to push on it a bit."

"You be careful," Artie said. "I told Pua the same thing—I no like da man." His voice had the inflection of Hawaiian Creole "pidgin" as he said it.

"Yeah, Artie didn't care for Peabody right off," Opal said, "but I thought he was charming. He really tried with Pua, but of course, he was outclassed. No one's good enough for Pua as far as I'm concerned, but she's lonely out there on her ranch with only her dog and nephew for company."

"Speaking of, Lei said Pua was getting out on bail soon. Probably Monday since it's the weekend now," I told them. "Do you need any help handling her place?"

"Nope, we've got it covered—and you've got some investigating to do," Opal said.

"Just be careful," Artie repeated. His blind eyes seemed to be warning me even more than his words.

# 16

I woke up early the next morning with the weight of Tiki draped over my head like a heavy fur hat. The deep, rumbling purr reverberating through my head wasn't the ocean breaking on the beach as it had been in my dream. Instead, it was a flea-riddled stray cat using my cranium as a pillow.

The realization almost made me fling Tiki off, but I thought better of it—she might dig her claws into my head and hang on. I was pleased that my attack cat was finally showing friendly signs, but the idea of fleas in my hair made my scalp crawl and itch.

"Hey, Tiki," I whispered cautiously. "What do you say I give you a bath? I bought some flea shampoo at Opal's. You're gonna love it."

Tiki's purr vibrated my entire head.

"Is that a yes?"

Very carefully, I reached up a hand to pet her, stroking her back while simultaneously removing my head from under her body. By twisting around and rising to my knees, I was able to keep petting as she lay on my pillow, stretched out contentedly, her eyes gleaming half-slits in the dim light.

"C'mere, pretty girl. Let's go over to the sink and get you clean." I eased my free hand underneath her body on one side and fisted the hand that had been petting her around the loose skin over her shoulders, getting a grip on the scruff of her neck.

Tiki yowled and lashed out with a paw, drawing blood. I shrieked as she leaped off my pillow and took up her spot under the table. Her tail lashed angrily. Clearly her trust had been betrayed.

I pressed my fingers over my wounded arm. "You need to have a flea bath before we can share a bed, understand?"

She growled again and added a hiss for emphasis. "Well, I'll wash my hair with the flea shampoo then. You can get used to the smell. I'll show you it's not so bad."

That's how I found myself climbing into Mr. K's lifted truck with my hair in a wet braid, swimsuit already on under my athletic shorts and a tank. A brand-new towel and change of clothes tagged along in a grocery bag.

"What's that smell?" Mr. K said after greeting me with a big smile and a quick hug that set my innards abuzz.

"New shampoo from Opal's. You like it?"

"Seems a little . . . strong." His eyes appeared to be watering, but he focused on getting the truck on the road. "You can always bring your shampoo along and shower after we go out, instead of before. That's what most surfers do."

"Okay. Got it," I said seriously, as if taking instruction already. "Where are we going?"

"Back toward Hana there's a fun spot called Koki Beach. Perfect for beginners."

I turned my head to look out the back window and could see two long surfboards in the truck's bed.

"I appreciate you taking the time to teach me," I said. "I can count on one hand the number of weeks of vacation I've taken throughout my career, and most of those were at Christmas so I could see Aunt Fae in Maine. Maine's pretty in the winter snow, but not a place to go surfing."

"I guess not, though serious surfers always find a way. I bet if you look online, there's a Polar Bear Surf Club in Maine, or something like that. You might have a new sport when you visit." Mr. K downshifted and swerved around a rock that had dislodged from an overhanging cliff and landed in the road. "Never a dull stretch of road around here."

I rolled down my window, enjoying the fresh breeze off the ocean and the way it dissipated the fumes from the flea shampoo. "It's so beautiful here."

"Kinda ruins you for living anywhere else," Keone said. "I've been all over the world as a pilot. Never planned to come home except to visit. Then, my dad passed away and Mom wanted the family around her. Once I came back, I realized there was nowhere I'd rather be than the eastern coast of Maui."

I held out a hand and a dangling hibiscus, crimson as blood, brushed my fingers as we passed. "I'm going to miss this when I leave." I hadn't meant to say the words aloud, but it was too late to take them back.

Keone glanced at me sharply. "You don't plan to stay." He smiled, a slow, wicked grin. "Only the people the island accepts end up staying, anyway."

"What do you mean?"

He shrugged those big shoulders. "We have a saying: 'the island decides.' People try to move here all the time. Most of them don't make it past the two-year mark. That's why I'm not too worried about New Ohia ruining our lifestyle. Those off-islanders can try all they like to change Ohia, but the island will only accept those whom it wants here."

"I hope you're right." An odd tightness gripped my chest. I wanted to be one of the people the island decided to keep—even though I wasn't planning to stay. Talk about *lōlō*.

"But it sounds like you won't be here long, anyway." His voice was casual.

"I—I'm not Postal Service. I'm Secret Service. My boss pulled strings to get me the job in Ohia." I told him my situation. "So, besides being weird about . . . things," my face heated, remembering when he'd touched me and how I'd reacted, "I'm not going to be here long enough to have a relationship."

"Is this your way of giving me the 'it's not you, it's me' speech?" Keone smiled. "It's okay, Kat. We're just going surfing, not getting married. At least not right away."

"Ha." I stuck my face out the window like a golden retriever to cool my cheeks. "You're funny." I changed the subject. "How do you feel about driving me to Kahului after we surf to help me investigate Fran Borland's murder? I have a lead I want to follow up on."

Surfing is fun.

This isn't a newsflash to those who've tried it, but it sure was to me. The right equipment is key, and the board Mr. K brought for me was called a "soft top." Ten feet long and made from floaty foam, its rough, textured deck made it easy for my feet to grip.

We practiced on the beach before getting in the water. I was physically fit enough to pop up into the proper stance and even had the arm strength for paddling out, so I may have had a few advantages as a first-timer. But those things didn't help with the timing of when to paddle for a wave, where to position myself, and the balancing act of keeping upright.

Keone helped by swimming beside me as I paddled the board. He coached me on when to turn the cumbersome thing around and pushed me into my first few waves to make sure I caught them. He was a dolphin in the water, and his confidence and enthusiasm assured me that I could master this, even when my first few attempts ended up in wipeouts.

Once I caught my first wave and rode it all the way to the beach —Keone cheering me all the way—I was hooked.

Koki Beach was the perfect spot to learn to surf. The waves were gentle, and it had a sandy bottom that was forgiving on the wipeouts. It also had a great view to aim for—a pair of coconut palms framing a little picnic hut on the beach. Off to one side, huge ocean birds circled a nearby atoll.

We lingered out in the ocean between "sets" (which I learned meant groups of waves). I pointed to huge, dark seabirds riding the updrafts off the mini island. "What are those?"

"Great frigatebirds. *'Iwa* in Hawaiian. They nest on that island."

"Ee-va." I tested out the word. "What does that mean?"

"The frigatebirds are known to steal fish from other birds, so they're called 'thief.' The English word 'frigate' refers to ships used in the 1700s to pursue other vessels, including pirate ships."

I watched the graceful, powerful birds circling the little atoll, and missed seeing a wave hump up behind me, its crest frothing.

"Look out!" Keone called. "Time to duck dive!"

But I was too late for that advanced maneuver and ended up taking a tumble. My board and I washed up on the beach, my bikini seriously out of place and sand in areas it really shouldn't ever be found. I rearranged myself into decency, and watched Keone body-surf a wave in to join me, one arm extended as I'd seen Pono do the other day.

"Never take your eyes off the ocean," he reminded me.

"I couldn't help watching those birds. And I can't tell whether you're a dolphin or a sea otter in the ocean. You seem to know it so well."

"Dolphin, definitely." His playful grin lit up his face. "'Kaihale' means 'house of the sea.' And the dolphin is my '*aumakua*.'"

I picked up my heavy board. "I think I've wiped out enough for my first day. Maybe you could tell me what an 'ow-ma-koo-ah' is on the drive to Kahului?"

"Sure."

I was really starting to like Mr. K's easygoing, upbeat attitude—maybe a little too much. He hadn't balked at taking me to "town" and pursuing a conversation with Fran's cousin, Gavin Peabody. "We'll grab some sushi on the way back," was all he'd said, a gleam in his eye.

I did the best I could to clean up and get ready for our trip to civilization, considering all I had to work with was a cold shower at the beach park and the mirror in the sun visor in Mr. K's truck.

"You look beautiful," he said, as I scowled at my sunburned face in the mirror.

I attempted to tug a comb through my sea-tangled hair. "You're funny. But then I told you that already."

"Some women don't need makeup and curling irons. You're one of them." He sounded completely matter of fact.

I could only tolerate the compliment because he was busy driving and not looking at me. I'd never been good with compliments. I cleared my throat awkwardly and changed the subject.

"So, what's an *'aumakua*?"

"Family protectors. Our ancestors can take different forms and return to guard, warn, or even reprimand us."

"Kind of like a 'spirit animal'?"

"No. We don't choose a personal *'aumakua*, though some people claim them. Each family has an animal, plant or even a place that has chosen them. The relationship is mutual and goes on for generations. We respect and protect our *'aumakua* in its earthly form as it holds the *mana*, or spiritual power and presence of our ancestors. And in return, it looks out for, protects, and gives wisdom to us. The Kaihale family's *'aumakua* is the dolphin, as I said, though Pono's branch claims the whale."

"I want an *'aumakua*."

"It's a Hawaiian thing." He smiled, taking any sting from the words. "But you can have a guardian angel. Maybe Tiki is yours."

I snorted. "Ha! I'm in trouble if that's the case."

A minute later I asked, "Don't you want to know what's fishy about Gavin Peabody?"

"I'm sure you'll tell me."

"He had the strongest motive to kill Fran of anyone the police have found, but he has an alibi."

"Doesn't that rule him out?" He had to put both hands on the wheel to dodge a tourist parked kitty-corner to a waterfall.

"Tourists! Do they think they're the only people on the road?" I exclaimed indignantly.

Keone laughed. "Been here less than a week and you're already grumbling about the tourists."

"I guess I am. But hey, this isn't Disneyland. It's like they abandon their brains to get a photo, and people can get hurt." I huffed and brought myself back to our conversation. "Anyway, another reason I want to check out Peabody is that Pua was dating him. Did you know anything about that?"

"No." Keone gunned the truck around a dawdling red Mustang with the top down. "But it seems like that might have gotten her into trouble."

"You're right about that. The cops think that gives her motive. So how shall we play this, to get maximum information from this guy?" I was interested to see what Keone came up with.

"I sit in the truck and wait for you as backup, while you exercise your amateur sleuth muscles," he said. "I'll be honest—I don't think this is a good idea, Kat. You could mess things up for the investigation without meaning to. Did the cops ask you to help with this part of things?"

"They've been grateful for the tips I've brought in so far," I said, defensive. "I want to clear Pua's name and find Fran's killer. I've got a feeling about this guy."

Keone shook his head and kept his eyes on the road. "Just be careful."

"You're not the first to tell me that," I said, remembering Artie Pahinui's warning.

# 17

Keone gave me a little finger wave as I got out of the truck in the parking lot of a two-story apartment building in Kahului. "I'll be right here. Give a yell if you need me."

"Chicken," I said.

"Too many cooks in the kitchen, is what it is." He winked. "Go get 'em, Kat."

This guy. I couldn't even get mad at him for not doing what I wanted.

I shut the truck's door with a bang and turned to face the building. A sun-blasted cube of concrete painted the color of rust, the building looked like it had gone up sometime in the 1970s and hadn't seen an update since. Crisping grass attested to Kahului's recent drought conditions, but a large plumeria tree beside the main entrance still had leaves and even a few hot pink, five-petaled flowers.

I walked up crumbling cement steps, the plastic bag containing the personal items from Fran's desk in the post office inside my backpack.

The main entrance to the building was a single glass door with a call box. I scrolled through the list of names, searching for G. Peabody and coming up empty. Peering inside, I noted an expanse of worn carpet and a wall of mailboxes. There were three doors, one marked STORAGE, one marked STAIRS, and one marked MANAGER. Bingo.

I hit the call button for Manager.

"Yes?" A male voice picked up on the first ring.

"Hello. I'd like to speak to Gavin Peabody about a personal matter," I said in my most businesslike voice.

"No soliciting."

"This is not a solicitation. It's about . . . Frances Borland." I held my breath.

The door buzzed loudly, releasing its lock. I opened it and stepped inside, immediately assailed by the smell of cooking onions. The lobby, if you could call it that, was stuffy and hot, and clearly had ventilation issues.

I headed for the door marked "Manager" and knocked. A man wearing an aloha shirt decorated with hula dancers opened the door. A thick gold chain was visible in his open collar. "What's this about?"

I'm of the opinion that the only good jewelry on a man is a watch and a wedding ring, so the chain was off-putting—as were the anatomically correct, naked hula dancers on the shirt.

"You wanted to speak about Fran?" Peabody frowned.

His outfit had distracted me to the point that I had to make an effort to remember my speech. I pasted a sorrowful look on my face and extended a hand. "I'm so sorry for your loss. I'm Kat Smith, the new postmaster."

"Peabody. Gavin Peabody." We shook.

Peabody's pumped-up arms and obvious hair plugs went perfectly with the gold chain and ugly shirt, but not with stylish Pua. I tried to picture the two together and couldn't make it work in my head.

"What's this about, Ms. Smith?"

"Oh my goodness, it's all been a bit much." I flapped a hand and my eyelashes dramatically. "Can I sit down somewhere? Perhaps a cold beverage?"

His teeth showed in a humorless smile. "Sure. Come have a seat in my office. Coke okay? That's all the machine out here is stocked with." He gestured to a vending machine with most of the labels crossed out.

"That would be lovely." I took a seat in a molded plastic chair just inside the office. In front of me was a desk topped with a very new-looking Mac computer. Peabody crossed the lobby and whacked the side of the vending machine several times. A can of Coke rattled down into the tray and he hooked it out. "Management secret," he said, returning to hand the cold drink to me.

"Thank you. It's such a long way out here . . ." I popped the top and drained half of the Coke, hiding a burp behind my hand. "I appreciate you seeing me with so little notice. I was the one to discover Fran, you know."

Peabody sat down abruptly, some of the color seeping out of his face. "Oh yeah?"

"Well. Part of her, at least." I cast my eyes down modestly. "I can't bear to talk about it."

"So, you came here then." Skepticism dried his tone. "To talk to me."

"No, to return some of Fran's personal effects. In case they were of sentimental value." I took the white plastic bag containing the magazine and other personal items out of my backpack and held it out.

Peabody recoiled as if I'd offered a snake. "I don't want anything of Fran's!"

I widened my eyes. "Really? Aren't you her next of kin? Her . . . heir?"

He scowled, waving away my offering. "It was nice of you to think of that, but whatever it is, I don't want it. Fran and I weren't close."

"How sad. She seemed very isolated. In fact, it was a surprise to find out she co-owned this building with you."

"How did you know that?"

I simpered and fluttered my eyelashes. "Little birds chirp in Ohia."

"I'm not surprised," he said darkly. "That's how I heard Pua got arrested for killing her—the coconut wireless."

"It also told me that you and Pua dated."

Peabody flapped a hand in a dismissive gesture I was beginning to recognize. "She wasn't my type." He refocused his gaze on me as if seeing me for the first time. I felt his eyeballs crawl over my body from the top of my head to the bottom of my Nikes. "You could be a model, with that height and those legs."

*EW.* How had Pua put up with this guy for six whole months? I had to get this interview back on track. "Are you sure you don't want Fran's things? They were left in her desk at the post office."

"No. Fran went her way, and I went mine. There was no love lost between us."

"So where did you think she went when she disappeared?"

"No idea. Nor did I care." His eyes narrowed suspiciously. "You seem awfully interested in Fran."

"Well, moving into her living space, taking her old job, and finding her body will do that to a person," I said. "I bet the news that you inherited her debt to the New Ohia development wasn't welcome, since you weren't close." I observed Peabody closely as I hit him with that left hook.

Peabody's heavy black brows flew up. "What?"

"Mr. Ching from New Ohia hasn't contacted you yet?" I clicked my tongue. "He told me he was going to right away. The payment for the unit she bought in the development is overdue. He told me about it when I let him know the sad news."

Bright color flooded back into Peabody's cheeks. "Thanks for stopping by, but I need to make some phone calls."

I was being dismissed. "Once again, I'm sorry for your loss. If I can help in any way, please let me know. I'm at the post office in Ohia."

"Bye," Peabody said pointedly, and reached for the phone on his desk.

Ichiban, a hole-in-the-wall Japanese restaurant, was located in one of the oldest shopping centers on Maui, according to Mr. K. The little shoebox of an eatery was sandwiched between a grocery called Ah Fook's Supermarket and a nail salon named Talons. A huge monkeypod tree in the parking lot spread gigantic, shading arms over the area, the only real clue to the shopping center's age.

"Our family used to drive out here from Hana to stock up on groceries once a month," Keone said. We were seated amidst an abundance of kitschy Japanese decor from the 50s. "Coming to Ichiban was a big treat."

"Nice that it's still here when so many other things have changed on the island." I picked up the printed paper menu that doubled as a placemat and examined it. "You said sushi, but I'm not really a fan. What else is good here?"

"The tempura is excellent," came Pono's distinctive bass voice. I lifted my gaze to see Keone's cousin and his partner Lei entering the restaurant. Lei was missing her usual badge, gun, and cotton blazer, but otherwise looked the same. She had an extremely cute toddler with dark brown curls riding one of her hips.

Keone, seated across from me, shrugged at my surprised glance. "I can't come into town without letting my cuz know I'm here. Once the word gets out, no telling what might happen."

Pono slid into the booth beside Keone as Lei flagged down our waitress. "I need a highchair, please." The lady nodded, leaving to fetch a wooden baby chair.

Lei turned to me. "Kat, meet Rosie."

"Hi Rosie!" I waved and smiled. I'd dare anybody not to when looking at that cherub face.

Rosie blinked big brown eyes and popped a finger out of her mouth to speak. "Hi, Auntie Kat."

I felt a sensation like a sweet breeze passing over my skin, tightening my chest—it was the cockles of my heart warming. I'd always wondered about that old saying, and now I knew what it felt like. "Oh my gosh, Lei. She's too adorable."

"I know." Lei's smile was huge. "And she has great verbal skills for her age."

The highchair arrived, and Lei took a few minutes to settle Rosie into her seat. She then handed the little girl a copy of the menu and a pack of crayons. Rosie bent her curly head over the paper and started coloring.

"I'm surprised to see you guys," I said. "Especially on a weekend."

"We were at the office doing some follow-up when Keone called." Lei said. "Murder never sleeps."

"What murder?" Rosie's piping little voice made all of us jerk as if we've been zapped with an electric prod.

"Nothing, honey. Grown-up talk," Lei said. "What are you drawing there? Is that a dinosaur?" The conversation steered back to more appropriate topics for young ears for a few minutes.

Once Rosie was sufficiently absorbed in her coloring again, Lei leaned over to me and said, "Keone let us know you were going to visit Peabody. Didn't I tell you not to stick your nose in the investigation?"

"I had some of Fran's things to return to him." I patted my backpack next to me. "He didn't want them, anyway."

"How did it go?" Pono asked.

"I found out that Gavin Peabody is a squicky individual who didn't care much for his cousin Fran."

"Squicky?" Keone raised his eyebrows, his dimple showing.

"Combo of squidlike and icky. Not a quality human," I said, with a meaningful glance at Rosie. "Pua was smart to dump him."

"I could've told you that," Pono said. "The dude hardly blinked when we gave him the death notification. Just asked what 'disposing of the remains' was going to cost him."

The waitress came by again, and everyone ordered sushi but me. I took Pono's advice and went with the tempura. Once our server left, I revisited the story of my jog through the New Ohia development for Keone and Pono.

"The one interesting thing I learned is that Peabody didn't know about Fran buying a senior unit in New Ohia. He was not pleased that Ching said he'd inherit her obligation to buy into the development."

"He will inherit plenty from her stock portfolio to either pay for the unit, or for legal assistance to get out of it," Lei said. "The lawyer handling her estate said it was worth several million."

My eyebrows rose. "Huh. Seems he really did have a motive to . . . do away with Fran," I said, carefully avoiding the "M" word, as Rosie reached over to help herself to some of her mother's sushi.

We were nearly finished with dinner when suddenly Lei's and Pono's phones went off simultaneously. They both looked at their devices and abruptly got up to answer them, leaving Mr. K and me to keep an eye on Rosie.

The toddler, who I guessed to be between two and three years old, was surprisingly articulate and good company. She had drawn a picture of a dinosaur that actually had a head and a tail, though the middle was somewhat indeterminate.

"What's your favorite dinosaur?" I asked Rosie.

"Brachiosaurus," she said with perfect pronunciation. "I like the herbivores best."

Keone and I looked at each other with our mouths ajar at the tot's brilliance.

Lei hurried back with Pono in tow. "I know this is outside the usual, but would you two mind taking Rosie home to our place in

Haiku? We have a call out to a . . . a situation in Ohia. I'm going to ride with Pono so we can head straight there to check it out."

Lei and Pono were homicide detectives. Murder was the only "situation" they checked out.

Someone had just been killed in my new hometown.

# 18

Lei called her husband about the change of plans. I would be driving Rosie back home in Lei's truck, then Keone and I would take his vehicle the rest of the way to Ohia. Because of the location of Haiku on the eastern coast of Maui, we'd be driving the classic "road to Hana"—the extra winding route. Keone assured me most of the tourists would be gone and the roads would be clear by the time night fell.

"I've got it memorized," he said. "We'll just whip around those turns once we drop Rosie off."

"Are you sure you trust me to drive your daughter home?" Nervous perspiration broke out on my upper lip as we settled Rosie into the car. I'd rather take a shift guarding POTUS all by myself than be solely responsible for Lei's daughter's welfare.

"Since when do I get a top-notch Secret Service agent to escort my daughter home from dinner?" Lei said. She was already in work mode, her mind a million miles away as she secured Rosie in a big, molded plastic thing with enough straps to resemble a seat on a space shuttle. "Bye, honey, I love you. Daddy is waiting for you at home."

"Bye, Mama." Rosie hardly looked up as Lei kissed her brow—she was playing with some kind of push-button toy.

Lei shut the back passenger door of her silver Tacoma. I got into the driver's seat.

"Just follow Keone. He's been to our house lots of times before," Lei said.

Mr. K was in his truck and positioned to turn onto the busy Hana Highway, waiting for me. I pulled up behind him and waited for the third truck in our little procession to pass by. We let Stanley, with his whirling cop light on the dashboard, surge out into traffic ahead of us. Cars cleared the road in front of them, and we were able to follow for a bit before we had to break off toward Haiku.

"You like dogs?" Rosie asked suddenly, from the rear seat. "D is for dog."

I glanced in the rearview. It was angled to monitor the toddler in her seat with a small bull's-eye mirror. She held up the toy to show me—it was an alphabet letter recognition game.

"I do like dogs."

"We have a dog. His name is Conan."

"Conan. That's a good name." I groped for a topic. "Do you like cats?"

"No." Rosie met my gaze in the mirror. "Because they don't like dogs."

"Oh. Well, I have a cat. Or, you could say, she has me." I sped up around a van loaded with windsurfers, keeping Mr. K in view. "I'm not sure Tiki likes anybody."

"Yah. Cats poop in a tray. It's gross."

I had no idea where Tiki pooped. That was a nasty thought, too.

Conversation ground to a halt. I pushed the button for the radio, and some mellow "slack-key" guitar came on. I recognized the style from Artie's playing. A glance in the mirror told me Rosie had gone back to her toy.

Eventually, we turned off the main highway onto a narrow road heavily bordered with tropical plants, lichen-covered trees, and thick ferns. Keone's taillights flashed as he made a left turn. I followed him into a driveway bordered by ti plants. A high, wooden wall surrounded the property, making visibility inside impossible. Keone leaned out to hit a button on the kiosk, speaking into it. A moment later, the gate rolled back, accompanied by the fierce barking of a very large and ferocious looking dog.

"That's Conan. He's happy I'm home," Rosie said.

He didn't sound happy, but I'd take her word for it.

I pulled up and parked next to Keone's vehicle. A tall man with dark hair and striking blue eyes arrived at the truck before I had a chance to turn it off. A huge Rottweiler and a slender young boy accompanied him. I turned off the vehicle as Lei's husband opened the passenger door, clearly eager to see that his daughter had arrived safe and sound. "Hi Daddy," she said.

"Hey, baby girl." He started undoing the many straps and buckles. "Let me get you out of this thing."

I rolled down the window but stayed inside Lei's truck, concerned about the Rottweiler's growling attention, currently split between me and Keone. "Hi, I'm Kat. Is your dog safe?"

"Sorry. That's Conan, he's all bark and no bite." Rosie settled on his hip, Lei's husband opened my door and made an introducing gesture between me and the dog. "Conan, this is our new friend, Kat."

"Hi, Conan." I extended a loose fist, palm down, for the dog to sniff. His head was the size of a bowling ball. After a thorough examination, he lost interest in me and trotted over to greet Keone.

"And I'm Michael. Michael Stevens. Most people call me Stevens." Lei's husband had a really nice smile. "Thanks so much for coming all the way out here to bring Rosie home. It's a big help."

"No trouble. We were headed back to Hana, anyway," Keone said, joining us. "Your place was on the way."

Stevens introduced us to Lei and Stevens's other child, Kiet. The boy was shy, but affectionate with Rosie. Stevens put her down and Kiet took his sister by the hand, leading her back into the house.

"Got time for a snack or drink?" Stevens cocked his head toward the house, where warm orange light poured from the windows. It was a sturdy-looking cement block dwelling, embellished with a wide and welcoming front porch.

"No thanks, not tonight. Kat and I need to get on the road," Keone said. "Good to see you again, man. It's been a while."

"We'll have you guys out for a barbecue or something," Stevens said. "Thanks again for giving our girl a lift."

"It was my pleasure," I told him, and it was. We got into Mr. K's truck, turned around, and made our way out of the compound. Rosie and Kiet waved goodbye from the porch, one on either side of the massive Rottweiler.

"What a great home scene," I said, feeling a tug somewhere deep inside—quite possibly my dried-up uterus reminding me that a clock was ticking on a life I'd likely never have.

"Sure is. Lei and Stevens have earned it. They've been through heck and back. Did you know that house is new? Some crazy perp burned down their old house. They barely escaped alive."

My eyes widened as Keone told me some of the challenges Lei and her family had been through. "The insurance didn't cover the cost of a rebuild and they wanted the new place to be fireproof, so friends and family pitched in on the construction. I put in some weekends myself."

I smiled at him. "That makes me like you even more."

"You like me, huh?" His teeth flashed in the dim light of the dashboard. "Good to know."

I stared out at the road to Hana, a mysterious dark path lit by the truck's headlights, its tropical splendor hidden by night. "Don't let it go to your head."

"Oh, that's not where it's going," he said, and thumped his chest. "Right here. That's where I'm feeling it. Among other places."

I hoped he couldn't tell I was blushing. "Just keep driving, Mr. K."

I was nodding off, curled up in my corner of the front seat, when we finally arrived at the Ohia Post Office. He turned off the vehicle. "You have arrived," he said in his GPS app voice, just like the first time he brought me here.

I yawned. "Thanks for the surf lesson. The whole day, really. It was great."

"You're welcome." Mr. K's voice shimmered with something soft and rich, but he kept his hands on the steering wheel.

My chest prickled in a good way.

He was hoping for a kiss.

Could I do it?

I wanted to. Oh, I really did. Maybe if I kissed him super quick, I could outwit the PTSD symptoms. I put a hand on Keone's arm and lunged toward him, just as he leaned toward me.

Our skulls cracked together.

I saw stars, but not for the reason I'd hoped. "Ow!"

"No kidding." Mr. K sat back, rubbing his forehead ruefully. "That was real smooth."

I spotted something past his shoulder, off in the direction of New Ohia. "What's that?"

He turned to look. "Some kind of event lighting?"

"I don't remember seeing anything over there during my jog, and there's nothing else unusual lit up nearby . . ."

"Think that's where the body is that Lei and Pono were called out on?"

"Can you drive us over to see?"

Keone's teeth flashed in the dim light. "If you give me a kiss. Just a little one. I can't take it if you—"

I silenced him by leaning over and putting my mouth on his.

It was a good kiss, but I pulled back before I could get the willies and spoil everything. "Now, let's go see what's happening in New Ohia."

He didn't answer—just turned on the truck and pulled out.

The entrance to New Ohia was just as classy at night. Subtle ground lights lit the palms at a dramatic angle along the carefully landscaped streets. Huge, portable stadium spotlights surrounded the entrance to the clubhouse that I'd explored with Jimmy Ching. Yellow plastic tape stretched between decorative palms, fluttering in the evening breeze.

Keone pulled onto the grassy, mowed shoulder behind a cluster of police cruisers. I was out of the vehicle and hurrying over to the barrier before I realized what I was doing. From where I stood, I could see a fallen cowboy hat and a flowing, snowy beard protruding from beneath a black tarp covering the body.

I knew who the victim was.

"Oh no." I covered my mouth with a hand, remembering the man who'd been one of the first customers I'd met in the post office.

I could see Doctors Gregory and Tanaka were preparing to move the body already. Lei and Pono conferred with them in the bright circle of illumination. I waved to get their attention. That didn't work, so I put my fingers in my mouth and whistled. Aunt Fae taught me how to call her deaf old dog, Scar, that way. It was a big sound.

All the cops, including the ones in uniform, spun to look at me and Keone, who stood beside me.

"Do you have an ID on the victim?" I hollered. "Because I know who it is."

Lei came striding over. By the flare of her nostrils and red of her cheeks, I gathered she didn't appreciate my wolf whistle summons. "This is an active crime scene. We just cleared out the gawkers, and now you two show up."

"Rosie was fine on the way home," I said, reminding Lei I'd done her a favor. "And like I said, I know who the victim is."

Pono arrived behind his partner. He gave Mr. K a terse head nod. "Cuz."

"Hey. She like come see what was up ovah heah," Keone said in pidgin, throwing me squarely under the bus.

I gave him a dirty look, then turned back to address the detectives. "Do you want to know who it is, or not?"

"You've been here how long?" Lei narrowed her eyes, then sighed, tossing up her hands. "Who is it, Postmaster Sleuth?"

"His name's Kermit Hubbard. He goes by Kermit. He's deaf," I said, spilling what little I knew about the guy. "Pua introduced us on my first day in the P.O. He's a local who lives in Old Ohia." I looked around. "Where's Jimmy Ching? He told me this whole area is under camera surveillance with AI, so he probably has the whole thing recorded somewhere."

Lei and Pono glanced at each other with one of their mind-melds—I'd said something they hadn't known.

Lei addressed me. "Okay, Kat. That's good info. Now go home and mind your own business, okay?"

I stepped back from the tape, feeling slapped. "You got it, Sergeant Texeira."

I spun on my size elevens and instead of heading for Keone's truck, I took off down the road toward my shack.

"Want a ride?" Keone drove up alongside me in his truck as I semi-jogged along the road out of New Ohia and to my little home, such as it was. I glanced over at him, illuminated by the lights of the instrument panel. Dang, he was cute. It was so annoying.

My temper was already cooling and I was starting to feel silly for taking off in a huff. Lei was well within her rights to set me straight, and I hadn't responded to gentler reminders.

We were only a half-mile or so from my shack, but it was dark out and the last thing I needed to do was turn an ankle. Also, someone had just been murdered nearby, and my Glock was still with the police.

"Thanks." I opened the passenger door and used the chrome support to hop in, buckling my belt for the short ride. "Sorry I took off. That was rude."

Mr. K's eyes gleamed. "I like that you know when to apologize."

"Lei hurt my feelings when she told me to step off, but it was nothing to do with you."

"It kinda was," he said. "You're putting a strain on things between me and my cuz with how aggro you're being about investigating."

I flushed. "Oh, wow. I didn't even think of that. I'm sorry."

"See? You know when to apologize." He grabbed my hand and kissed my knuckles super quick, then let go. "Was that okay? Did that bother you?"

"Uh. No." It was like he'd licked me with lightning too fast for me to feel anything but fire—and want more. "That was . . . nice."

"*Nice*." He snorted. "Nice is lame."

"For me, nice is . . . as good as it ever gets." I didn't say anything more because I had no idea how to have this conversation with him, and we were already pulling up in front of my shack.

On the porch, illuminated in the headlights, sat Tiki. Her yellow eyes were slits of malevolent doom. "Uh-oh. I'm home late."

"She looks pissed," Keone said.

"She's probably hungry and worried about me." I opened the door and hopped out of the vehicle, eager to get away—away from touching or not touching, holding hands or not holding hands, a hug or no hug, fast kisses or slow kisses, even the possibility or expectation of kisses. And most of all, I was eager to get away from how I always messed up relationship stuff. "Thanks again for everything." I slammed the door.

Mr. K rolled down the window, not letting me get away that easy. "What are you doing tomorrow? It's Sunday so the post office is closed."

"No idea."

"I'll pick you up for lunch and a hike," he said. "I've got a place you need to see."

"Sure. That sounds nice."

He snorted. "Delete that word 'nice' from your vocabulary, woman."

"Okay." I focused and dug deep. "That sounds . . . delicious, nutritious, and exciting, Keone."

"Much better. Now go turn on your light and check the shack. I want to make sure it's clear and you're safe inside before I go."

Mr. K was being bossy, protective, *and* gentlemanly. Baby Rosie taught me today that when I had that fuzzy, tingly feeling, it was the warming of the cockles of my heart. But this . . . *nope*. Mr. K being bossy, protective, and gentlemanly didn't get to me *at all*, no sir, not me, Kat Smith, the oldest virgin in the world and a Secret Service agent whose job it was to protect others.

I headed for the porch and approached Tiki with caution. The headlights from Keone's truck showed rage in every bristling hair on her blotchy calico body.

"Hey, girl. I'm sorry I'm late." I sidled past and palmed my key, unlocking the door. "I'll give you an extra hot dog with dinner, okay?" She flicked her tail as if she understood. I took a few steps inside, pulled the dangling light bulb cord, and lit the place up. I peeked into the bathroom then returned to the doorway and gave Keone a thumbs-up.

"All clear," I announced loudly in my Secret Service voice. "Thanks again for a wonderful day, Mr. K."

He flashed his lights, pulled out, and drove away.

Nope, I didn't feel a bit sad to see him go. I was perfectly fine here by myself, with my loving feline companion to guard me against any killers still lurking in the neighborhood.

I was sliding into my sleep tee, a towel wound around my head from a shower, when the attack cat gave a loud hiss followed by a yowl. Tiki squatted menacingly under the table, her tail lashing and her eyes fixed on the door. Someone was on my porch.

# 19

“That’s not spooky at all,” I said aloud, hunting around for a weapon in my backpack. I found my thumb-sized pepper spray, formerly attached to my car key in Washington, D.C. It would have to do. “Good girl, Tiki. You can tell someone’s coming better than a dog.”

Right on cue, a knock sounded.

I stood to the side of the locked door in case the intruder decided to plug me through the wood. Holding the pepper spray in one hand and the broom in another, I called out, “Who is it?”

“It’s me, Lei. Sergeant Texeira.”

I released my breath, set the broom aside, and put the pepper spray on the table. “I’m not dressed for company, Lei. I’m in my pajamas.”

“It’s just me. Pono’s waiting in the truck.” Lei’s voice sounded weary. “It’ll only take a minute.”

I unlocked and opened the door. The porch wasn’t illuminated, but the bulb inside illuminated Lei’s face. She looked tired, with dark circles under her eyes.

“You look beat. Don’t tell me you and Pono have to drive all the way back to Kahului tonight.”

"Thankfully, no. The local PD is putting us up at a cottage they own in Hana." She was holding a brown paper bag. "Can I come in?"

I gestured to Tiki, whose growl seemed to rumble the timbers of the floor. "I can't vouch for your safety. I'll step out there." I moved out onto the porch and mostly shut the door. A crack of light was enough to see by. "I really need to put in a light out here."

"Yeah, you do. Preferably a sensor light. A woman alone can't be too careful with what's been going on." Lei handed me the paper bag. "In light of that, I had a rush job put on this. Ballistics are clean on your weapon."

I clutched the paper bag containing my Glock to my breast, hugging it like a teddy bear. "Thanks. I never expected safety to be an issue in Ohia."

"Hopefully a temporary situation." Lei rested her hands on her hips. "I'm sorry for giving you attitude earlier. You've been a big help. Pono reminded me of that."

"Thanks." I hugged the gun tighter. "I've been a bit—overenthusiastic about the investigation, though. Keone reminded *me* of that. I don't want to muddy the waters."

"The tips you gave us were solid for this latest murder. Jimmy Ching couldn't be found tonight, but there are some security staffers who were able to give us a download of the surveillance footage. We're planning to review it tomorrow."

"That's good."

"And your ID of the victim was helpful too." Lei cocked her head at me. "Turns out Kermit Hubbard is a registered sex offender. Has quite a nasty history."

A chill swept over me and raised goose bumps. "He was so . . . cute, for lack of a better word. The beard, the cowboy hat, his concern for Fran. I'm shocked."

"I'm not." Lei's brown eyes were dark with the memories of all she'd seen as a cop over the years. "Anyway, I thought you'd sleep better with your weapon close by, given the body count out here."

"You're right. I will sleep better. Thanks, Lei. I really appreciate that—and the information about Kermit."

"Keep it confidential." Lei yawned suddenly. "Pono's probably already asleep in the truck. Speaking of, thanks for taking Rosie home. I should have said that sooner. Pono reminded me of that too."

"Seems like those Kaihales are better at getting along with others than we are."

"You're right about that." She smiled. "See you tomorrow, if our paths cross." She lifted a hand and headed for the idling truck, whose lights were down so as to not blind us.

"Tomorrow, huh," I muttered. "Should be interesting." I would stop in on the Pahinuis, my investigation partners, and see what they knew about Kermit Hubbard. Was his death related to Fran's? It seemed like too much of a coincidence for it not to be, but what was the connection?

I stepped back inside, locked the door, and put the gun on the table. I unwound the towel from around my head, suddenly so tired I could hardly keep my eyes open.

Tiki came out from under the table and repositioned herself in front of the Murphy bed, looking hopeful. "We talked about this, Tiki. You can't sleep with me until you've had a flea bath."

She turned on her sputtering motorboat purr. Her bad eye was almost recovered, and the food I'd been feeding her had plumped her up a bit. But she was still a semi-feral cat with many unknown parasites. "Tell you what. I'll make you a bed right beside me."

I went into the bathroom and fetched my terry cloth robe. She seemed to like being next to me, so maybe she'd accept that as a substitute. I set the fuzzy robe on the floor right beside the bed, then plumped and shaped it into a cozy hollow. I sprinkled kibble over the inside of the nest. "Here, kitty kitty."

Tiki narrowed her eyes, turned up her nose, and slinked under the table. She lay down with her back to me and made a "hmpf" sound. I already missed her purr.

"Okay. Maybe tomorrow you'll be ready for the bath." That was hard to imagine, but I could dream. I slid into bed and placed the loaded Glock under my pillow.

Lei was right; I was going to sleep better with my weapon—and my attack cat—close by.

My eyes fell shut, and I was gone.

I woke to a beam of light coming through the bullet hole in the wall beside my pillow. I peeked over the side of the bed. Sometime during the night, Tiki had gotten over her snit and climbed into the bed I'd made for her out of my robe. My heart cockles were definitely warmed by the sight of that ornery cat curled up like a striped cinnamon roll on my bathrobe.

Also, she wasn't sleeping on my head like a flea-ridden Russian *ushanka*. I'd worn one of those on a mission—incredibly warm and exactly how Tiki felt. Great in Russia, not so great in Hawaii.

I was making progress with my cat.

Tiki heard me rustling and opened one yellow eye, then the other. Her rusty-voiced complaint sounded exactly how I feel without coffee on board.

"Yep, it's that time again. Time to go out, greet the day, and help find a murderer," I said. "With a pause in the middle for lunch and a hike with Mr. K."

That last part made my heart do a little skip and jump.

Had I really kissed him last night?

Yep.

More relationship progress!

Tiki hopped out of her nest and took up her spot under the table, studiously ignoring me as I got out of bed. I folded the mattress up and out of the way, then put on a pot of Nectar of Life. "Sure glad Fran left this coffeemaker behind," I told her. "Along with her favorite mug."

The mug had a chip in it, but it was otherwise perfect for me. The design declared, "DO NOT SPEAK TO ME UNTIL THIS MUG IS EMPTY."

"Fran and I had some things in common," I told Tiki. The cat continued to ignore me, still officially piqued that I hadn't allowed her access to my pillow.

I opened the front door of the shack. "Oh, my goodness."

The morning sky was breathtaking. Sunlight framed the perfect crescent of Ohia Bay, illuminating the puffy clouds sailing along the horizon. The palm trees lining the beach and the old pier were gilded with a golden glow. Mynah birds cackled and hopped in the finally dry parking lot. Turtledoves cooed. The waves surging up the beach across the road were a gentle lullaby. A clump of yellow ginger blooming among the hibiscus beside the shack flavored the air with the tropics.

I took out my brand-new beach chair, unfolded it on the stoop rock, and sat down to enjoy a little slice of paradise. My coffee was soon ready and I sipped from Fran's mug, enjoying the view. I may not have ever imagined my life as a Secret Service agent taking this turn, but I couldn't be mad it happened if mornings like this were a part of it.

Fifty yards away or so, Opal appeared on the front porch of the store, gently leading Artie by the hand. Her cap of silver hair gleamed, and she wore one of her crazy patterned shifts and yellow Crocs. She and Artie took seats in the wooden rockers on the porch, and she leaned toward him, talking and pointing. He nodded. She was likely describing the day to him, so he could see it with his blind eyes. A pang tightened my chest—their love was so gorgeous.

Opal spotted me and waved. "Good morning, Kat! Great day, isn't it?"

"Sure is." I wanted to update them on Kermit Hubbard's death, and this was my chance—before the store opened. But I hated to pollute their sweet start to the day with bad news. Still, they would want to know, and better they heard it from me. I slid my feet into my new, black flip-flops and headed over, taking my coffee with me.

Opal pointed to my mug. "It's a little spooky seeing you drink out of that thing. Fran used that every day."

"I think of her as a friendly ghost I'm trying to help." I downed a healthy swig of coffee for emphasis. "Speaking of ghost—can you keep more secrets with me? I've got news."

"We're finding Fran's killer together," Artie rumbled. "Spill."

I sat on the front step in front of their rockers. "What do you know about Kermit Hubbard?"

Opal's brows shot up. "What's going on with him?"

I didn't answer, not wanting to prejudice her with the news of his murder.

She sighed, then turned to Artie. "You don't like him. Tell me why again?"

Artie shook his head. "That man has a darkness in him."

Opal nodded, turning back to me. "Kermit moved to Old Ohia five years or so ago from the mainland. Texas, I think. He's a regular at the store, but we don't socialize outside of that because Artie doesn't care for him. Honestly, he mostly keeps to himself. Said he moved here to retire. He has a little fishing boat that he takes out from Hana, and sometimes gives us fish to sell if he's brought in extra. Seems harmless enough."

"Maybe now, but that's not his history." I told them what Lei told me. "Those records are public, so you can look him up. But the big news—he's dead. He was killed in New Ohia sometime yesterday."

Opal gasped, but Artie didn't look surprised. The big man shook his head. "I saw that coming."

"What do you mean, Artie?" I asked.

"I mean that the darkness took him in the end, as it does to those who give in to it."

I shivered, just a tiny bit. Opal elbowed her husband. "Stop sounding like a fortune cookie, Artie."

He chuckled and shook his head. "But it's the truth."

"Do you want to see what the runes say about Kermit's demise?" I asked Opal. "I'm curious."

"Nope." Opal was definite. "It's too soon."

"Okay then. Do you think Hubbard's death is connected to Fran's somehow?"

"I don't know, and I don't want to think about that right now. Sorry to cut you off, Kat, but we need to get dressed, get the store open and coffee on before the regulars show up." Opal stood up and took Artie's hand.

"I understand." I stood and stretched. "As for me, I'm going to the beach. See what the waves have left me this morning."

"There's going to be something for you," Artie said in his mysterious way before Opal tugged him through the shop's door.

Back at the shack, I refilled my mug and changed into my bikini, not surprised that Tiki had disappeared again. She'd finished the kibble I'd put out the night before, and almost emptied her water bowl, too. I'd be seeing her again this evening, and I looked forward to it.

Sunday morning in Ohia was very quiet. Was everyone sleeping in, or going to church? Aunt Fae would want to go when she visited. Maybe I should explore the town more fully before I took my beach walk. There couldn't be much more to see, but I was curious.

Wrapped in my beach towel and wearing my flip-flops and hat, I turned left out of the parking lot instead of crossing the road to the beach. I walked up Hibiscus Drive, which slanted gently uphill. The streets were all named for Hawaiian flowers. I noticed Plumeria Street, where Ms. Maka from the Ulupalakua Store lived. Maybe I could spot her house.

Yeah, I'm nosy. I own it. I'm Kat Smith, the Postmaster Sleuth. Yesterday, it was New Ohia. Today, I'd explore Old Ohia.

I turned right and walked along the shoulder—there was no sidewalk. The small yards were mostly fenced and neatly kept. Here and there, I'd find an outlier with old, rust bucket cars, loose chickens and barking dogs, or overgrown gardens buzzing with bees and butterflies. The houses were small and square, built of wood with corrugated roofs. I'd learned the style was called "plantation," which apparently referred to the camps of workers' cottages built during Hawaii's agricultural era.

I spotted something yellow fluttering at the corner of one of the lots up ahead and instinctively sped up. I wished I'd worn my Nikes, the rubber sandals slapping against the bottoms of my feet. Sure enough, the yellow glint was crime scene tape threaded around the outside of a chain-link fence. The fence encircled the yard of a little house much like the rest, except for a rather large boat and black Ford truck parked in the driveway.

Stanley was pulled in tight against the Ford.

I put my hands on my hips. This had to be Kermit Hubbard's house. Lei and Pono must be in there searching the place!

Right on cue, the front door opened. Lei emerged, her wild curls confined in a hair net, booties on her feet, and blue rubber gloves on her hands. She was struggling to carry a heavy-looking computer and monitor.

"Whoa, let me help!" I used a bit of my beach towel to open the front gate and hurried up to Lei. "Let me take the monitor, at least."

"Well, if it isn't Kat the Curious."

"Guilty," I said.

Lei looked in danger of losing her grip on the equipment or I'm sure she wouldn't have let me assist. I whipped off the towel and caught the monitor carefully by the edges, using the fabric to keep my fingerprints off the glass.

Relieved of that unwieldy burden, Lei was able to navigate the steps and make it to Stanley's truck bed, where she placed the computer body and cords in a plastic bin. "Pono has a towel back here, we'll pad it with that. I'm taking this in for our tech department to analyze."

"Makes sense."

We stowed the gear as best we could, padding it from the bumps of the upcoming trip back to Kahului. I retrieved my towel and rewrapped it around my body. "Find anything interesting inside?"

"Wouldn't you like to know," Lei teased. She didn't seem mad at me this time. "We'll be here a while. What brings you out to Plumeria Street?"

"Believe it or not, I was just taking a walk around the neighborhood before going to the beach. Wanted to explore the town a little—I haven't seen much of it besides the post office and New Ohia."

Lei smiled, indicating my outfit with a gesture. "I believe you. No woman in her right mind goes sleuthing in a bathing suit."

I smiled. "I was also looking for a church. Is there one here?"

Lei raised her brows. "Your outfit is questionable for that, too."

"I was thinking for when my Aunt Fae comes to visit."

She relented. "There is one. Go right on Hibiscus Drive, and it's at the top of the hill. It's a lovely spot overlooking the village. Has an interesting graveyard, too."

"Well, look who it is." Pono emerged, carrying a couple of paper evidence bags. "Haven't seen you in hours."

I shook my head. "I swear, you guys, I was just out for a walk." I pointed to the bags he was carrying. "Got anything incriminating in there?"

Pono just grinned. "I like your persistence, Kat." He stowed the bags, which looked like they contained square or rectangular shapes, in the bin with the monitor. DVDs? VHS tapes?

"Well, I'll just . . . go to the beach then," I said. "Let me know if I can help with anything."

"Take care," Lei said, but she was already headed back into the house.

What was in there? "Dang it." I wanted to know.

I flip-flopped my way back to Hibiscus Drive, where I paused to look up the hill. Over the crest of the rise, I could just make out a small white steeple that marked the church Lei described. But now was not the time, and this was not the outfit, for exploring the church and its grounds.

I turned and headed down toward the beach. Though my mind was buzzing with curiosity over the items Lei and Pono pulled from the house, I had to find a way to let it go. It was going to be a busy week at the post office, and my day off would be wasted if I wasn't careful.

"Shoot, I forgot to ask them about the surveillance footage of the crime scene in New Ohia," I muttered, looking both ways before crossing the Hana Highway. "But never mind. They didn't seem in the mood to tell me anything, anyway." I parked my slippers by a lava rock, tossed my phone and towel on the sand, and set off to walk the shingle beach before hopping in the ocean for a swim.

I was getting downright spoiled. No one ever seemed to be around when I went for a morning beach walk. I loved seeing the pristine sand, the tideline etched just above where the gentle waves foamed.

Out to sea, clouds were forming on the horizon—it looked like a rain squall might be rolling in. Riding the winds over the bay were two large frigate birds. Keone had called them *'iwa*. They swirled gracefully, their long, black wings hardly moving.

I was so busy looking at the birds that I tripped over a piece of wood and landed on my knee, burying it in the sand. "Ow!"

The sand was too soft to push up on, and I struggled to regain my footing with my knee sunk. I dropped to my butt and rolled to one side, frowning at what tripped me.

The item in question was a piece of lumber, new and out of place —and one end was stained a rusty brown.

"What the . . ." Without touching it or getting any closer, I squinted to inspect the two-by-four. Near the stained end, I spotted a few long, silver hairs caught in the splinters. "Son of a beehive, this might be the murder weapon from last night!"

# 20

I glanced up from the two-by-four to see where it might have come from. Clearly visible from my vantage point on the ground, a series of footprints led straight down and stopped about ten feet from the piece of lumber. Just below, the high-water mark had smoothed and darkened the sand. The perp must have come down to the beach to dispose of it and thought they threw the murder weapon into the ocean. But it was dark, and they didn't quite make it. I scrambled clumsily to my feet, looking around, but the beach was empty.

I had to alert Lei and Pono to this discovery.

I hurried back to where I'd tossed my towel and phone. My hands shook as I scrolled to Lei's number. Thankfully, down here by the water, I could get a few bars of service. I called her cell phone.

"Kat, this had better be good." Lei sounded hot and annoyed when she answered.

"I think I found the murder weapon. That's pretty good, don't you think?"

"What is it?"

"Piece of lumber. Bloodstained on one end."

"Where are you?"

"At the beach."

"Don't touch anything." She hung up.

I snorted. "You didn't need to tell me that," I said to the empty air.

Lei and Pono walked toward me on the beach, still in their booties, gloves, and hair nets. Pono carried a camera, and Lei a large evidence bag. On any other day their outfits might have been funny in this setting, but adrenaline made my heart pound as the truth of what happened last night settled over me.

Someone clubbed Kermit Hubbard in New Ohia with a handy two-by-four, likely grabbed from one of the construction sites. Then, less than a hundred yards from my shack, the murderer tossed the piece of wood they'd killed a man with onto the beach.

My little slice of paradise was corrupted. The whole place was, frankly. I'd been safer guarding the Secretary of State on his last trip through a terrorist-riddled Middle East.

"Why don't you sit down, Kat?" Pono said. "You look a little washed-out."

I folded up abruptly, landing on my behind in the sand. I wrapped my arms around my legs, suddenly cold.

"I tripped over it. That's how I found it," I told them, and pointed to the piece of wood. "The murderer thought they were throwing the club they'd killed Kermit with into the ocean, but the waves didn't come up high enough to take it away."

Pono walked to where I'd identified the killer's footprints. The size was hard to gauge because the sand was so soft, but I'd guess the perp had feet close to my size elevens, which likely ruled out a woman. He took photos and followed them to where they disappeared at the grass beside the road.

Lei crouched by the two-by-four, inspecting it. She waited until

Pono came back and photographed it in situ, then picked it up by the clean end and slid it into the paper evidence bag she carried.

"Thanks, Kat," was all she said, before turning to walk back to where they'd parked the truck.

I couldn't stop shaking despite the sun on my skin. Pono was on the phone with someone, but I paid no attention, instead watching one of the *'iwa* catch an updraft and float out of sight.

Pono returned and sat beside me in the sand. "You okay?"

"I'm creeped out. The perp was so close to my shack." I hugged my bare legs tighter.

"Yeah. True." Pono brown eyes were kind. "But you've been in hairier situations than this with your Secret Service duties, right?"

"Right." I stiffened my spine, grateful for the reminder. "Why was Kermit in New Ohia at night?"

"That's a good question." Pono stripped off the booties and hair net. He set the items aside. "We're going to analyze his phone, and we've finished searching his house. And if it's any consolation, you probably weren't home yet last night when they threw the weapon down here."

"That does make me feel better for some reason."

"I hoped it would. I also called Keone to see if he could keep you company, since Lei and I have to take this stuff back to the station in Kahului. He's on his way."

"Oh." My nose and eyes prickled—was I going to cry? So embarrassing. "That's not necessary."

"He told me he was taking you for a hike. It's no trouble for him to come early." Pono pulled the gloves off and set a warm hand on my shoulder. "This is a lot for anyone to deal with."

I nodded. I waited to see if I'd freak out because Pono was touching me, but it felt good. It felt as if I had a brother, something I'd always wished for, and that brother was looking out for me. "Thanks, Pono. You're a good guy."

He snorted. "Don't tell anyone, or you'll ruin my reputation."

I might as well see what info he'd give up while he was being generous. "Was there anything on the surveillance video?"

"Nothing too useful. We think whoever did it knew about the cameras, because they wore a hat, gloves, and baggy clothing. Couldn't tell much."

"Did . . . Mr. Hubbard speak to the murderer? Did he know what was coming?"

"Nope. Hubbard was standing outside the clubhouse, staring in the windows. Looked like he was waiting for someone. The perp came out of the bushes, whacked him a couple of times, and ran away."

I digested that. "I was hoping you'd have the whole crime wrapped up from the video and that would help us solve who killed Fran, too. Jimmy Ching was so proud of the security."

"Pono!" Lei called from the truck. "Let's get this evidence back to the station!"

"Keone will be here in a few minutes." Pono stood up.

"Have you found Jimmy Ching yet?" I called after him. I knew I was pushing my luck, but it was worth a shot.

Pono shook his head as he walked away. Ching was still in the wind. The project manager had to be Suspect Number One on Lei and Pono's list.

I stared at the dents and disturbances in the sand where the piece of wood had been, including the knee gouge and butt shape from when I had fallen. Suddenly, a rogue wave swooshed up and erased the marks as if they'd never been.

The murderer had been hoping for that, but they hadn't been that lucky.

I sat listening to the wind rustle through the palm fronds as I waited for Keone. My mind wandered to my conversation earlier this morning with Opal and Artie about Kermit Hubbard's death. I shivered again. Artie's words about finding something at the beach had absolutely come true, and that was almost as creepy as my discovery.

Almost. But not quite.

I was still sitting in the sand with my arms around my knees, gazing out at the horizon, when I heard the rumble of Keone's truck drive up. It hadn't taken long for me to memorize that sound.

I turned my head and forced a smile as he approached, towel in hand. "You didn't have to come. I'm totally fine."

"I'm fine, too. And glad to see you, Kat." Mr. K draped the beach towel over my bare shoulders.

I don't know where his big blue towel, printed with fish shapes, had come from. Maybe from a sunbeam in the backseat of the truck's cab, maybe from his clothes dryer. Didn't matter—the thing was toasty warm as if heated by one of those fancy towel racks in a five-star hotel.

"Mmm, this is so nice." I shut my eyes and snuggled into it. When Mr. K sat in the sand next to me, put an arm around me, and pulled me in for a side hug . . . well, I was totally okay with it. I sighed and relaxed, resting my head on his shoulder. I waited for those freaky feelings, but they never happened.

Keone gave me one more squeeze and then let go. "Since our schedule has changed, you want to go surfing again? Getting in the ocean always knocks the bad out of my mood."

"Yes." I stood up, keeping the sun-warmed towel wrapped around me. "That sounds perfect. Let's go rip up the curl and banzai the hang ten."

"Just no, on the surfer slang. You're not ready, Grasshopper." Keone dusted the sand off his butt. "I think we need something more positive today." He gave me a hand, hefting me to my feet. "Hey, I haven't had breakfast. Let's grab something at the general store before we go to Koki Beach."

"Sure." I appreciated that he hadn't asked me a thing about finding the murder weapon.

Keone and I crossed the road and entered the general store, which smelled of delicious baked goods with a top note of Kona coffee.

I sniffed loudly. "Opal, what's cooking?"

"Artie always makes a big coffeecake for the after-church crowd on Sundays, and we order in malasadas from Komoda's," Opal said.

"Oh, broke da mout!" Keone exclaimed.

I frowned. "That's not very nice, Mr. K."

He laughed, and so did Opal.

"It's pidgin, Kat," Opal explained. "Means 'delicious' or 'good eating.'"

"In that case I need a malasada right now," I said. "I heard Dr. Tanaka say Dr. Gregory has been eating too many of them and that's why she couldn't get his coverall over his belly. They must be tasty."

"You've been warned. One is never enough." Opal pointed to a big pink bakery box beside the cash register. "Want one to go, or for here?"

Before I could answer, Keone came up to the checkout with a nylon swim shirt and a wrapped bar of wax. "I'm taking Kat out surfing again," he said to Opal.

I pointed at the nylon shirt. "What's that?"

"That's a rash guard, you'll need it this time."

"What does that do?"

"Protects your skin from the surface of the board. I'm putting you up on my old longboard today. It's not as easy to ride as the soft top, but you're picking it up pretty quick. I don't want you to get too used to how floaty that starter board is."

"What's the wax for?"

"Don't you know that surfers wax their sticks?" Opal said with a wink. "I've picked out the best malasada for your first experience."

She handed me a light brown pastry on a napkin. The orb was halfway between a baseball and a golf ball in size, soft but slightly crusty, and dusted with sparkling granulated sugar. It smelled like it came from a bakery in heaven, if heaven had a bakery. Everything I had been through that morning seemed to catch up with me all at once. The fact that I was starving hit me, and my stomach gave a loud gurgle of anticipation.

I took a bite and shut my eyes, moaning in ecstasy. Thick,

creamy coconut pudding broke across my tongue from the middle of the perfectly textured, soft doughnut shell.

"What is this amazement?" I exclaimed when I could speak.

"That must be a haupia pudding malasada." Mr. K eyed my pastry enviously. "Do you have any more of those, Opal?"

"Nope. That was the last one. But I have one with poi inside."

"I'll take it."

Soon, we were both making ecstatic noises as we finished the malasadas, gone in just a few bites. Keone glanced at me with his twinkly eyes. "Now you know what 'broke da mout' means."

"I sure do. Gimme another one. Don't care what kind," I begged Opal.

We grabbed coffees to go to complete our breakfast, Keone insisting on paying for everything. I pointed across the street as he wrapped up the purchase.

"We'll talk more later," I told Opal, "but I found the murder weapon on the beach this morning."

"What!" Opal exclaimed.

"Yep. Tripped right over a two-by-four with blood on it. That was after I ran into Lei and Pono searching Kermit Hubbard's house on Plumeria Street, purely by accident. It's been a busy morning." Keone pretended to browse a nearby rack of sunglasses while I briefly filled her in.

"Well, Artie did say the ocean would have something for you." Opal shook her head. "He's seldom wrong."

"That's not creepy at all."

A group of locals entered, yelling for coffeecake and malasadas. Opal waved us off. "Talk later, Kat."

Out at the truck, Keone squinted a look at me. "Why were you telling Opal all that info?"

"The Pahinuis and I are trying to find out who killed Fran and clear Pua's name. I guess that's turned into trying to find Hubbard's killer, too. I don't know how much you want to get sucked into investigating with me, though, in case it's a conflict of interest with Pono."

"I guess I have to think about that. I want to know what you're up to, but I kind of don't at the same time. This is the aspect of you that I consider 'Trouble' with a capital T."

"You are not wrong."

# 21

Just as Keone promised, the ocean at Koki Beach was the perfect place for me to wash away the angst of tripping over a murder weapon ditched a hundred yards from my shack.

The sun on the water, the focus and energy required to catch the waves, and the vigorous trouncing they kept giving me pulled me right out of my head. I fell off Keone's longboard from the front, from the side, from the other side, from the tail . . . and it invigorated me in a way I can't imagine anything else would.

Well, there was one other activity I could imagine doing with Mr. K to get my mind off murder, but that was still only in the imagination stage in my experience. Maybe that's where it always would stay, but I could dream, right? Because Mr. K was dreamy, especially on a surfboard.

Keone rode the soft top that I used in my first lesson, and he did all sorts of tricks on it: walking all the way up to the nose to hang his toes off, standing on one leg like a ballet dancer, turning around and riding it backwards, taking off with the fin first and then flipping it around halfway down the wave.

I came up from one particularly bad wipeout and squirted water at him with my mouth. "Show off!"

"You bet. I want to impress my woman."

I avoided responding by pushing the board under the lip of an oncoming wave. I hugged the nose close as I swam through it, a more advanced technique Keone called "duck diving."

Mr. K was calling me "his woman"?

Too soon for that. He was moving too fast for me.

Maybe he just meant it in a playful, friendly way. I didn't have to know right now.

The rash guard was a great idea. It stopped my bikini from slithering around where it shouldn't and kept my stomach from getting irritated by the surf wax on the top of the board.

I could really see what the function of the wax was, too, as I stood up to take off. My toes gripped the sticky bumps of wax and found more purchase than they would have on the hard, slick fiberglass otherwise. That didn't mean I wasn't still wiping out most of the time.

We came in from surfing, rinsed off, changed, and headed to Hana for the food trucks. We were both starving for a more substantial meal than a couple of malasadas. Keone steered me to a Mexican/Hawaiian food truck called Fish Taco, where a friend of his cooked up fun combos I'd never had before. We ordered mahi-mahi tacos and ceviche.

"This is a killer breakfast. You know the best places to eat. These tacos have ruined my mouth." We were seated with our elbows on a picnic table, digging in.

Mr. K laughed. "Nice try."

"I've been all over the world and eaten all kinds of food at all kinds of restaurants," I told him, dead serious. "And the food I've had at these trucks is some of the best I've ever had. Not to mention that spiritual experience that is a malasada."

"Well, you're going to love this hike just as much as the food out here. I'm taking you to the Pools of ʻOheʻo and Pipiwai Trail. It's a part of Haleakala National Park, and we drive past the entrance every time we come back to Hana from Ohia," Keone said. "You might have seen pictures of it, because the trail goes through a bamboo forest that is one of the most Instagrammed paths on the planet."

"Sweet." I finished my tacos and took a long swig of lemonade. "You're assuming I'm fit enough to both surf and hike in the same day."

"I know you're fit enough for that, and a lot more besides."

I shouldn't have liked the way he smiled at me, and it shouldn't have made my dirty mind go where it went . . . but oh well. That happened.

We bought bottles of water for the hike and Keone insisted I slather on sunscreen, then we headed out. As we drove toward the entrance to the Pipiwai Trail, with its iconic waterfall and bamboo forest, I seriously hoped I was done with murder for the rest of the day.

The trail that led from the Pools of ʻOheʻo (also known as the Seven Sacred Pools, Keone told me) went uphill through a forest of guava trees and alongside the stream that fed waterfalls into the famous pools. The soil was rust red clay dotted with lava rocks, and the going was slow due to slippery mud and tangled roots.

"All of this is part of the volcano's breakdown over time." Mr. K reached up to pluck a guava off one of the overhanging trees. He handed it to me. "Ever had one of these before?"

"Nope. Seems like a nice palate cleanser after the fish tacos." The yellow fruit was about the size and shape of a lemon, but the resemblance ended there. I took a bite, and my teeth sunk through the thin outer skin into ripe, tangy, pink innards filled with seeds. "Mmm. This doesn't taste anything like that guava juice they give you on a plane."

"True dat."

We kept going and passed a few tourists, mostly coming back down the trail. I could see why they began their hike earlier than we had. Though the air wasn't particularly hot, it was humid and was probably cooler earlier in the day. I bundled my ocean-tousled hair in a ball and poked a stick through it, then took off my T-shirt to hike in my bikini and shorts. Keone didn't say anything about my change in outfit, but he hung back to walk behind me from then on, which gave me a little smirk. *Ha.*

Making our way through a gulch, we encountered an old cattle gate. Apparently, there were still loose cows grazing in the park. Shortly after, we crested a small rise to find the most enormous banyan tree I'd ever seen filling the hollow of the land below us.

"What the—is that a single tree?"

"Yep. I thought you'd like it." Keone grinned.

"You bet I do."

We descended to the base of the tree and passed a couple of tourists with their phones and cameras out, posing for photos. "Want me to take a picture of you?" Mr. K asked.

"Sure." I vamped a little, then posed with one hand high on the trunk and the other on my hip. The trunk was bigger than three Volkswagen buses put together, banded with long roots and branch extensions that held up limbs the length of a city block. "Aunt Fae will like that one," I said, looking at the photo. "I'll send it to her when I get a signal."

"Let's get a selfie." Mr. K put an arm around me, and we both smiled for the camera.

"Nice to see you making friends."

I knew that dry tone, though I hadn't spent more than a day in the company of its owner.

"What!" I spun to see Pua Chang standing under one of the enormous banyan branches. A young man twice her size stood just behind her, regarding us with a vacant stare. I assumed he must be her nephew. "Pua! You got out!"

"Thanks to a good lawyer, I was released yesterday," Pua said with dignity. "So, you've met Keone Kaihale, one of our most eligible bachelors. Wasting no time, I see."

I bristled a bit at her tone.

"I had to snatch Kat up before someone else did," Mr. K said, rescuing me from the awkward moment. "So glad to see you're okay, Auntie Pua."

Keone stepped forward to give her a hug, but the nephew raised a hand the size of a dinner plate and shoved Keone back hard enough that he tripped, barely keeping his footing on the muddy ground.

"No touching," the nephew growled. "Touching bad."

"No, Sonny. Keone is a friend," Pua said, putting a restraining hand on the young man's arm. "Remember? We can hug friends." She turned to me with a strained smile. "Kat, this is my nephew. His name is Roland Chang, but everyone calls him Sonny."

"Hi Sonny." I stepped forward with my hand out. "Nice to meet you."

"Friend," Sonny boomed. He grabbed me up in a bear hug so tight that it pushed the air out of my lungs.

I could not stop my panicked reflexes from kicking into gear. I stomped on his instep with my Nike, kneed him in the balls, and twisted his hand up behind his back so he arched away from me in agony.

Sonny howled.

Pua screamed.

And Keone waved his hands in front of my face. "Stop, Kat. Friend!"

I let go of Sonny's thumb, breath sawing through my lungs as the raw terror receded. "Oh, son of a beehive. I didn't mean to hurt you, Sonny," I panted. "I can't handle being touched when I don't know it's coming, and sometimes even when I do."

The guy was doubled over his family jewels. Pua scowled at me as she patted his back. "He's a big boy, but he doesn't know his own strength. Apparently, neither do you."

Sonny gradually straightened up. Tears rolled down his face as he pointed at me. "You not friend!" He made a sudden darting move, and I dropped into a defensive stance. He thought better of trying to take me on and hid behind Pua instead.

I straightened. "I am a friend, but not one you can hug. I'm sorry, Sonny." I felt terrible for confusing him. "Some people you don't hug, no matter what. I am one of them."

"Not friend!" Sonny didn't sound like he'd accepted my apology. He glanced away, muttering and wringing his hands.

"This was an important lesson, I guess. Maybe we can storyboard this social situation with his therapist when he's calmer, but he can't process when he's upset," Pua said. "I'll see you tomorrow at work, Kat." She took Sonny by the hand and tugged him away. He paused to give me a dirty look before following his aunt up the incline.

"Not friend!" Sonny bellowed over his shoulder, getting in the last word.

I headed out from under the banyan tree and broke into a jog, weaving up the path until it leveled out. I had to discharge the aftermath of adrenaline, and shame swamped me. I was still messed up! I thought I was getting better!

"Kat." Keone caught up with me and touched my shoulder, just a light tap.

I whirled around. "Aren't you afraid I'm going to karate chop you for touching me?"

"I'm not afraid of anything you'd do to me," he said gently.

Tears flooded my eyes. "I feel terrible." I covered my face with my hands. "That poor kid."

"Well, Sonny's a big guy who shouldn't go around squashing women without permission," Mr. K said. "I saw how tightly he grabbed you. Yeah, you could have expressed yourself differently, but I don't think this was a bad thing in the end. And as Pua said, it's a valuable lesson for him. Maybe we can go to their house and practice different hugging scenarios with him and the therapist."

I whooshed out a sigh. "Yeah, okay."

We resumed walking at a slower pace and crossed a metal bridge connecting two high cliffs, a stream winding below.

"Wow, this is beautiful," I gasped.

The bamboo forest began on the other side of the bridge. The air was filled with the musical creak and squeak of the giant stems, crowned with feathery tops like the leaves of celery stalks. The light was dim and green, and if it was possible, it would have *smelled* green, too.

We stepped off the bridge and up onto a boardwalk suspended above the muddy ground. I stopped, shocked by who was approaching me this time.

# 22

Mattie Ramirez of the Red Hat Society was a distinctive figure even without her purple outfit and scarlet topper. She strode energetically toward us, a pair of hiking poles pumping at her sides, her gaze fixed somewhere in the distance. A pair of earbuds added to her focus. She would have brushed right by Keone and me on the raised plastic boardwalk if I hadn't held up a hand.

"Mattie? Ms. Ramirez?"

She stopped, turned, and pulled out an earbud, searching for the source of her name. She recognized me and smiled. "Well, if it isn't the new postmaster! What was your name again?"

"Kat. Kat Smith. Looks like you're getting a nice workout."

"You too," Ramirez said with a wink, running an appreciative eye over Mr. K as he stood beside me. "Who's this hunk o' honey?"

"Keone Kaihale. Pleased to meet you, ma'am." Mr. K went to shake her hand, but she hugged him instead and patted his shoulder when she finally let go.

"Don't call me ma'am, sweet cheeks. Unless we're role-playing, then I've got a few uses for that title."

A grown man can still blush, and Mr. K looked adorable with red along the tops of his cheekbones and ears. I suppressed a grin.

"Well, you two have fun up at the waterfall. Your timing is perfect—most of the tourists went early and it was deserted when I got there," she said.

"You do this hike often? You must really be fit," I said. "I guess those hiking poles work as well as your cane for stability."

"Oh, heck yeah. Better even. Trouble is, I need both hands to maneuver the darn things." She waggled the poles. "I have a problem with vertigo. Gets me at the darndest times, and I don't want to fall and break a hip." She leaned in conspiratorially. "Did you hear about that nasty child molester getting offed in New Ohia? Good riddance, I say."

"Uh . . . I did hear about it." I cleared my throat and fumbled for my water bottle, stuck in a loop on my shorts. I definitely didn't want to discuss recent events with this busybody.

"Heard he got whacked with a two-by-four and they're looking for Jimmy Ching," Ms. Ramirez said with satisfaction. "Two bad apples gone from Ohia in one fell swoop."

How had all that gotten out so fast? Had Opal passed it on? I didn't think anyone other than me, Keone, the detectives, and the Pahinuis had known about the piece of wood I'd found.

Mattie's sharp brown eyes took in my expression. She flapped a hand and chuckled. "My nephew works security for New Ohia and saw the whole thing on the video feed."

"He shouldn't be talking about an open investigation. It could muddy the waters for the detectives," I said. "And you shouldn't be passing it on, either. What if they wanted to withhold the murder weapon as part of their strategy?"

Mattie straightened up, offended. "Well, aren't you the expert." She lifted her nose in the air and spun on her heel. "Be seeing you behind the counter, Ms. Smith."

Ouch. Nice way to remind me I was nothing but a public servant. Off she went, at a speed I'd be hard pressed to keep up with.

"Aunties like that don't like being told not to gossip," Keone observed.

"Ya think?" I elbowed him. "She sure liked the look of you."

"Let's get moving." Mr. K wasn't enjoying his brush with sexual harassment.

"Okay, but you go first this time. I want to take in the view." I thought I'd add insult to injury.

Keone snorted. The red hadn't yet faded from his ears. He took off up the boardwalk at a blistering speed. Soon I was jogging to keep up, barely able to glance around at the majestic bamboo forest.

We were at the waterfall in no time. I gasped as we approached the roaring, three-hundred-foot plume of water that poured over the cliff and pelted spectacularly into a small pool at the bottom. Just as Mattie Ramirez had said, no one was there. The place seemed to vibrate with energy.

"We're not supposed to go in, but since no one's around . . .?" Keone raised a brow at me.

Still wearing my swimsuit, I was ready for action in thirty seconds flat. I shucked off my shorts and Nikes and left them in a pile out of range of the spray. "I wouldn't miss it for the world. That waterfall is calling my name."

We approached the fall, and I was soaked and shivering long before we got to the water. "Chicken skin," Keone said, touching my arm.

"We call those goose bumps where I'm from, and it's a tad nippy, even for a girl from Maine." I ducked under the waterfall without further ado.

The pure power of it hit me like a freight train—the pressure of the water pushed down and surrounded me in an overwhelming sensory explosion.

I whooped with exhilaration when I burst back out.

Keone was right behind me, hollering too.

I turned and hugged him, thankful for the amazing experiences of his island home that he'd so generously shared with me. It was a tender hug with some friction here and there that I might've liked a bit more than I should've, but I wasn't going to jinx things, so I let go quickly.

We floated lazily in the small pool for a few minutes before making our way to the edge and climbing out. "I better get back to the shack before dinnertime. Tiki wasn't a happy camper last night when I came in late."

"How're you two getting along?" Mr. K had a thin hiking towel tucked into his pocket. He handed it to me before using it himself.

"Thanks. You're a real gentleman." I dried myself briskly. "We're making slow but steady progress. I got her to sleep on my bathrobe next to the bed last night instead of my head. We're working our way up to a flea bath."

Keone laughed. "I'd like to see you try that!"

"She'll come around," I said with more confidence than I felt. "I have to do something about all the pests she's carrying in and out of our place."

"How about one of those pills that kills the fleas and turns the cat toxic if they bite?"

I tapped my lips thoughtfully. "I've never had a pet, so I've never heard of that."

"Usually prescribed by a vet. You should trap Tiki and take her in for an exam, for her own good. Make sure she's fixed, too. Last thing you need is a batch of feral kittens."

"Tiki would never forgive me."

Keone shrugged. "Animals don't hold grudges."

"You don't know Tiki." I rolled my eyes. "She's a special case."

We picked our way across the wet, slippery rocks around the pool and back to the trail.

Mr. K spoke from behind me. "Speaking of special case. I thought about what you said about helping you investigate . . . and I've made a decision."

I had to pause in the middle of the bamboo forest boardwalk to turn and give him my full attention. Whatever Keone decided was going to have a big impact on the progress of our relationship—and on my ability to poke around town effectively, as an outsider without wheels.

I cocked a hip and fluttered my eyelashes, hoping to sway him to join Team Postmaster Sleuth. "So, are you in?"

"Nope," he said. "I can't help you."

I deflated like a tire with a slow leak and quit the eyelash flapping.

Keone folded his arms on his chest, his voice serious and his gaze direct. "I respect why you want to solve these murders. But for me, it's different. My family and friends are everywhere here. My cousin is a homicide detective working these cases. The more I know, the more I have to answer to others about what you're doing."

My stomach sank like a boulder in a bayou. "Dang it. I was really hoping I'd have your help."

"I'm sorry, Kat. I know you're disappointed, but the less you tell me about what you're up to, the better."

"It's going to come between us, eventually." I felt as certain of this as winter arriving early in Maine. "Plausible deniability. That's what you want."

"It's not what I *want*. It's what I *need*. This island is too small, and the coconut wireless never stops."

"I get it." I turned and started back down the boardwalk, blind to the beauty of the bamboo dancing around me. I was no longer having fun. Wow, things can sure change fast between a guy and a girl and a murder investigation.

"Kat." Mr. K called my name.

I stopped, but only because I knew he was going to touch me if I didn't.

I didn't turn around. I stared down the boardwalk, waiting for him to say whatever he needed to say from behind my back.

"I still want to do what I can to keep you safe. And I won't try to stop what you're doing, unless I think something is too dangerous."

That sparked my temper and I turned to give him a glare over my shoulder. "You seem to think I'm some little lady in need of protection. Dude, I AM the protection. That is the definition of what a Secret Service agent does."

His voice was soft as he said, "But you're Postal Service now."

I didn't care to be reminded. I didn't choose any of this. I started walking again and didn't look back.

I went fast, hoping to lose Keone, but that wasn't possible. The man was at least as fit as me. But he didn't try to talk to me, so I didn't have to run. The way back down from the waterfall was easier —all downhill. I grabbed a few more guavas along the way and stuck them in my pockets for later.

What was the point of being with this guy, anyway? We had nothing in common. He was Hawaiian, and I was a *malihini* who wouldn't be here long. I was also messed up, as today's situation with Pua's nephew clearly showed. Regular dating wasn't going to go anywhere. I was meant to be alone with my attack cat, living in a shack, with the knowledge that the postmaster before me had lain in a shallow grave behind my dwelling for the last six months.

Not that I was feeling at all sorry for myself.

We reached the end of the hike in silence.

"Want to go for a quick dip?" Mr. K pointed toward the Pools of ʻOheʻo swimming area as we exited the trail. "I don't know about you, but I'm pretty sweaty. Might be nice to rinse off."

I wanted to be alone, but I wanted to cool down even more. What difference would a few more minutes make? "Okay."

I followed Keone along a split in the trail to the series of waterfalls that splashed pool to pool, all the way to the sea. The biggest pool, directly below the Hana Highway bridge, had a series of bluffs edging it on one side. People were climbing them and jumping in—some with flaps and screams, some with graceful leaps, some with belly flops or cannonballs.

Mr. K clambered sure-footedly to the highest outcrop on the cliffs, one I hadn't seen anyone else attempt. My heart pounded as I climbed after him, motivated by nothing but stubbornness. I'd just told him "I am the protection"—I couldn't wimp out now. I would jump off whatever he did, even if it killed me.

At the very top of the cliff, Keone walked to the edge and looked down.

Jade green water rippled far below. There was no way to tell how deep it was, or how close the rocks at the bottom were to the surface. Other visitors, all around the various bluffs, stopped what they were doing to watch.

He turned back to me. "I've been coming here since I was a kid. I know just where to jump, but I'd rather you went in at the main spot for your first time." He pointed back down to a lower jump point, around fifteen feet in height from the water.

I narrowed my eyes at him. "No. I'm jumping where you're jumping."

He sighed gustily. "Well, when you get to the edge, it will seem like you can't clear the trees growing out from below. Jump outward as far as you can. Point your toes on the way down and hold your nose, otherwise you might burst an eardrum."

And then, just like that, he hurled himself forward into space, letting out a yell that bounced off the cliffs, and disappeared.

# 23

I ran to the edge, looking for Keone. I almost fell, windmilling my arms and scrambling back from the ledge. The drop off the cliff into the pool had to be forty feet, at least.

Mr. K bobbed up from his jump, way down below. His head seemed tiny as he shook the water out of his hair, letting out a whoop. He swam to one side and treaded water. “Come on in, Kat! Just remember to jump out as far as you can so you clear the trees.”

I was so busy fixating on how far away the water was to notice the trees, but now that I did, I gulped. Twenty feet down, they protruded out from the cliff face another six feet or more. My brain filled with images of being impaled on the branches before smashing my brains out on the rocks.

“Serves me right for getting myself into this,” I muttered.

The longer I looked down, the worse the scenarios were that played through my mind. I needed to go—and go *now*—before I chickened out. I'd overcome a thousand obstacles in training the same way. “Nothing to it but to do it.” I backed up as far as I could, then sprinted to the edge and jumped with everything I had.

“I AM THE PROTECTION!”

My voice rang off the cliffs as I flew forward and plummeted down, eventually remembering to pull my legs in, point my feet, and grab my nose before I slammed into the water. Because that's what it felt like—being slammed feet first into a concrete block.

I sank all the way to the rocky bottom and pushed off, rising on a rush of bubbles to the top and bursting out of the water. The gust of adrenaline completely blew my angst away.

Keone was right there beside me in the water, cheering. "Awesome, Kat! Everyone in Ohia heard you. I got the message, too. Loud and clear."

"Good," I said primly, and dog-paddled for the edge of the pool. "Let's do it again."

Later, at the truck, he handed me one of his beach towels and said, "I'll be busy all next week flying back and forth from Kahului to Hana. But I'm off Wednesday night, if you want to go out to dinner."

"You asking me on a date?" I rubbed my wet hair with the towel, then wrapped the terry cloth around my body, tucking the edges in over my breasts.

"I guess I am." Mr. K's gaze was following what I was doing with the ends of the towel.

I waved my hands. "Eyes up here, buddy."

He laughed.

I laughed.

I couldn't remember right now what I'd been mad about, but I was sure it would come back to me later, once the adrenaline rush left my nervous system wiped out. "Wednesday night, dinner. Okay. It's a date."

"We'll go to the steakhouse in Hana," he said. "They make you sit down with menus, they bring the food, and they have drinks with umbrellas in them. It's crazy. We'll have to wear actual clothes."

"Not sure I can deal with that level of fancy." We climbed into the truck to head back to Ohia.

It had been a very full day, but it turns out it wasn't over yet.

When we pulled up in front of the shack, a whole group was gathered on the porch of the Ohia General Store.

A party was shaping up—Artie Pahinui held court on the porch with his guitar, surrounded by a gaggle of Red Hat ladies and other townspeople. As soon as Mr. K and I rolled to a stop, Opal and the others waved us over.

"Join us! We're having a celebration!" Edith Pepperwhite, the lawyer who looked like a lawn gnome, called us over.

"What are you celebrating?" I shouted back, tucking the ends of my towel in around myself as Keone came around the front of the truck and opened the door for me.

"Pua getting out of jail!" Opal hollered from the porch. "She'll be here in half an hour. Come on over!"

"Sounds fun," I yelled back. I turned to Keone. "You want to go? I'm sure you're invited too."

"Nah, I need to get on home. Got a super early flight tomorrow." He gave me a hopeful smile. "Got a kiss for your surf instructor?"

We stood sheltered within the open door of the truck, but still highly visible. I was acutely aware of the watching eyes on the porch of the general store, so I gave him a quick peck on the cheek.

"C'mon, Kat. Give him a better kiss than that!" Edith yelled, and the other Red Hat ladies whooped.

"I don't want to jinx it," I whispered to Keone. "I don't want to freak out on you, especially in front of other people."

"How about I keep my hands where they are, and you lay one right here." He tapped his lips.

What full, warm, soft-looking lips they were. Surely, I could . . . I leaned in and closed my eyes. His arms still propped on the truck, I felt him drift toward me, his mouth gently meeting mine.

"Whoo-hoo! That's more like it!" Opal yelled.

I broke away—laughing, embarrassed—but also a little happy because I'd stuck with it. In fact, it was so nice that I'd forgotten the audience, even if they hadn't forgotten us. I stepped away from the shelter of the truck. "Thanks for a wonderful day, even if you won't help me investigate the murders."

"I gotta draw the line somewhere, Trouble."

"Ugh." I rolled my eyes. "See you Wednesday."

"Six o'clock," he said, slamming the door behind me. "Remember to wear a clean shirt."

"I might surprise you with a dress."

"Don't tease me like that. My heart can't take it." He grinned as he circled the front of the truck and climbed in. Dang, the guy was cute. No fair. I waved goodbye as he pulled away, and he threw a 'shaka' gesture to the ladies on the porch. They hooted some more and he beeped his horn, driving away into the warm evening.

"Meeeooooow." Tiki yowled loudly from the stoop rock. She'd arrived while I was distracted, and her tone warned of repercussions if I didn't feed her soon.

"I'll be over in a minute," I yelled to the party on the porch, and quickly attended to the needs of my feline companion before she took a chunk out of my leg.

By the time I'd appeased Tiki, gotten myself showered and dressed, and joined the party on the porch, Artie was taking a break from playing. Opal had rolled out a long sheet of pink butcher paper and the ladies were writing "WELCOME BACK PUA" on it with pens and crayons. Reggae music played in the background, and someone had filled a washtub with ice and stocked it with beer and wine.

"Ready for some *pupus*?" Opal asked me.

I frowned. "Why would I want poo-poos? Doesn't sound good."

"Ha! That's Hawaiian for appetizers." Pearl rolled toward me in her wheelchair with a big tray on her lap. "We've got sashimi, *limu* on rice crackers, and *haupia* squares. So *'ono*."

I gazed down at a plate containing slices of raw fish, small pale crackers with seaweed on them, and cubes of something white and jiggly. "I'll have one of each, thanks."

"Grab a paper plate from my side pouch." She had stashed a stack in the pocket under the arm of her chair.

I helped myself to one of each, and a toothpick to spear them. Edith walked up, carrying a stack of napkins, which she tucked in the pocket under the other arm of Pearl's chair. "What'll you have to drink? We have beer, wine, sake, or kava."

I decided to stick with what I knew. "Beer, please."

She bustled off to fetch it, while I stared doubtfully at my paper plate. Clara elbowed me, Josie at her side with a slim green oxygen tank in tow. "How many of these things have you tried before?"

"None."

"I suspected as much." She eyed me over a pair of half-glasses on a beaded chain that looped around her neck. "Best to dip the fish into some shoyu with a little wasabi. Pearl? You forgot the sauce!"

"Oh shoot. It's in my other pouch." She fumbled around and produced a small Tupperware tub. She peeled the top off. Brown liquid sloshed inside, along with a round pellet of some bright green paste. "Here's what you do: poke your piece of fish with a toothpick and swizzle it around. Be sure to get a little of the wasabi on it, but only a little."

"Why?" I followed directions, swirling a chunk of the dark red fish in the sauce, then dabbing the green paste until I had a nice goo.

"You'll see." Her dark eyes sparkled behind cat-eye specs bedazzled with rhinestones. "Put the whole thing in your mouth to really get the feel of it."

I did. "Whew!" Heat from the green paste blasted up my nasal passages, obliterating any flavor from the raw fish. Seconds later, the burst of heat passed, and I could taste the fish's sweet, salty flavor and a smooth, pleasant texture. "Hmm. I like it."

"*Limu* next! Foraged just this morning," Clara said. "Then the *haupia*—it makes a nice finisher."

The compressed rice cracker with seaweed on it was okay. The white cube turned out to be a firm, coconut-flavored pudding. "I had this today already, in a malasada!" I exclaimed, stabbing another jiggly cube of haupia. "This has . . . broken my mouth for anything else."

Everyone laughed as I accepted a beer from Edith.

"I'll get that right someday." I glanced around. "Where's Mattie? Mattie Ramirez? We ran into her on our hike in the bamboo forest today."

"Oh, she couldn't make it," Clara said. "Had some business to take care of." She pointed. "There's Pua now! And she brought Sassy and Sonny Boy!"

I wasn't excited to see either of Pua's companions, but hopefully we'd get along a little better this time. We certainly couldn't do any worse than what happened earlier at the banyan tree.

I put a smile on my face and took a big swig of beer as Pua pulled up in her Honda SUV, her nephew in the passenger seat and her evil white dog on his lap. I hung back and let the Red Hat ladies, the Pahinuis, and other townspeople greet Pua first. I kept a wary eye on Sonny, who stayed in the car during the first crush of greetings. He held Sassy on his lap while she barked savagely through the closed window, spit flying from her fangs. It seemed Pua had her own version of Tiki to contend with.

Finally, Pua came up onto the weathered boards of the porch and approached me, a plastic cup of pale yellow liquid in her hand. "Sake," she said, lifting it toward me. "Always served warm."

I fanned myself with a hand. "I'm warm enough, thank you. This is hitting the spot." I lifted my bottle of Primo Beer. "I'm so glad you got out of jail unscathed."

Pua frowned. "Says who? I was fingerprinted, dressed in an orange jumpsuit, and spent the night in a jail cell. Not something I plan to forget. Or forgive." She narrowed mean dark eyes, an effect I remembered from our early interactions.

I cleared my throat. "I think the police felt they had no choice because of the physical evidence they found on the body. It also may have flushed out the real killer—did you hear about what happened to Kermit Hubbard?"

Pua opened her mouth to answer, but another person from the town bumped her on the elbow and gave her an enthusiastic hug. When she had a free moment, I caught her eye once more. "I'll see you at work tomorrow, Pua. We'll catch up then."

"Sounds good." She forged into the crowd and was soon surrounded like a queen by her courtiers. Dressed in a red designer dress with kitten-heeled Louboutins, she looked like a queen, too. Imagining Pua Chang in prison orange was difficult. That night must have been excruciating for a woman like her.

With the guest of honor present, Artie picked up his guitar once more. Surrounded by the mellow flow of conversation and music, I felt my eyes begin to shut on their own. It had been a very long, physical day, and with every sip of beer it caught up with me more.

"Clara!" I called. She was dressed in a flowing palazzo pantsuit in an African print that complimented her glowing skin. She floated over to see what I needed. "I'm fading. You seem to know your way around this food—can you help me put together a plate to take home?"

"Sure!" Clara had a smile that lit up a room. "Let's go over to the *pupu* table and load you up." Clara handed me a doubled paper plate that was so piled with food that I needed both hands to hold it. Soon, I was waving goodbye.

I crossed the parking lot to my shack. Apparently, I hadn't locked the door of my humble abode. I was sure I'd left the light on inside, too. But when I set my loaded plate down and opened the door, I was met with darkness. I stumbled forward, pulled the string for the light—and stopped short.

On the small Formica table sat a green coconut. I might have taken this as a friendly gesture, if it hadn't also had a hatchet wedged into it, pinning on a note that read: "GO AWAY OR DIE."

# 24

"Oh, crud on a cantaloupe." I spun around and whipped open the bathroom and closet doors. Nothing. The place was empty—there was nowhere else for an intruder to hide in the shack.

I dropped the Murphy bed and retrieved my Glock from under my pillow. Not the best place to keep it, but my crude hiding place had worked well enough. Whoever had come in while I was at the party—all thirty minutes of it—had not found it, and that was good.

I expelled and checked the magazine, making sure there was a round in the chamber. Satisfied with the readiness of my weapon, my brain went into threat analysis mode:

1. The person who left this little scene was likely someone at the party. They'd known the shack was empty, where I was, and that I was distracted.

2. They only had a half-hour in which to enter, set up the display, and leave.

3. They did so with dozens of witnesses only fifty yards away. Someone may have seen them enter or exit.

4. Tiki was not actually that great at attacking intruders—OR, she knew the person.

5. The rusty stains on the blade of the hatchet might be blood,

potentially Fran's. I never found out how she was killed, so this could be the murder weapon.

6. I needed to secure the premises, stay alert, and stay armed from now on. I had an enemy who had just declared war.

I pulled my phone out of my pocket. Alas, no bars. I needed the cops. They would also need statements from everyone at the party about their whereabouts and what they'd seen. I decided on a bold move.

"Go big or go home, Kat," I muttered to myself.

Careful not to touch anything, I retreated to my porch, letting out a gigantic bellowing scream. "HELP! Everyone, come over here! I need HELP!"

The response was gratifying.

The entire party froze, then streamed down off the porch toward me, Pua Chang leading the charge. Even Artie Pahunui, walking with his stick in one hand and the other on Opal's shoulder, approached.

"What's happened, Kat?"

"Are you okay?"

Questions came at me from all directions.

"No, I'm not okay!" I yelled. "Someone threatened to kill me, and that might be Fran's murder weapon right there! Anyone with phone signal, call 911!"

Some fumbled for their phones, others clustered in the doorway to gape at the little tableau that had been left for me. Pua stood beside me and shook her head, dropping her phone back into her pocket. "I think we have to call from a landline."

Artie and Opal arrived, the crowd parting to let them through. Opal clapped a hand over her mouth in shock. "That's awful, Kat! Artie, there's a green coconut with a note held to it by a hatchet with stains on the blade. The note says 'go away or die.'"

Artie blinked his blind eyes. "The killer is here," he declared in his resonant voice.

A shiver tripped down my spine. The hairs on my arms and the back of my neck stood up. Artie was never wrong.

I clapped my hands to get everyone's attention. "Nobody move. Everyone except Artie and Opal, stay right here. Opal, go back to the store and call 911, then call this number." I handed her my cell phone. "That's Lei Texeira, the detective on Fran's case. She needs to know what happened." Restless murmuring rippled through the crowd. I drowned it out with my best Secret Service crowd control voice. "Everyone here needs to make a statement to the police about their whereabouts and what they saw between the time I arrived at the party and my discovery. We might be able to solve Fran Borland's murder right now."

In the distance, Opal disappeared into the general store to call the police. The partiers, the mood gone somber, milled around in front of my shack, muttering to each other in little pods.

"All right, everyone." I forced a smile. "I know this has been a shock, but it's important that you don't talk amongst yourselves about this until the police have a chance to get your statements. No reason we need to be uncomfortable, though. How about we all go back to the general store and have some more *pupus*?" I pointed to my loaded plate. "Might as well eat dinner."

"Sounds good, Kat." Edith Pepperwhite waved a gnarled hand. "C'mon, everyone. Let's take this party back to where it started."

Truth was, I didn't want to have to keep looking at the threatening display, nor did I care to have the town peering in at my sad little lodgings and speculating amongst themselves. Yeah, that was sure to happen, but it didn't have to happen right in front of that bit of nastiness on my kitchen table.

I closed the door, locked it, and picked up my loaded double paper plate. I was behind the crowd now, following them back to the general store. As my eyes scanned the people in front of me, two sets of eyes stared back—Pua's nephew, Sonny, and the dog. The two were still sitting in the SUV, but on the driver's side now. When had they gotten out? I hadn't seen them mingle at all.

I forced my face to relax. I smiled at the young man as I approached the SUV. "Hi, Sonny," I said with a little wave. Sassy jumped up, putting her paws on the open window ledge, and yapped shrilly.

Sonny stared back at me, expressionless. “Not friend,” he said.

Well, I guess I deserved that. I continued past the front of their SUV.

I reached the porch and looked for a spot to sit down. My legs had gone a bit rubbery with the aftereffects of adrenaline. But there was one more thing I needed to do. “Can everyone grab some refreshments and then sit separately? I know you want to talk, but it’s important that—”

Edith interrupted me. “Kat’s right. We shouldn’t talk about or speculate on what she found in her house until the police get here and we talk to them. That said, we are perfectly fine and within our rights to hang out here, get comfortable, and talk about other things—like how great it is that Pua has Bennie Fernandez as her defense lawyer!”

Edith scooped me on the leadership moment, but that was okay. I didn’t want to ride herd on half the town of Ohia anyway. I sat down on the top step leading into the store and stared down at my plate filled with unfamiliar foods. My appetite was gone. All I could think about was the green coconut, the hatchet, and the note telling me to go home or die.

Opal put a hand on my shoulder, and I jumped at her touch. “I have a cell phone signal booster inside. I got Sergeant Texeira on your phone if you want to talk to her. The regular cops stationed in Hana are on their way.”

“Yes, please. I’d like to speak to her.”

Opal handed me the phone and removed my plate without a word. I stood up and slipped inside the dimly lit cave of the store, heading for the door marked PRIVATE. I wanted to get as close to that signal booster as possible, but also away from listening ears.

Once inside the little storage room, I sat down on Artie’s comfortable chair and put my cell phone to my ear. “Hello? Lei? Can you hear me? Kat here.”

"Hey Kat." Lei sounded tired. "I hear you've found something nasty in the shack."

"Yeah." My eyes prickled. There must be particulate matter in the air. "I think Fran's murder weapon might have been given to me as a warning."

"Tell me what happened. Don't leave out a thing."

I did so, stopping frequently to answer clarifying questions. "Are you going to be able to come out?"

She sighed. "Not today. I'm home, finally. But I'll call the first responders and tell them what I want collected from the folks at the party. Don't touch the items on the table, or anything else if you can help it, until the team has dusted for prints. I'll come out with Pono tomorrow and collect the evidence."

"Sounds like I need to spend the night somewhere else."

"I guess so. I'm sorry, Kat. This is a bummer."

"Yeah, it is." I rubbed my tired, sore, prickly eyes. *I was not crying . . . there was dust in them, by golly!* "I'll see if Opal has an idea where I can go for the night."

"Get some rest and see you tomorrow." She ended the call.

I stared at the phone for a moment. I could call Mr. K. He would probably want me to update him. But suddenly, telling him the latest seemed like just too much. Right now, I wanted to curl up somewhere (safe) and sleep for a thousand years.

Opal appeared in the doorway. "The Hana cops are here, and they want to speak to you."

Guess that thousand-year nap was going to have to wait a while longer.

Artie and Opal invited me to spend the night at their place, and after the day's marathon of events, I went down hard on the little futon they set up for me in the living room.

Opal woke me at eight forty-five in the morning, much later than

I planned to sleep. I leaped up off the futon and jogged next door to feed a cranky Tiki. Drifts of fingerprint dust covered everything, but I didn't have time to address that now. I threw on my "work uniform" of a polo shirt and jeans, dragged a brush through my hair, and tied on my Nikes. I avoided looking at the macabre display on the table waiting for Lei and Pono and headed out the door.

I beat Pua into the post office, but not by much. I was still trying to impress Pua Chang—I'm a big enough girl to admit it. But surely it wasn't fair that she walked in five minutes behind me, smelling like a tropical bouquet, polished and perfect in an outfit that cost more than my whole month's salary. How did she afford her wardrobe? I hadn't a clue. I'd never felt more like a ginormous, unkempt Great Dane beside a pretty toy poodle than I did this morning.

"Hey, Pua." I closed the instructional binder when she poked her head into my office. "I'm so glad you're back. I couldn't wait on people on Friday without knowing the procedures."

"Yes, let's make getting you trained our priority, in case I'm arrested again." She gave a tinkle of fake laughter and click-clacked her pumps over to the counter. "Let me show you the basics on posting a package for a customer. We have five minutes before I unlock the front door."

"It's great you think I can learn that in five minutes," I said dubiously.

She slanted me a cool side-eye. "You're a smart woman, Kat. Anyone can see that."

My heart cockles fluttered. Being called smart is my favorite compliment, bar none. "Okay. Lay it on me."

Sure enough, she showed me in five minutes flat, then flipped up the counter divider and headed for the front door, where several customers already lurked behind the glass. They weren't there to mail stuff—they wanted the scoop on recent events and to clap eyes on Pua to make sure she was okay.

That kinda warmed my heart, too. Dang it, I was in danger of falling in love with Ohia and its quirky, gossipy people. Leaving was going to hurt. While I wanted my situation in D.C. to get sorted, I was also starting to dread my departure.

Pua was as gracious as a hostess in a receiving line, unlocking the door and welcoming her adoring fans. I got to ring up a few customers buying stamps to justify their visit. One even leaned in to ask me about the "dead body with a message carved on its butt" that had been left on my table. Yikes! A mere coconut with a hatchet and a threatening note seemed mild now. It's amazing how passing news along verbally can distort a message. I was glad to set the record straight.

"And if you hear of anyone bragging about threatening me, or anything truly useful, call Maui Police Department," I told them.

Finally, the initial surge ebbed. Shortly after, Chad arrived with the mail van. I carried all the stuff in with his help, then Pua and I put on our gloves, dumped out the bags, and got to sorting.

"Can you focus on organizing the packages?" Pua asked. "You're stronger."

I like being called strong almost as much as I like being called smart. "Sure!" I headed for the unruly mountain of boxes and slippery plastic delivery bags.

If I didn't know better, I might think Pua was buttering me up. But why?

I began sorting the packages, writing the customer's address numbers on the side in Sharpie. Then I made a yellow tag to insert into their mail slot, so they could retrieve the package at the counter when they checked their box.

"We never got to finish our conversation last night," I said. "Did you hear what happened to Kermit Hubbard?"

"Oh." Pua shuddered delicately, but her swift hands never stopped moving. "A terrible thing."

"He was a registered sex offender. Not sure if that's relevant, but it seems like it might be."

"Shocking," Pua said, but didn't seem at all surprised.

"Did you know I found the murder weapon used on him?"

Her busy hands stalled. She seemed to go still all the way to her core. "That must have been stressful for you," she said at last.

"It was. A piece of lumber from a construction site in New Ohia—the perp pitched it onto the beach hoping the tide would take it out, but the waves didn't cooperate." I blew out a breath. "The cops would have chalked it up to a crime of opportunity, but the whole thing was caught on video. Kermit was hanging around outside the clubhouse, waiting for someone. Out of nowhere, the perp ran up and whacked him on the head from behind. He never saw it coming." I watched Pua carefully as I reached for the next package.

"How awful! Could they tell anything about the murderer on the video?" Her voice was tight, and her hands slowed.

"No. That's the funny thing. The person must have known about the cameras in New Ohia because they avoided them and wore a hat, baggy clothes, and gloves. The police couldn't even make out gender."

"Ah." Pua seemed to relax, and her sorting increased in speed. "Not too many people know about the cameras. Maybe that will help them in the investigation."

Pua Chang knew something about the murder. I'd bet my new Nikes on it.

# 25

As soon as I saw Stanley pull up beside the post office, I told Pua I was taking a break. She nodded, knowing I had to unlock my place and let the detectives in to remove the threat left on my kitchen table.

I exited the back door of the building just as Lei was hopping down from the chrome step, dodging a puddle. It seemed to rain every night in Ohia and the parking lot was perpetually muddy.

Lei's curly hair was rolled into a ball and pierced by a chopstick. The bone hook pendant I'd glimpsed her holding occasionally encircled her neck, hung on a coconut fiber cord. Her big brown eyes were kind as she looked me over.

"You up for a hug?" she asked unexpectedly. "You look like you could use one."

Suddenly, I couldn't think of anything I needed more. Okay, maybe a kiss from Mr. K, but a hug from Lei was a close second. I had a feeling she didn't give them out often. "Yes, please."

Lei had strong arms, and her powerful squeeze made up for her small (compared to me) size. I shut my eyes, receiving the extended physical touch without a problem. Maybe I was getting over my weirdness, at least a little.

"You've had a rough landing here in Ohia," she said, letting go.

I stepped back. "Yes, I have, but I've made some great friends here. I found a glass ball on the beach on my first day—that's supposed to be good luck."

"I can tell you're a glass half-full kind of *tita*, because you also found a body and a murder weapon," Pono said, joining us.

"*Tita*? What's that?" I smiled at my second favorite Kaihale. Pono wore a navy blue polo shirt and Oakleys clamped around the back of his head, with a fresh buzz cut so short I could see his scalp.

"Pidgin term. Means a tough local chick who is not scared to fight and doesn't take crap from anyone."

"Wait. I thought I was a *haole malihini*. A white newcomer."

"That too." Pono smiled. "But I see full-on *tita* potential in you."

"I guess that's a compliment?"

"Sure is." Lei turned toward my front door. "I take it you've kept the place locked since the discovery?" She was pulling on nitrile gloves as she spoke.

"Yep. I spent the night at Artie and Opal's. Besides a quick stop this morning to get ready for work, the place should be exactly how I left it last night." I pulled the ring of keys I'd received from the main office out of my pocket. I'd added my deadbolt key to the ring. I stepped up onto the porch and threw the bolt open. "*Voilà*." I opened the door with a push and the rickety door flew inward, banging against the wooden wall.

Tiki, who must have been sleeping in her makeshift robe bed, shot into the air with a yowl and landed on the table, just behind the macabre coconut. Her patchy fur puffed up so that she was double her already enormous size, and her yellow eyes narrowed to slits. She lifted a paw, set it on the axe handle protruding from the coconut, and hissed.

"Whoa," Lei said, from behind me. "I think we found the perp."

Tiki looked offended. She took her paw off the handle and growled, preparing to jump and maim whomever she could reach.

I took a careful step back, my hands raised in a surrender gesture.

"Hey, girl. Sorry for waking you up. We're going to take that stuff off the table, okay? It's not adding to our shack's ambience."

Tiki sat back on her haunches, lashing her tail. Black fingerprint powder flew hither and yon. She lifted a paw and licked it, shooting a glare at me.

"That's it, Tiki. No reason to be mad. Why don't you come on out and go hunting? Maybe you can find the murderer for us," I soothed. "You're upset I stayed at Artie and Opal's last night . . . I get it. But after the nice detectives get this stuff off the table, we'll have a nice, quiet evening together."

"You are so pussy whipped!" Pono chortled at his own joke.

Tiki took that as her cue and leaped down off the table, zooming past me and hissing at Pono as she passed.

"She heard that," I told him. "She understands everything."

Lei shook her head. "Yikes. Talk about a tough roommate situation."

Lei pulled out a large paper evidence bag and shook it open. "Pono, can you make out the evidence log?"

"Yup." Pono removed a pad from his back pocket and uncapped a cheap Bic pen. "Go ahead."

"One large fresh coconut, no prints on it per visual examination and police report. One hatchet, also no prints." Lei took hold of the handle and removed the weapon, examining it. "First responders took swab samples of the stains on the blade—negative for blood." She touched a dark spot. It seemed tacky, like tar. "I think this might be sap. Very sticky and hard to clean off. I'll have our lab do a closer analysis." She handed the hatchet to Pono, and he bagged it, securing the paper bag with an attached log sheet and a tiny handheld stapler. I was impressed by their smooth operation, but they'd clearly worked a lot of scenes together.

Lei went on with her running monologue. "One threat letter, handwritten, no visible prints—but we'll also test for prints back at the lab. If the perp staged this scene with uncovered hands, they could have wiped the coconut and the hatchet clean but would not have been able to remove their fingerprints from the paper itself."

"Sounds like the hatchet wasn't Fran's murder weapon," I said.

Lei glanced at me. "Nope. There was no visible cause of death on Ms. Borland's body. The ME ruled it undetermined."

"What? She wasn't murdered?"

"Her body was too degraded to determine cause of death. There were no obvious wounds."

"But wait, why did you arrest Pua then?" I frowned.

Lei didn't answer, turning back to the table instead. "Did you find anything else out of place?"

"No. Not that I did much of a careful search. Once I discovered the threat, I knew one of the partygoers had to have planted it. Stopping them from leaving was my priority." I put my hands on my hips. "What did they say in their statements? Was anyone seen coming in or out of my place?"

Lei continued to ignore me, turning on a high-powered flashlight and scanning over and under the table.

Pono seemed to take pity on my situation. "We had our reasons for arresting Pua Chang."

"I work with the woman every day and deal with her friends and fans too," I said shortly. "If there's something I should know about her, please tell me."

Lei finally looked up. "We did what we did, and someone else did what they did. What does that tell you?"

I fisted my hands on my hips. "Nothing clear. The murders are connected? Pua wasn't the killer because she was in jail when Kermit was whacked? Help me out here." I pointed to a giant, hand-size hairy brown spider that Lei's flashlight had illuminated under the table. "I'm in a scene straight out of an Indiana Jones movie, and that spider is big enough to take on Tiki." I shuddered. "Can you guys help me kill that thing before you leave?"

"Cane spider. They're fairly harmless," Lei said. She unlatched the back window and propped it open with a stick. It didn't have a screen. Pono picked up the broom I'd bought at Opal's and gently shooed the spider, which ran with terrifying speed out the window.

"We try not to kill them. They're good for keeping down mosquitoes and other insects," Pono said, pulling the window shut and latching it. "Natural bug control."

I made a face. "No thanks. I'll live with the attack cat and the pooping geckos—but I draw the line at pet spiders."

"Have you heard of the Big Island Changs?" Lei gave a small lift of her chin, and Pono closed the door of the shack, presumably so we'd have more privacy. Gloom fell over us in a green tinted shroud, the only remaining light filtered through the foliage outside my one window. I reached up and yanked the string of the bare bulb that lit up the room. I was going to have to make a spider sweep before bed —I couldn't unsee the cane spider they'd chased outside.

"My boss, the head postmaster in Kahului, told me that the Changs are a major crime family in Hawaii. He said that's why Pua has never been promoted to postmaster—she'd be in a position to commit mail fraud if she were in charge of this outpost."

"I can't say more at this time, but . . ." Lei hesitated, choosing her words carefully. "There's more going on here than meets the eye."

"This is so frustrating," I said.

"I know." Pono touched my shoulder with a big hand, and I jumped away. I hadn't seen it coming. "Sorry. My bad," he apologized.

"Yeah, I'm . . . tactile sensitive." I grabbed one of the two metal folding chairs beside the table and sat. "Is there anything else you can tell me about what's going on?"

"The witnesses at the party claim to have not seen anyone come or go from your cottage," Lei said. "All those interviews, and nothing useful was learned."

"Someone is lying." I had a flash of memory. "You know who might have seen something? Pua's nephew, Sonny. Roland Chang. He and her dog were sitting in her car during the half-hour in question, facing my shack. He was in the passenger seat, then in the driver's seat when I saw him next. I never saw him or the dog join the party. He had to have seen whomever came and went from my place."

Lei and Pono exchanged a glance. "I don't remember seeing his name in the statements. We'll follow up on that," Lei said.

"He's got a cognitive disability. Pua tries to keep him from getting too agitated. I'm sure he was upset by the events, so maybe they skipped talking to him because of that."

"We can swing by Pua's on the way back to Kahului," Lei told Pono, "and talk to the kid then."

"Do you know anything new about Kermit's murder? Or where Jimmy Ching disappeared to?"

Lei fixed me with a squinty eye. "Shouldn't you be getting back to work? I know we need to."

I sighed, my shoulders slumping. "Okay. Be like that." I headed for the door and opened it, stopping short.

Jimmy Ching had just pulled into the post office in his big, shiny white SUV. "Lei! Pono! There's Ching!"

Pono brushed past me, headed for the development manager like a big, burly, heat-seeking missile. "Jimmy Ching! Maui Police Department. We need to speak with you."

Ching wore his usual blue polo shirt with the New Ohia logo and a pair of chinos with boat shoes, no socks. A monogrammed bracelet of heavy gold links adorned one wrist, and his hair was freshly barbered. "Hey. I've been meaning to return you folks' calls."

I could practically see the steam coming out of Lei's ears as she followed Pono across the parking lot. "Hands on the vehicle," she barked. "Spread your legs."

"What is this about?" Ching wasn't following directions, so Lei spun him around and slammed him down on the hood of his car. The man emitted an outraged bellow as she frisked him.

"He's clean," she told Pono.

Customers from inside the post office congregated on the porch area to goggle at the sight of Jimmy Ching getting his comeuppance. Even Pua Chang emerged to watch.

"Would you like to meet with us somewhere private, or shall we drive back to Kahului to speak at the station?"

"I want my lawyer present, so I'll drive myself to the station and you can follow," Ching said. His face was flushed with anger. "If you're wondering where I was when Kermit Hubbard was killed, I was on Oahu meeting with funders."

"We'll need proof of that, and we have some other questions for you," Lei said. "Kahului it is."

Ching got into his vehicle, whatever he'd been planning to do at the post office forgotten.

Lei lifted a hand in farewell, and Pono gave me a 'shaka' as he got into Stanley. The two detectives pulled out and followed Ching's vehicle.

"Well, that was exciting," Pua said.

"I hope they nail that guy!" said one of the customers. A general mumble of agreement followed. "New Ohia sucks!"

I turned back and locked the door of my shack so I could return to work. Tonight was going to be a mellow evening cleaning up fingerprint powder and rebuilding my relationship with Tiki—or so I hoped. A quiet night alone with my cat seemed like an elusive dream at this point.

# 26

The rest of the afternoon was seriously anticlimactic but passed quickly as a steady stream of postal customers ebbed and flowed from the building. Pua and I never had time to discuss the scene with Ching, and my mental faculties were kept occupied practicing the new skills I was learning in basic postal retail service.

As soon as Pua locked the front door and we began our four p.m. closing procedures, I texted Lei: *What's the scoop on Ching? Did you arrest him?*

No reply.

I tidied my work area and Pua returned. "I texted Lei about Ching, but she hasn't answered."

"I'm not surprised." Pua still looked as fresh as she had when she arrived that morning. I, however, felt hot, bothered, and frazzled. She looked me over. "Do you have any plans for tonight?"

"Just cleaning up the fingerprint powder all over my place and taking a cool-off swim at the beach."

"Why don't you do that, and then join Sonny and me for dinner?" Pua smiled. "You look like you could use a home-cooked meal, and I've had a nice Hawaiian-style beef stew slow-cooking in the crock pot all day."

"Oh man." My mouth watered at the thought. I hadn't had a chance to eat anything but a granola bar in hours. "I'm on it. Oh yeah."

"See you at five thirty, then?" Pua quirked a well-groomed brow. "I'll come back and pick you up."

"Yes, please and thank you."

We locked up the building and went our separate ways; Pua drove off and I returned to the shack. I pulled on rubber gloves, put my phone in a bowl, and turned on my Classic Rock collection. To the sounds of "Carry On Wayward Son," "Hot Blooded," and "I Won't Back Down," I sang, dusted, and swept. I cleaned the place in no time, chasing out another cane spider and a couple of geckos while I was at it.

"Natural bug control," I grumbled as I shooed them outside. "Keep out, I don't need your help!"

Soon the shack was sparkling from top to bottom, and I still had half an hour to jump in the ocean. I threw on my bikini, jogged across the road, and ran into the surf for a quick cooldown. Remarkably refreshed after twenty laps across the pristine bay, I trotted back to the shack to be confronted by Tiki sitting on the porch.

It was five p.m. on the dot, her time to return and demand a meal. The cat glared balefully at me and lashed her tail.

"Hi, honey, I'm home," I singsonged. "You hungry? I've whipped up a special bowl of kibble for you already." I sidled past the attack feline and unlocked the door. I was building a new habit of keeping the place locked, by golly. I didn't want any more surprises inside my shack, though getting in through that latch on the back window would hardly be a challenge—I needed to fix that.

Tiki fired up a monologue of rusty-voiced meows mixed with guttural growls as I opened the door and pulled the light cord, illuminating our spanking clean hovel.

"I can bring home the bacon, fry it up in a pan, and never-never-never let you forget you're a caaaaat," I sang, imitating the old Peggy

Lee song, one of Aunt Fae's favorites. I gestured to Tiki's bowl, already topped up with Purina. "Cuz I'm a wo-man!"

Tiki stared at me like I was nuts.

Which, maybe I was. But at least the cat wasn't mad anymore. She advanced to squat in front of her bowl, muttering as she ate.

I hopped in the shower, then pulled on clean yoga pants and a well-washed T-shirt from my Secret Service training days. The logo was worn so faint it was almost gone. My clothing was never going to impress Pua, so why try? I braided my wet hair and put on fresh socks and my Nikes.

"Sorry, Tiki. I know I told you we'd have a quiet girls' night at home, but I've been seduced by the possibility of a bowl of hot beef stew." My stomach growled loudly at the thought. "I'm sure I'll be home early, anyway. I just can't miss out on this chance to show Sonny I can be a friend."

That reminded me—because of the flurry with Jimmy Ching, Lei and Pono weren't going to be able to ask Sonny who he might have seen go from the party into my place. Maybe I could ask him about it.

Pua pulled up in her car with Sassy and Sonny in the passenger seat. "See you later, Tiki. Hold down the fort," I said and locked the cat inside, leaving the light on so it seemed like I was home. I didn't want any more surprises like the message I'd found on my table, no sir. I wasn't taking any chances.

I hurried to the car and opened the back door, slipping in behind Sonny and Sassy, who was barking loud enough to drown out fireworks on the Fourth of July. "Thanks so much for inviting me to dinner. I'm starved."

Pua shushed Sassy, who finally stopped yapping. "It's the least I could do to celebrate our first full day of work together."

She must have been talking to Sonny about being nicer to me because he smiled. "Hello, Kat."

"Hi, Sonny." I extended a closed fist for Sassy to sniff. "And hi,

Sassy." The little hellhound turned up her nose, but at least she didn't bite me.

Pua put the car in gear and pulled out. We drove along the narrow, bumpy road toward their property. "You did well at the counter today," Pua said, breaking the silence.

"Thanks. You were right about the basic functions not taking long to learn." I cleared my throat. "I was surprised Jimmy Ching showed up like he did."

Pua glanced at me in the rearview mirror and gave a short negative nod. She didn't want me talking about the developer in front of Sonny.

Sonny frowned. "He not a friend."

I decided keeping my mouth shut was a good idea, and we drove the rest of the way in silence. Pua went faster than I ever would have on the extremely rough road, dodging potholes and dangling tropical vines with aplomb. Soon, we turned up into the valley where her little homestead rested in the lee of the mountains, snug as a bird nest in the notch of a tree.

Once again, I saw movement on a ridge. "Look! Wild goats!"

"Not so wild," Pua said. "They come down often to forage. Sassy barks and lets us know when they're trying to get into the garden."

"Then I shoot them," Sonny said. The grin he gave me over his shoulder was disturbingly bloodthirsty. "Them good eating."

"Now, Sonny," Pua said mildly. "They are pests, though," she explained to me. "They nibble everything down to a nub."

We reached the gate and Sonny got out to open it without being asked. Sassy hopped out and ran to the house, then took up her position on the top step to bark at us as we approached. Pua pulled in and parked in a lean-to carport. The place wasn't ostentatious by any means, but everything was tidy and well-maintained.

"I didn't get to tell you before, Pua. I love your little farm."

Pua smiled. "We love it too. Come on in and pay no mind to Sassy. She will have to know you for a year, or ten, before she stops barking."

"It's fine. I don't take it personally, especially since my cat hisses and growls at me every time she sees me."

"Tiki is a tough one, that's for sure." Pua unlocked the front door and opened it. A draft of delicious cooking aromas wafted out the door to wrap around me. "Come on in."

I stepped forward into the house, trying to ignore that Sonny was walking right on my heels. His uneven, heavy breathing warmed the back of my neck.

"Sonny," Pua barked. "Boundaries. Eighteen inches from another person, minimum, please."

"Okay." He backed up and I stifled a sigh of relief. "Kat my friend now."

"That's right," Pua said. "Did you set the table before we left like I asked you to?"

"Yes, Auntie."

"Good. Let's go dish up—I can hear Kat's tummy rumbling from here."

Indeed, my stomach was gurgling embarrassingly. "I sure am ready for some of whatever you've got cooking."

"A nice meat and veggie stew with stuff from my garden. I hope you like it."

I followed Pua and Sonny into the kitchen and stopped in surprise.

The rest of the house was decorated in 1950s Hawaiian plantation style, but the kitchen was brand new, sparkling clean, and ultramodern. Sleek blond Danish cabinets, blinding white counters, and gleaming appliances were all pulled together by a white marble floor. "Wow, Pua! This is a showplace!"

"Thanks. A gift from my family." Pua approached a shiny red enameled Crock-Pot, the source of the mouthwatering smells. "I'll serve up our bowls here and we can carry them into the dining room. Sonny, can you get the rolls?"

"Sure, Auntie." The young man opened a warmer section of the oven to reveal pale purple rolls.

I pointed. "Why are they purple?"

"Those are taro rolls. Kind of like sweet potato rolls on the mainland. You're in for a treat if you've never had them before."

"Looking forward to it," I said. "I'd like to wash my hands first. Should I just use the sink here?"

"No, we have a powder room. Off to the left of the entrance." Pua took the lid off the Crock-Pot and ladled stew into large white ceramic bowls.

"I'll be right back."

I headed out of the kitchen, surveying everything curiously as I made my way to the restroom. That little closet of a lavatory was decked out with gold-plated fixtures and a state-of-the-art Japanese bidet with flashing lights and a butt warmer. I was too scared to press any buttons and get sprayed where I wasn't ready for it, but the setup was impressive for sure.

Where was the money coming from for all of this?

"A gift from my family," Pua had said. The infamous Big Island crime family was sending her money. Was it simple generosity? Or something more?

Pua's homemade stew was as delicious as it smelled. The taro rolls, dipped in the broth, were fragrant and soft; the purple poi that gave them color, a subtle enhancement. I tore through half of my bowl and three of the rolls and was reaching for a fourth when Sassy broke into stranger danger barking.

Pua and Sonny exchanged the kind of glance that spoke of surprise and concern, not what I expected to see between a caregiver and a mentally challenged young man. Sassy ran out from under the table, yapping up a storm.

"Go see who's here, Sonny," Pua directed.

The flash of intelligence I'd glimpsed in her nephew's eyes disappeared. "Okay, Auntie," he said in his usual monotone, getting up and thumping off down the hall.

"Probably a delivery," Pua told me, dipping a bit of taro roll into her stew.

"Wow, they bring stuff all the way out here?"

"All the time."

Sassy stopped barking. I heard the rumble of voices, and Sonny returned with Gavin Peabody in his wake.

Pua's face went immobile. "Gavin," she said frostily.

Peabody held a bouquet of grocery store carnations that hadn't weathered the drive well. He still wore that gold chain, but at least his shirt wasn't pornographic this time.

"Pua, honey. I was in the area . . ." Peabody's voice trailed off as he noticed me. His grin faded. "Ah. The nosy Ms. Smith."

"Mr. Peabody. Hello." I waved from my spot at the table. "Just in the area, huh? This is pretty remote for a drop by visit."

"I wanted to see if Pua was all right after her . . . ordeal."

"You mean when I was arrested and spent a night in jail," Pua said. "For a crime I didn't commit."

"Yeah. That." Peabody held out the flowers. "For you."

Pua curled her lip delicately but took the carnations. "Since you came all this way, you might as well have some stew. Come with me and I'll put these in water and get you a bowl." She led her erstwhile suitor down the hall toward the kitchen.

Sonny resumed his seat at the table and picked up his spoon, slurping loudly. I cocked my head, trying to listen to the conversation in the kitchen. Though I could hear a murmur of voices, I couldn't hear well enough to tell what they were saying.

"Do you like Mr. Peabody, Sonny?"

"Who?" That vacant look filmed the young man's eyes.

"Gavin. Mr. Peabody." I pointed toward the kitchen.

"He's a friend." Sonny scooped his last spoonful of soup. His utensil scraped the bottom of the bowl with a sound that sawed my funny bone and made me shiver.

I finished my stew, antsy as a gecko on a hot tin roof. "Do you want more, Sonny? Let me take your bowl and I'll get you seconds." I wanted an excuse to eavesdrop on Pua and her boyfriend.

Sonny reached for another taro roll, and I took that as permission to retrieve his dish as well as my own. "I'll be right back."

I walked on light feet in my socks—heel-toe, heel-toe—to the door of the kitchen and lurked there just out of visual range.

"I can't believe you had the nerve to come out here," Pua hissed. "After what you did."

"And I can't believe you had that nosy witch over to dinner!" Peabody sounded angry. "And what is it you think I did, anyway?"

"Fran. You killed Fran." Pua said it as a statement. "And they arrested me for *your* crime."

A tremor passed over me—a "goose stepping on my grave," as Aunt Fae would have called it. If my ears had been an elephant's, they would have been flapping.

"I did no such thing!" Peabody whisper-shouted. "I thought she left town, just like everybody else. Was that why you broke up with me? We had a good thing going, you and I. In more ways than one."

"I don't need you for my operation anymore," Pua said. "I've got a new conduit for what comes through the post office."

"Yeah, I can see by this kitchen that you're doing just fine."

"How dare you," Pua said.

"And how dare *you*," came Sonny's voice behind me.

*WHAM!* A burst of red stars, then an all-black nothing.

# 27

Waking up from a bash to the head is a bummer.

The black gradually receded to gray, then to the warm red of illumination behind my closed eyelids. The blessed silence of unconsciousness gave way to a rumble of arguing overhead. The peaceful darkness filled with electric pulses of pain that emanated from my head, sizzled along my nerves, and took up residence in my teeth.

Yeah, my teeth pulsed with pain in time with my heartbeat.

OW. Son of a BEEHIVE.

I'd experienced this particular discomfort before—I was bashed on the noggin by an insurgent while on duty in Beirut. I'd only been out a few seconds then. I'd also hit my head running an obstacle course and knocked myself out. Less exciting, but no less painful and debilitating.

I lay perfectly still, playing dead for a moment as I performed a threat assessment:

1. I was lying flat on my back with a head injury, and I appeared unconscious. Check.

2. I wasn't tied that I could tell. Check.

3. A light was on overhead, blooming bright behind my eyelids. Check.

4. The voices arguing over me were those of Pua, Peabody, and Sonny. Check, check, and check.

Sonny sounded different, not speaking with his usual stunted sentences. “We need to get rid of her,” he said. “She overheard you.”

“Kat doesn’t know what she heard,” Pua said. “We can pretend you had an anger episode and struck her.”

“She’s smart. She’s been watching me. You never should have brought her over to the house, Auntie. I told you that.”

“Well, I’m sorry. I wanted to—"

“You wanted to take her in like a stray and feed her. But she’s no stray. This Kat has claws.”

“Ha, good one.” Peabody’s voice.

“You saw what she did to me before, Auntie. She’s big and she’s dangerous.” A foot poked me in the shoulder. Sonny was standing over me, studying my face. I could smell stew on the air and hear his adenoidal breathing.

“I still think the best thing to do is pretend you overreacted, Sonny. And you did, hitting her on the head like that,” Pua said peevishly.

“We can pretend the killer who took out Kermit Hubbard did her too,” Sonny said.

“Okay, I’m out of here,” Peabody said loudly. “I’m not going to—”

I heard a thump that sounded like someone hitting a watermelon with a tire iron and Gavin Peabody landed on top of me so hard, I couldn’t help letting out an “oof!”

“Now you’ve done it, Auntie,” Sonny said. “We’ve got two bodies to get rid of.”

I concluded my assessment: Threat Level Five—I was in extreme and imminent danger.

Except it was Sonny and Pua who planned to murder me. Even unarmed, I could take them.

Downgrade to Threat Level Three and continue to gather info on the murders—this was my best strategy for the moment.

I kept my eyes closed, my face slack, and my mouth ajar, breathing shallowly. Peabody, heavy as a cement wheelbarrow, squashed my rib cage. He reeked of hair gel and Old Spice, so mouth breathing was a good idea anyway.

"We aren't killing them." Pua's voice had gone high with stress. "I just clocked Gavin to buy us some time."

"And how will buying time change the fact that both of them know too much?"

Yep, Sonny was the dangerous one. Clearly his disability had been an act. How could I have missed that for so long?

"There's no way we can get away with a double murder," Pua protested.

"Yes, we can. We'll set Peabody as up as Kermit Hubbard's killer and do a murder-suicide scenario with him and Kat."

"Wait a minute. What do you know about Kermit's killing?" Pua was having a hard time keeping up with her nephew.

"Kermit was no angel. That guy was observant. He realized I wasn't disabled and he tried to blackmail me. I arranged a meeting to pay him off, and . . . gave him what he deserved." Sonny's lack of emotion was chilling.

My breathing sped up and my eyelids twitched. I forced myself to relax and be still.

"Did you kill Fran too?" Pua's voice vibrated with emotion.

"I heard you fighting, and I sneaked up on her when she went inside the shack and lay down on her bed. She'd been drinking so it was easy to smother her with a pillow. Then I packed her stuff like she left and hid her body. It worked, too. For a while." He paused. "She was standing in your way, Auntie, and you had to do all her work. I thought for sure you'd get the promotion with her gone, and we wouldn't have to be so careful with the shipments." A few seconds of silence, then Sonny blurted, "Kat's eyelids are moving! She might be waking up. Hand me the butcher knife."

"No, Sonny!" Pua screeched. "This is a brand-new marble floor! Not here!"

"Okay, but we've got to do them both. The longer we wait, the more likely they wake up and cause trouble."

"We can tie them up and take them wherever you think is best, but we're not butchering anyone in my kitchen. Blood is notoriously hard to get out of natural stone," Pua said.

Of course, she was only thinking of her fancy new floor. Boy had I been wrong about Pua Chang, too.

"I'll get some rope." Sonny stomped off.

I heard a rustle, and then Pua's voice in my ear. "Kat. I know you're awake. Here's a knife for you to cut the ropes with." I felt something slim and cold slide into my hand—a paring knife. "Make your move when you think it's best. I'm sorry things got so out of hand. I didn't know Sonny was . . ." She stopped. Her voice came from above me, louder and clearer. "I was checking their vitals."

"Well?" Sonny sounded impatient. "Did they save us the hassle and die?"

"Both are still alive but unconscious. Where do you want to set this scene up?" Pua's voice was as matter-of-fact as if she were planning a party. "I don't want it anywhere connected to us."

"We should take them to New Ohia and stage it there. Jimmy Ching is in Kahului, so he won't interfere. It would be good to keep the spotlight on that shady place—that's why I did Kermit Hubbard there."

"But what about the cameras?" Pua took hold of my wrists. Her touch was soft and deft as she pressed my palms together, concealing the knife. She wrapped rope around my wrists and tied it, keeping it loose enough that I palmed the blade easily.

Meanwhile, Sonny heaved Peabody off me, and I heard a moan as the man's head hit the floor. "Shut up, Peabody. You always were a whiner."

A slithering noise followed as Sonny dragged Peabody down the hall.

I cracked an eye to see what was going on. Pua had taken the avocado-colored wall phone down and was punching buttons. "Pua?" I whispered.

"I'm calling 911," she hissed. "I have to stop Sonny."

"Give me the phone." With Peabody off me, I could move freely. I stood, despite my swimming, thumping head. "It should take him a bit to get Peabody into the car."

"Auntie!" Bellowed Sonny from the front of the house. "Make sure Kat's legs are tied, then hurry up and help me. He's waking up!"

"Coming, Sonny!" Pua handed me the phone, her eyes wide with fear, and hurried down the hall.

I spoke rapidly into the handset when the operator came on. "This is Agent Katherine Smith of the Secret Service." I rattled off my identification number. "I'm at Pua Chang's house, just outside of Ohia. This is a landline, so the address linked to the number is my location. Her nephew, Sonny, has taken me and another person hostage and is threatening our lives. Pua is in danger too. Send units ASAP, then call Sergeant Lei Texeira and Detective Pono Kaihale and notify them of the situation. This attack is linked to the murders of Fran Borland and Kermit Hubbard." I hung up the phone to the protesting squawks of the operator.

I eased the knife down between my palms to my wrists. It only took a minute to cut the thin hemp with the razor-sharp paring knife. Freed, I slid the knife into my pocket and ran for my backpack in the dining room. I grabbed the thumb-sized pepper spray I kept in the outside pocket. I hadn't brought my Glock, but I sure hadn't seen these events coming.

I trotted on stocking feet to the front door, which had been left open a crack. I peered through and could see across the porch to where Sonny and Pua were wrestling with Gavin's bound body. Sassy, thankfully, had followed Pua outside or she'd have given me away.

The man was kicking up a storm, thrashing and struggling against the ropes around his hands and feet. "Help!" He bellowed. "Help!"

"I told you to shut it!" Sonny yelled right back and whacked the man on the forehead with the butt of an old-fashioned Smith and Wesson revolver. Gavin Peabody went limp at the blow—twice in one day, poor guy!

Pua, trying to hold his feet, lost her grip. Peabody, only halfway inside his car, slithered out of the back seat of the SUV and hit the gravel with a thump.

"Dang, Auntie." Sonny sounded disgusted. He waved the pistol. "I'm losing patience with this whole mess."

"I'm sorry," Pua said contritely. "Gavin's heavier than he was when we were dating."

Sonny stuffed the pistol into the back waistband of his pants and reached for Peabody's shoulders. "Grab his ankles and we'll try again."

This was my chance.

I shoved the front door open and charged out onto the porch and down the steps. I ran with one arm extended, the tiny spray can of Mace ready, the other arm in a blocking position.

Sonny's mouth fell open and he dropped Peabody's top half, reaching for the weapon. Before he could get the gun out of his waistband, I squirted him in the eyes with the pepper spray and rammed him in the solar plexus with my elbow.

Sonny flew backward into the SUV. My momentum carried me forward and I followed him into the backseat. Tears streaming down my face from the spray, I clambered on top of him and held him down with my forearm to his throat. "Give me something to restrain him," I yelled at Pua.

Pua's dark eyes were calculating as she considered her options—then she bent and untied Peabody's legs. She handed me the rope he'd been secured with.

I flipped Sonny around, pulled his arms behind his back, and tied him tighter than a pig on a spit at a barbecue. He was still retching and weeping as I secured his feet with the rope from Peabody's hands. I shoved him into the backseat, made sure the childproof lock was on, and slammed the door on him.

I turned to face Pua. "It would be better for you if you cooperate and let me bind you."

"You'll tell them I helped, right?" Pua picked up the frantically barking Sassy and sat on the porch steps.

"Of course. I couldn't have got away without you." That was an exaggeration, but she was starting to realize the depth of trouble she was in, and I didn't want her overthinking it.

I spotted the spool of light gauge hemp Sonny used to restrain Peabody and me. I pulled off a length and cut it with the paring knife, securing Pua's hands behind her back and her ankles together.

Sassy took offense at this mistreatment of her beloved person, and grabbed me by the pant leg. She tugged, growling, until Pua scolded her. The dog hopped into her mistress's lap and licked Pua's face as she hung her head.

"I didn't realize . . . you know. That Sonny was . . ." She was still unable to say the words.

"A murderer," I finished for her.

"Yes."

"But he was your partner in moving drugs and cash through the post office for the Changs."

She nodded.

"Gavin helped you, too."

She nodded again. "But we never killed anyone. Drugs are a victimless crime."

"Whatever you need to tell yourself. I'm getting some ice for Peabody. I'll be right back." I hurried into the house, raided the freezer, and bundled ice into a dishtowel. Peabody was still out, his mouth ajar and making snoring noises when I returned. I didn't like him enough to do more than set the bundle of ice on the knot emerging on his forehead. I still had questions for Pua.

"Did you know that Sonny killed Fran?"

"I . . . I thought Gavin did it. Fran and I had an argument the evening she disappeared. She'd been drunk all day and I was covering for her. I got sick of it, you know."

I rejoined Pua on the steps and took out my phone, thumbing to my recording app. "I'm taping this, okay?"

She shrugged, defeat in every line of her dejected form.

I made a statement about the date, time, location, and who we were, then continued with the interview.

"I confronted Fran the day she disappeared," Pua said. "I told her I'd been documenting her behavior on the job. I gave her a choice to quit or retire, or I was going to give the head postmaster photos, video, and everything else I'd been collecting." Pua blew out a breath. "Fran had been drinking on the job that day. Discreetly, but enough to make her drunk. She slapped me and . . . well . . . I slapped her back." Pua stared down at the little white dog on her lap, dignified despite her bound position. "That must be how my hair got caught on her ring, the evidence they found on her body. Anyway, Fran stormed off, but I still had another hour before I could close the post office. Sonny was waiting for me in the car because we had errands to run that day. Afterward, we went home as usual, but he . . . he must have . . . hurt her . . . and hidden her body during that hour."

"Why did you and Sonny pretend he was handicapped?"

Over in the SUV, a rhythmic thumping had begun. Sonny was kicking the back door of the vehicle with his feet. We could hear his muffled shouting, but both of us ignored it.

Pua shook her head. "I guess there's no point in keeping any more secrets, but I want you to know I never participated in killing anyone. If I'd known what Sonny was up to, I'd have put a stop to it."

"I believe you," I said. I didn't, really, but I wanted her to keep talking.

"I took Sonny in as a toddler from my brother and his girlfriend who were in the drug scene. He'd had early exposure in utero and was born addicted. He had cognitive impairment, and at three years old when I got him, he didn't speak at all. He didn't begin talking until five, and even then, it was limited."

Off in the distance I heard the wail of sirens. "The cops sure take their sweet time getting out here," I grumbled.

"It's always been tough to get what you need in Ohia," Pua said. "That includes things like special services for Sonny. Over time, he adopted this handicapped persona as a way to cope with his differences. I didn't push him to show his real abilities because I thought he needed that psychological crutch for some reason. I guess he felt safer letting others make their assumptions. Later, when he began helping me move product and cash through the post office for the family, it was useful to have people underestimate him."

"Yeah. I bet." I thought back to the night of Pua's welcome home party. Sonny had to have been the one to leave that macabre warning on my kitchen table, but it never occurred to anyone, including me, that he was the culprit.

Several MPD cruisers and one big, purple truck roared up the narrow road toward us. I exhaled a sigh of relief at the sight. "Thanks, Pua. I'll tell everyone how you saved my life. That will count for something."

She nodded. Tears slipped down her cheeks, and Sassy licked them off.

Together, sitting side by side on her porch steps, we waited for the cops to arrive.

# 28

The next morning, I lay in bed with my eyes shut, the dull thump of a headache reminding me of last night's misadventures.

"Ugh," I moaned, feeling sorry for myself. If only this headache was from overdoing a night of partying instead of surviving a thump upside the head. But then again, I'd not only survived, I'd brought down a murderer and a crime operation that had been run through the post office—so that was something.

Tiki jumped up and landed on top of me with a weight that knocked the breath out of my lungs. She was almost as heavy as Gavin Peabody. "Tiki. I told you. No bed until you have a flea bath."

Tiki fired up her purr in rebuttal. The sound vibrated through my whole body, as comforting as a kettle boiling on the stove.

Or a tractor passing by in low gear.

Or maybe a motorboat on its way to a tropical beach.

Anyway, it was nice. I let her stay there on my chest, purring. I might have also been afraid to move in case her mood changed.

A knock on the door of the shack shook the flimsy walls of the place. Tiki leapt off me to take up her defensible position under the table.

I sat up gingerly, cradling my head. "Who is it?"

"Ms. Smith? It's Phil Hanoi. The head postmaster from Kahului."

I looked around wildly for my phone, which wasn't good for anything but keeping the time in my shack. I found it on the floor beside the bed, dead as a doorknob. It never got charged last night. I'd seriously overslept.

"Mr. Hanoi. Give me a moment," I stuttered.

"Take your time. I'll let myself into the post office—I'll be working here today. The police called me at home last night about the . . . the situation with Pua, and I'm here to help."

"Thanks so much," I said. "I'll see you shortly."

His footsteps retreated.

"Wow," I told Tiki. "Unexpected."

I hurried to get showered and dressed in my work clothes. I made the mistake of looking at myself in the mirror—the bruising and swelling had migrated south to make puffy, purplish bags under both of my eyes. I looked like I'd been in a bar fight.

Make-up wasn't going to do much for my appearance, and my scalp was too sore to drag a brush through my snarled locks. What I was looking at was going to be as good as it got, and that wasn't good at all.

I plugged my phone in (better late than never) and made myself a cup of reheated old coffee. I downed it quickly with two Tylenol and headed out, locking the door of the shack behind me. I left Tiki inside—she was still finding her way in and out, and there was a part of me that didn't really want that particular mystery solved.

As I headed for the back door of the post office, Opal hailed me. She and Artie were sitting on the front porch of the general store, enjoying the sunshine as was their morning routine. "You okay, Kat?"

"Not really." I didn't have the time or the bandwidth to fill in my friends. "I'll check in with you guys later. My boss is already here at the P.O."

"Okay. See you soon." Opal waved.

I took a deep breath and opened the back door of the post office.

My first glance was at the big wall clock. It was eight fifty-five a.m. —I wasn't late after all. Mr. Hanoi stood in front of the locked front door, fumbling through a fistful of keys and muttering to himself. He jumped at the sight of me. "Ms. Smith! I didn't expect you so soon. I should have made it clear—you're not to come in today."

"Oh really?" I put a hand gently over the crusty lump on my head. "Are you sure you don't need help?"

"I'm sure we don't need a lawsuit from an employee who was attacked by another employee who was arrested for drug trafficking and money laundering in the workplace," Hanoi said, breathless.

"Ah. I was out at Pua's place until late last night, making my statement and helping the Maui Police Department sort things out." I put a hand on the wall to steady myself. "Turns out you were right about Pua Chang. I'm really glad to see you here."

"And I'm glad you're all right. Well, relatively so," he said dubiously, eying me. "Don't worry, I have another employee on the way out to help. The cops are coming out today to do a thorough search of the premises for evidence related to Pua's case. I don't want you anywhere near any of it."

"I appreciate that." I said, leaning heavily on the counter.

Mr. Hanoi nodded sagely. "That's why they pay me the big bucks. Now scat, it's high time I spent time with the public. I was letting my office chair reshape my posterior, and we can't have that." He made a shooing gesture.

I scatted.

I locked the back door of the post office as I left, sighing with relief that I wasn't going to spend the day on my feet. The painkillers I'd swallowed hadn't kicked in yet, but I hoped they would soon as I teetered across the parking lot to join Opal and Artie on their front porch.

"My boss gave me the day off," I said, leaning on the porch support.

"You look terrible, honey. Let me get you a cup of fresh brew and a leftover piece of coffeecake." Opal bustled off.

Artie extended one of his giant hands to me. "Sit down with me, Kitty-Kat."

The sweet name brought tears to my eyes as I put my palm in his massive one. It felt like being engulfed in a cozy catcher's mitt. I took one of the wooden chairs worn shiny with use beside Artie.

We sat there soaking in the sunshine. I felt none of my old fear as he held my hand, which I'd worried would be back in spades after last night's unpleasant events.

Opal came out, carrying a little bamboo tray loaded with a warm, crumbling piece of coffeecake and a steaming mug. Both smelled heavenly. "I called that boyfriend of yours. He's on his way."

"Keone Kaihale's not my boyfriend, and he has flights today. You shouldn't have bothered him."

Opal rolled her eyes. "Do you think he wouldn't want to come check on you after last night?"

I sighed. Apparently, I was in a relationship, whether I thought so or not. "What did you hear about what happened on the coconut wireless?"

Opal summarized the gossip, ticking off points on her fingers: "One, Sonny is not disabled and is both Fran and Kermit's killer. Two, Pua Chang has been laundering money and drugs through the post office. Three, Sonny and Pua tried to kill you and Gavin Peabody, who's an accessory in their scheme. Four, all three of them were arrested last night."

"That's about it." I picked up a chunk of the coffeecake and stuffed my mouth, making chipmunk cheeks as I chewed, then swallowing with a gulp of coffee. "I've got a pretty bad headache."

"Glad you have the day off. You need to rest." Opal patted my shoulder.

I finished my breakfast as Opal unlocked the general store's door. "You better get back home before customers show up. Once they see your face, they're going to want to hear the whole story from you."

I set the cup and plate aside. "Thanks, you guys."

"No need to thank us. We're your *'ohana* now," Artie said.

"That means what again?"

"Family."

I didn't have time to get choked up because right then, Mr. K's big green truck roared into the parking lot. I'd be lying if I said the sight of it didn't give my sluggish circulation a boost. I stood up, but hardly made it down the porch steps before he reached me. He wore his white pilot's uniform and looked tastier than my coffeecake. "Are you okay?" he asked, his eyes filled with concern.

"I'll be fine." My voice was muffled by his shoulder as he scooped me up into an enormous hug. "Just a crack on the head. I'm taking the day off."

"Good. I'll take you home." And with that, he swept me off my feet and into his arms.

I believe I mentioned once or twice that I'm six foot one and wear a size eleven shoe. No one has ever lifted me off the ground except to throw me in a martial arts bout. Also, I have severe PTSD related to touch, and can't tolerate being held for more than a minute or two. Even so, I was fine with the current situation. I looped my arms around Keone's neck and enjoyed being carried over the dirt parking lot to my shack.

Once on the porch, I fumbled the key out my pocket, stuck it in the deadbolt and turned, pushing open the front door. Keone carried me over to the Murphy bed where Tiki sat on the pillow, guarding it.

"You're supposed to have a flea bath before we share," I told her.

She slitted her eyes and lashed her tail.

Mr. K gently, so gently, set me down on the bed. Tiki reluctantly made room for me.

"Yes, you're supposed to have a flea bath. But I guess I can make an exception today."

She flicked her ear in agreement.

Mr. K turned one of the chairs away from the table and sat on it, facing me. "You didn't freak out just now. While I was carrying you."

"Nope."

"That's a good sign."

"I guess it is."

We smiled at each other like idiots.

He cleared his throat. "I have news."

"I thought I was the one who had news."

"You mean Pua and Sonny?" He flapped his hand. "That's yesterday's news."

I pushed up onto an elbow. "There's more?"

"Yep. Jimmy Ching turned up dead at the airport early this morning. My flight was canceled for the investigation, so I have the morning off to spend with you."

"I think you better put on a pot of coffee," I said. "We're going to need to have our wits about us to solve this next one."

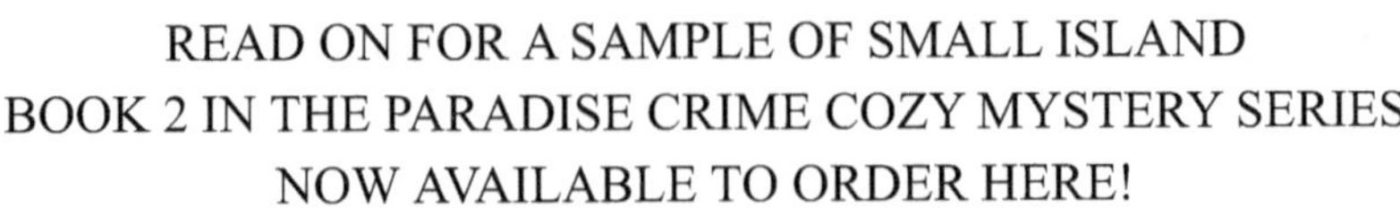
READ ON FOR A SAMPLE OF SMALL ISLAND
BOOK 2 IN THE PARADISE CRIME COZY MYSTERY SERIES
NOW AVAILABLE TO ORDER HERE!

## 29

# SMALL ISLAND

## A PARADISE CRIME MYSTERY BOOK 2

BY TOBY NEAL

I was still nursing a goose egg on my head and a couple of black eyes from catching my last murderer when it was time to hunt another one. Just another day in paradise in the tiny town of Ohia, on Maui.

"You should be resting," said Keone Kaihale, fondly known by me alone as Mr. K. My super-hot (maybe, someday, in my dreams) boyfriend was wearing his white pilot's uniform, which should be a guarantee that I'd be thinking about things other than death.

Which reminded me of death.

There had been a lot of it in the tiny town of Ohia lately.

"I'll rest when I'm dead," I said, continuing the theme. "Tell me what you know about Jimmy Ching's murder." I swung my legs to the side of the bed he'd carried me to, having decided I needed to rest my head injury. Tiki, my semi-feral cat, hissed and lashed her tail in disapproval at my movement.

For once, she and Mr. K were on the same page as he declared, "I'll tell you, but only if you stay in bed."

"And I'll stay in bed, but only if you fix that pot of coffee I asked for."

"Deal." He got up and went to the counter of the little galley kitchen to wrestle with my coffee fixings. I admired his well-developed lats, deltoids and glutes, clad in clingy white polyester trimmed in gold braid.

"The airline shouldn't dress their pilots like that if they didn't want women objectifying them," I said.

Keone winked over his shoulder. "You can objectify me all you want, babe. It's the aunties in town I worry about."

I snorted a laugh. "I take it you're talking about our local Red Hat Society."

He gave a theatrical shudder. "One of them actually pinched my butt the last time I ran their gauntlet."

"They're a force to be reckoned with, all right." Pearl, Mattie, Josie, Clara and Edith basically ran the part of town known as Old Ohia and were working on taking over the recent development of New Ohia, too. "I'll defend you next time."

I clutched my aching head and lay carefully back down, not daring to take up more than an inch or two of pillow while Tiki claimed it. She'd extracted payment in blood on more than one occasion. "Talk while you caffeinate, please. Tell me everything."

"Not much to tell. I showed up at the Hana Airport early, per usual, to take my plane back to Kahului and begin the day's runs. The Hana police were already there and had closed the airport to travel for the day."

"Did you see the body?"

"Nope. It was covered with a tarp and crime scene tape blocked it off." Keone poured water into the coffeemaker, and it belched in appreciation. "But I know a guy."

"Of course you do. You're related to a guy." Keone was the cousin of Pono Kaihale, a detective with Maui Police Department and the partner of Lei Texeira, a sergeant I'd come to know through the murders we'd solved.

"Not Pono this time." Keone pushed the button and came back to sit on the chair in front of the bed. "Pono and Lei barely got home from dealing with your situation last night."

"I remember." I yawned to illustrate my point.

"They're coming out to investigate the latest body, but they hadn't arrived yet when I was there. The Medical Examiner was also on his way. No, the guy I know is Mama's uncle. He works after-hours security at the airport. He's the one who found the body."

"Ah. And your great-uncle told you about it."

"He knows I have an interest in these things." Mr. K's eyes gleamed. "Ever since I met a certain Secret Service agent turned postmaster who's informally known as the Postmaster Sleuth."

"Uh-huh. Go on." I hid a grin behind Tiki's bulk as my cat glared doom daggers at Keone.

"Uncle says it looks like Jimmy came early to catch my flight to Kahului, and someone whacked him. Literally."

"Wait a minute." I sat up too fast and my head pounded. "Ow!"

Tiki, startled, yowled and jumped off the bed to hide under the table, taking a swipe at Keone's leg as she went by.

"Ow!" Keone yelled, grabbing his calf. "What was that for?"

"Tiki was disrupted and someone must pay when she's disrupted." I reclaimed the pillow the cat had occupied. "Can you shake this outside? I'm worried about fleas."

"I smelled your hair, Kat. You don't have to worry about fleas," Keone said, but he obligingly opened the door of the shack and took my pillow outside to shake it.

Apparently, he'd noticed I'd been washing with cat flea shampoo as a preemptive measure. Darn.

I sat up on my elbows and enjoyed the sliver of view I could see through the open door: past Mr. K's lovely rear, beyond the post office building's muddy parking lot, a coconut palm swayed over the beach, and the sun shone over the sparkling Ohia Bay. An *'iwa*, or frigate bird, circled the water looking for fish, and a rainbow dropped from a cloud to touch the old pier.

All that was visible from my bed through the door of my shack.

But the whole situation requires a bit of explanation.

My name is Kat Smith, and I'm a Secret Service agent who ran into a spot of trouble with a handsy Congressman I was protecting. I am (temporarily, I hope? Or not?) posted in the teeny tiny hamlet of Ohia on Maui as the postmaster until the witch hunt for my badge dies down.

Since I'd been here, hardly a week, I found the body of Ohia's former postmaster. She'd been dead six months and I solved her murder, plus that of a shady character from Old Ohia named Kermit Hubbard. But in spite of it all, I am falling in love with this place and its quirky people, and—let's be honest—its over-the-top, ridiculous tropical beauty.

And I wasn't just talking about my view of the beach, as Keone came back inside holding my freshly fluffed pillow.

"Here. Let me." Mr. K lifted my shoulders and tucked the pillow behind my sore head, patting it into place as he did so. "You look so cute."

"Don't lie to me," I said with dignity. My face was worse for wear and my hair looked like I'd combed it with a tree branch. "Try another compliment."

"Honestly, you're gorgeous," he said, "because you're brave. And smart. And resourceful. And kind. Plus your legs go on into next week." He patted one of my limbs.

"Oh." My eyes prickled suspiciously. "Can I trouble you for a cup of that coffee? Cuz I'm not going to let you make me cry."

"Crying is good for the soul. Gets rid of cortisol, the stress hormone." Keone went to the coffeemaker, which had finished burping out a pot of coffee. He poured me a cup in my favorite mug, the one that boldly declared DO NOT SPEAK TO ME UNTIL THIS MUG IS EMPTY.

I loved that mug. It had belonged to Fran Borland, the former postmaster, who'd lived in this shack before me. I thought of her as a friendly ghost that would rest easier now that her killer was behind bars.

"Tell me more about the dead body," I said.

"You sure I can't distract you with compliments?" Mr. K deployed his dimple.

"Nope. We have another murder to solve," I said.

Keone rolled his eyes, then settled into his chair with his mug balanced on his stomach and the air of a man settling in to tell a proper story. "Well, Mama's uncle is named Kawikikaialoha Kaihale, but we call him Uncle Wiki for short. "Wiki" means 'fast' in Hawaiian, my *malihini* warrior woman."

"I like that nickname better than you calling me 'Trouble,'" I said.

"You've earned both names."

To that, I could only agree.

To keep reading, order your copy of SMALL ISLAND now!

# ACKNOWLEDGMENTS

Dear Reader!

Thanks so much for coming along on this first adventure with Kat! First and foremost, for those who love to check a map (you know who you are!) Ohia is an imaginary town located on the eastern coast of Maui, between the villages of Hana and Kaupo, roughly a mile past the Pools of Ohe'o for those in the know of the area. Inspired by reading about Louise Penny's beloved Three Pines and Jana DeLeon's Sinful, I wanted to create a place peopled by colorful characters that encapsulated both the small town charms and big issues of Hawaii.

Ohia is a place where I want to live, quite frankly. I don't have to fact check every street name; only keep track of my own inventions from book to book. I get to play god there, and it's one of the most enjoyable things about being an author. Kat's shack reminds me of some of the places I lived in growing up on Kaua'i in a simpler era, as I wrote about in my memoir, FRECKLED.

As the pandemic ground on with isolation and bad news, and I shepherded my main mystery and thriller series starring Lei and Sophie to a pause point, I craved something lighter.

Funnier.

Something that would make me chuckle and smile as I wrote, not just flip pages like mad because of the tension.

I hope that, in this first in series cozy mystery, I've achieved a balance between smiles and tension.

I hope I've given you an escape from the troubles of the outside world. That's what I wanted for myself, in writing this series.

If you liked the story, PLEASE LEAVE A REVIEW. It makes such a difference in helping readers find the book, and I lurk around and read them on the days when the writing gets tough, and I wonder if I can go on. Without you, dear reader, I'd just be a redheaded lady wandering the beach, telling stories to my dog.

Thanks, and forever aloha,

Toby Neal

P.S. Thanks so much to new editor Laura Adamawich, who brought this manuscript along from rough to readable. Thanks always to Angie Lail who gave it a great polish at the end, and also to my ARC readers who help me find those tricky typos. You all are the wind beneath my writing wings!

# ABOUT THE AUTHOR

Kirkus Reviews calls Neal's writing, *"persistently riveting. Masterly."*
Award-winning, USA Today bestselling social worker turned author Toby Neal grew up on the island of Kaua`i in Hawaii. Neal is a mental health therapist, a career that has informed the depth and complexity of the characters in her stories. Neal's mysteries and thrillers explore the crimes and issues of Hawaii from the bottom of the ocean to the top of volcanoes. Fans call her stories, *"Immersive, addicting, and the next best thing to being there."*

Neal also pens romance and romantic thrillers as Toby Jane and writes memoir/nonfiction under TW Neal.

Visit tobyneal.net for more ways to stay in touch!

or

Join her Facebook readers group, *Friends Who Like Toby Neal Books,* for special giveaways and perks.

www.ingramcontent.com/pod-product-compliance
Lightning Source LLC
LaVergne TN
LVHW010609100826
845148LV00014B/2903

* 9 7 9 8 9 8 5 7 0 6 8 8 8 *